A FAMILY MATTER

BOOK 1 OF THE SIXCRYSTAL STATION SAGA

OX AARONSON

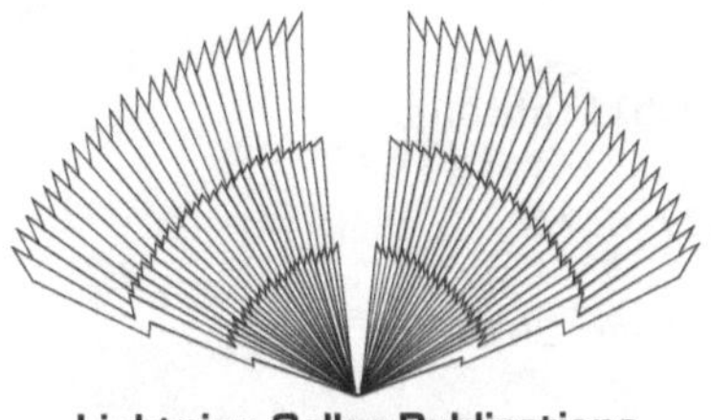

Lightning Cellar Publications

A Family Matter by Ox Aaronson

ISBN: 978-1-943305-03-2

Library of Congress Control Number: 2019905059

Published by
Lightning Cellar Publications
P.O. Box 6372
Lancaster, CA 93539-6372

First Edition, October 2019

20191012

For Phil,
who is a super genius

Chapter 1

"Family is not about genetics. Family is
about loyalty. And Nostraspace is run by
family."
> —Guido Mancini, mythical first Don of
> Nostraspace, as dramatized in *All Our
> Beginnings* by Thomas Ivanov

Multicolored light pierced the darkness as a screen
lit up. An insistent whine cut into the night, and
the shadow of a hand fell across the lighted screen.
With a firm slap, the hand came down on the screen and
silenced the alert. As the hand withdrew, it turned
the screen so its light illuminated a round face
poking out from under bedsheets. The face had high
cheekbones and a sandy moustache flecked with gray, and
bleary green eyes that blink tiredly at the message on
the screen.

On Polairmo, most everyone owned a Deep Space
Communicator, though few used them for their primary
function. This screen, however, had the DSC living up
to its name and functioning as it was designed to. It
contained a terse note from deep space, addressed to
Alexander Romano-Bennetti, sent to an address known
only to family and close friends. The message bore
two authentication badges—one that confirmed that the
message came from the known address of the Don, and
the other affirming that the message had originated
from Sixcrystal Station, the Don's private residence

in an orbit perpendicular to Polairmo's around the twin suns. It read, simply: <u>One of your cousins is in trouble. Be on the next shuttle.</u>

The man in bed sighed. "Lights."

The ceiling began to glow, illuminating a spacious bedroom with six real-wood panels on the walls and a large bed with a real-wood headboard. Beside him in the bed, wrapped in silky red sheets, lay a small woman with pixie features and rumpled blonde hair, breathing the shallow breaths of one in an untroubled sleep, her eyelids fluttering as she dreamed.

The man studied her features for a moment before sliding out of the bed, naked, and standing up. He was broad-shouldered and bowlegged, with a prodigious belly that drooped in front of him. He set the DSC down on the aluminum side table and padded silently into the bathroom. He stepped into the shower, where a blue light disinfected him from head to toe, and then a red light worked up and down his body to rebalance his skin and hair's natural oils. Finally, a quick rinse with water, followed by a blast of air to dry him off.

He stepped out and over to the closet beyond. "I've received a summons to Sixcrystal," he told the wardrobe.

The status panel on the wardrobe blinked purple and green for a moment as it considered, then the door slid open, revealing three outfits. The first was a simple light-gray uniform, the second a straightforward pair of tan pants with a white shirt and green vest, the third an elaborate formal outfit, complete with red cape and enough frills to hide the young lady in the bed.

He selected the second outfit, dressed, and then considered footwear options with a grimace. Again, he went neutral, choosing a pair of soft-soled shoes that slid on like socks.

He collected the DSC off the nightstand as he crept back through the bedroom. He slid open the bedroom door and stepped into the hall. "Lights out," he ordered.

The bedroom went dark behind him, and he stood in the dim hallway for a moment, synchronizing his DSC with the in-clothing hardware. When he finished, he slid the DSC into the inner pocket of his vest and moved down the hall into the main section of the house.

A woman in a black servant's uniform was on her hands and knees on the living room floor, fussing with a cleaning drone. She didn't look up, but said graciously, "Good morning, Sir Alex."

"Good morning," Alex answered, not stopping. "I've been summoned to Sixcrystal. I need to leave right away."

"Work or family?" the servant asked.

"Message doesn't say," Alex answered, pausing before exiting the room on the far side. "There's a young woman in my bed. When she wakes up, could you make sure she's taken care of?"

"Of course, Sir Alex," the servant said. "Do you remember her name, or should I pretend you were in such a rush you neglected to tell me again?"

"Such a rush," Alex said, slipping into the entryway.

The cleaning drone came to life and rolled away from the servant as Alex left.

Alex stepped out of the house and into the brisk air. The stars shone down on the still-sleeping city, patches of haze snaking through the streets as the skyscrapers turned the planet's strong winds into raging torrents of air.

The Bennetti compound sat on a private hectare in the middle of the city, immaculate landscaping lining the path to the street. Alex fumbled with his collar to get it to begin transmitting his authorization, and the street gate slid open for him.

The street itself was still silent. Planetwide, Polairmo had very little exterior lighting, and the only illumination came from a handful of windows that were lit in various buildings around him. A car shaped like a blunt cone on three wheels rolled silently up to the front of the house. Alex touched the access button, and the door swung up. He took the only seat inside. A console in front of him lit up with the address of the tube station. He tapped a green confirmation icon, and as soon as the door had closed, the car was rolling.

Safely en route, Alex took his DSC out of his pocket. It was a palm-sized blue box, one side of it all screen, the other side recessed buttons without labels. His fingers danced on the buttons, and it switched into local mode. He read the various messages he had received overnight, then he switched to the news feed. He scanned headlines, lingering on a story about the execution of a regional governor who had been embezzling, but quickly moved on to looking at a directory labeled "family."

The DSC AI began a cross-reference search for him, noting the most recent contact from each individual in the file and cross-referencing news stories for each. He began with Interstellar-language sources but was soon looking at sources written in several different alphabets.

Alex read intently until the car pulled up at the tube station. He turned off the DSC and returned it to his pocket. The car parked in the "Government Vehicles Only" spot directly in front of the escalator. Alex trotted up the steps, transmitting his ID to bypass security, and went straight past the public gates and to a waiting tube train. It sat on the boarding platform, a series of five windowless silver cylinders, each with a ramp leading to a thick hatch. The front two cars' hatches were already closed, ramps pulling back.

Alex headed up the ramp for the third car and entered just before the hatch began to swing shut. Thirty rows of blue seats, two on each side of a center aisle, stretched back with only about fifteen other people on board. Alex selected a seat against the edge of the car and closed his eyes to wait.

The back two hatches also swung shut, ramps retracting, and the entire platform began to slide back toward the tube. The tube itself was barely larger than the train, about seven meters in diameter. The tube rotated and hissed, and an opening rose like a curtain behind the train. The platform deposited the train inside the tube. Enormous anchors clattered as they released, and then the platform pulled back, empty. The tube rotated again, closing as it had opened. Soon a rush of fans sent blasts of air throughout the station, and the employees all clutched their clothes and possessions to themselves.

Inside, the car bucketed and shook as the vacuum returned to the tube, and then all went silent. A large screen at the front of the car put up a countdown. 3-2-1. The train shot forward with such force that Alex's face stretched backward slightly.

Once the acceleration had stopped, he stood up, looked all around himself, and then sat down again. He pulled out the DSC and resumed his research.

The tube train arrived at the spaceport in less than an hour. It was already almost midday on this part of the planet, and Alex tapped his foot as the platform performed the same dance in reverse to remove the train from the tube. He was the first out of the third car as the hatch opened, hopping onto the still-advancing ramp. The spaceport station was a crowded mass of people, with thirty-six tracks that all had tube trains arriving and departing. The crowd moved and undulated like a living organism, and Alex wended his way through the mass.

The crowd grew thinner as Alex approached the government offices. The sign above the main window listed guidelines for four classes of travelers: Outgoing In-System, Outgoing Jumpgate, Incoming In-System, and Incoming Jumpgate. A small queue had formed at the window, and Alex walked right past it. He thumbed his collar, and the glass doors beside the window unlocked and slid open for him.

The government offices were standard-issue aluminum from floor to ceiling. Rows of aluminum desks with aluminum chairs lined the main floor. People in slate uniforms shuffled around with tablets in their hands, barely looking up.

"We're holding the shuttle for you," a woman called from a desk halfway down the third row, her nose still pointed at whatever she was working on.

"Thank you," Alex said, picking up his pace across the floor and out the door at the rear of the office.

The shuttle sat in an enclosed courtyard. It had a squat, rectangular body with a cockpit off the front shaped like a flattened cylinder. A ramp extended down from the main body under the cockpit, between the landing gear, leading up to the lower airlock in the shuttle's belly.

The ramp started rising as soon as Alex was on it, and he had to duck for his last few steps to avoid hitting his head. As soon as he was in the airlock, the hatch in the floor slid shut, and Alex was able to step onto it for a little more personal space.

The shuttle was standing-room only, with about 300 people crammed on board. They were mostly in green military uniforms, a handful in slate government uniforms, two in light-gray Secret Services uniforms, and two others in civilian attire. One was a white-haired woman with a brass-handled walking stick who leaned against a bulkhead. The other was a slender young man in stretchy black clothing that left nothing of his anatomy to the imagination. The young man noticed Alex and snaked his way through the crowd.

"Alex!" he cried in a light tenor voice. "Are you my Capo on this job?"

The young man had blue eyes, brown hair, and skin so pale and smooth he didn't look a day over sixteen. His movements were catlike and graceful as he slithered up next to Alex.

Alex looked down into his eyes. "I don't even know what the job is."

The young man laughed the airy laugh of an otherworldly creature. "Well, neither do I, but when the Don says 'Come to Sixcrystal Station now,' you come to Sixcrystal Station now."

The old woman with the cane pushed off the bulkhead and approached Alex and the young man. She moved with a shuffling gait. Her dark-brown eyes had a penetrating wisdom behind them, though her body gave away nothing but frailty.

"Is one of you Alexander Romano-Bennetti?" she asked.

Alex nodded. "I am."

The old woman folded both hands onto her walking stick and gave a slight bow. "I'm supposed to report to you. Ellemarie Hayden. Ms., she," she said, giving her preferred honorific and pronouns.

"Nice to meet you," Alex said. "Sir Alexander formally, just Alex when we're on the job. He. This is Marco Guillermo, Mr., he."

Marco and Ellemarie folded their hands and bowed to each other.

Alex turned to Ellemarie. "Since you at least know who you're reporting to, do you have any information on our mission?"

"None," Ellemarie said. "They've had me in the spaceport hotel for a couple of weeks, and this morning my guard told me we've got a job and we're moving." She indicated a burly man with a shaved head in a green uniform that lacked any rank insignia.

"I recognize him, too," Alex said. "Never worked with him, though. Is he good?"

Ellemarie shrugged and leaned forward confidentially. "He's Casphar. If you can get used to the accent and the attitude, he's fine. Never once let me escape."

"I imagine you're easy to underestimate," Alex said.

"Well, he never did," said Ellemarie.

Marco slid closer to Ellemarie. "If you warranted a suite and a personal guard, you must've done something really good. I want to hear this story."

Ellemarie grinned with tight lips. Then she blinked in surprise and looked out the window of the rear airlock. "Oh, we're in space already!"

Alex turned and looked out the window, too. "You don't travel much by gravity drive, do you? You don't feel any motion unless things are going very, very wrong. Come over here, the view is amazing."

Alex, Marco, and Ellemarie moved over to the rear of the ship, a couple of soldiers parting for them as they approached the window.

Polairmo receded behind them. They had already turned away from its twin suns, so they saw the planet half lit, the daytime side mostly ocean and puffy clouds, the night side alight with city lights, despite the outdoor-lighting ban.

The trio watched in silence as the planet shrank into a tiny point of light and then became lost in the glare of the twin suns.

"How long does it take to get to Sixcrystal Station?" Ellemarie asked.

"These shuttles are fast," Alex answered. "A little less than two hours."

"Then I'm going to need to sit down," Ellemarie said, and shuffled toward a bulkhead.

• • •

Sixcrystal Station hung in the murky darkness of deep space. It got its name from its distinctive architecture: six domes, each at right angles to the others, forming a sort of distended cube on a frame of narrow tubes. Each of the eight corners of the cube had a docking port that extended out from it, green and red marker lights glowing on them. One dome always pointed at the suns, the opposite always pointed toward deep space, and the other four each caught the low-angle sunlight of dawn.

Alex stood looking out the window at the rear of the airlock, his gaze fixed on the expansive station.

Suddenly the rough-hewn gray hull of a battleship blocked the view.

Alex stepped away from the airlock. Ellemarie

was still leaning against the bulkhead just on the other side of the inner airlock hatch. Her eyes were closed, and her mouth worked as if she were asleep, but her feet continued to hold her weight even as she supported her right side with her walking stick.

Marco stood against the bulkhead beside her. He held his DSC in his hand—his was larger than Alex's and bright pink—watching a movie of two men having sex.

Alex walked over to them and spoke quietly. "We're docking with the battleship now. We should let the regulars off first and then wait to see who's here to escort us."

Ellemarie didn't open her eyes, but she nodded. Marco sighed exaggeratedly and slipped his DSC into a small pouch on his waist. "On with the fun."

Outside, the shuttle was backing gracefully toward a docking ring on the side of the enormous battleship. The shuttle looked like a tiny fly approaching an elephant as it slid behind the battleship's port sensor array, which reached out from the side of the ship like a giant ear. Automatic guidance lined up the shuttle's airlock with the docking ring, and the little ship mated with its much larger cousin.

The clicking of docking clamps announced their arrival to everyone on board. People shuffled toward the back, and as the rear airlock door opened, they filed out. Alex, Marco, Ellemarie, and the big man in the rankless uniform stayed back.

Alex walked up to the latter. "Alexander Romano-Bennetti. Sir Alexander, he."

The big man folded his hands and bowed. "Vassily Cheremetov. Sergeant, he." His Casphar accent was thick, and his brusque manner typical of Casphar military.

Alex folded his hands and bowed back. They then joined the other two and placed themselves at the back of the exiting throng. As the crowd cleared in front of them, a tall man with white hair and a handlebar moustache stood just on the other side of the airlock, looking straight at them. His green uniform was crisp and flawless, the colonel insignias on his collar polished to the point that they glistened in the artificial light.

"Were the four of you planning on getting off that there shuttle?" he barked, his voice high and sharp.

"The Colonel himself," Marco whispered. "Must be important."

"Mind your manners," Alex growled at him.

Marco responded with a wink. "Oh, Colonel Brawley loves me and you know it."

"The Colonel has questionable taste," Alex muttered back. Then a huge smile replaced the gruff visage, and he folded his hands and bowed. "Colonel Brawley! Great to see you again!"

"Sir Alex, if you'll pardon my saying so," Colonel Brawley barked back, "you and your team had better get your asses to Conference Room 1 immediately if you don't want the Don to use them for target practice!"

Alex marched off the shuttle, the others following. As he passed Brawley, he said simply, "I haven't been briefed."

"The Don will do that," Brawley snapped. "This is your team."

Alex nodded and headed down the corridor. All four moved as though they knew the way. Brawley fell in behind them.

The corridors were, like everything else, standard government aluminum. Soldiers moved purposefully up and down them, none of them paying any mind to the group of civilians. The door to Conference Room 1 slid open as they approached.

A long aluminum table with eight chairs was the only thing in the room. Three floor-to-ceiling windows commanded a view of exactly nothing. Once all five were inside, the door slid shut, and one of the walls converted to a videoconference screen.

The Don stood in his formal reception area in the Noon Dome, the light from the suns coming from directly overhead and casting shadows under his eyes and chin. He was about sixty, with gray-white hair and the same broad, round build that Alex had. He wore a formal blue cape and a yellow ruffled shirt over black trousers, and he leaned against a bench that sat beside one of the many trees that grew on Sixcrystal Station.

The videoconference screen made him somewhat larger than real life. His hazel-and-gray eyes sized up everyone in the room before he spoke. "Thank you, Colonel Brawley."

Colonel Brawley snapped his heels and folded his hands in front of his chest, then stepped out into the corridor. As soon as the door closed, the Don continued.

"I trust I don't need to tell anyone that this is strictly need-to-know, and anyone who leaks any of it will be wishing I'd just ordered them executed."

Alex and Marco both nodded immediately. Vassily smirked before snapping his heels and folding his hands. Ellemarie glanced around at the others before looking at the Don on the wall and nodding as well.

"Good," the Don continued. "Dale Carsoni is currently Capo of an undercover team on Reggit."

A picture of Dale Carsoni appeared in the upper-right corner of the wall. He also had the broad build of the Don's relations, but with darker skin and black hair and a clean-shaven face.

"Is there a problem, Alex?" the Don asked.

Alex unarched his eyebrow, and his expression went neutral. "No. No problem. It's just that Dale wasn't on my list of cousins who might be in trouble. He was at Angie's wedding on Areehgab last week."

"His mother was posting to social media for him," the Don explained. "Part of his cover. The rest of the family was instructed to drop his name casually in their own posts and when talking to the press."

"Fooled me," Alex said.

"Good," the Don said. "Then hopefully it's fooling the Casphar as well and they don't suspect him."

Vassily tensed but remained at attention. Alex looked over at him briefly and motioned toward a chair, but he shook his head almost imperceptibly.

"With him," the Don continued, "are Secret Services Agent First Class Melanie Coltrane"—another photo appeared under Dale's, showing the broad, dark face of a middle-aged woman with a military haircut—"and a private citizen, Kiera Twight."

Kiera's picture appeared last, revealing a slender yet attractive woman with long black hair and deep, dark eyes over a hooked nose.

"Oh, that's not fair!" Marco said. "Kiera's a terrible thief. Why does she get all the best assignments?"

The Don glared for a moment, and Alex reached over and smacked Marco's side with the back of his hand.

"Based on monitoring of Casphar media and communications, we think the team initially pulled off their assignment, but they've been incommunicado for six weeks now."

"What was their assignment?" Alex asked.

"Need-to-know," the Don responded, puffing his upper lip out slightly as he said it.

Alex nodded and resumed an "I'm listening" pose.

"Your mission is very simple: Get in there and bring them out."

"I cannot go in Casphar space," Vassily said, his Casphar accent coming through stronger than before. "Casphar marines not allowed resignation. I am still Casphar marine as far as Casphar concerned."

The Don pointed a finger directly at Vassily. "You are a Nostraspace citizen now, Sergeant, and if they have any problems with your credentials, that's an act of war as far as I'm concerned. Your knowledge of Casphar worlds, culture, and military procedure will be invaluable on this job."

"Are we going in under our real names?" Alex asked.

"No reason not to," the Don answered. "And it eliminates the risk of traveling under forged credentials."

Alex turned to Vassily. "We'll all have your back, Sergeant."

"Now, I want to make this very clear," the Don went on. "Dale Carsoni is not your target. The entire team is your target. I want the entire team back. 'Unharmed' is the preference. 'Kicking and screaming' is an option. Do not leave corpses behind. Is that clear?"

"Perfectly," Alex answered for the team.

"Then I will leave you to make plans. Good luck."

The videoconference wall blinked back to bare aluminum.

Alex motioned for the team to take seats. Alex placed himself at the head of the table, Ellemarie taking the far side, and Vassily and Marco sitting across from one another on the sides. "All right, everyone, assets. I need to know who you are and who I'm working with. By now you've probably noticed that I'm Sir Alexander Romano-Bennetti. I hold the rank of Secret Services Agent Alpha Class, and I'm 32nd or 33rd in the line of succession based on the most recent published orders. My training is covert ops and society. Marco I know, but I want him to introduce himself to all the rest of you."

Marco blinked and grinned slightly in Vassily's direction. "Marco Guillermo, Mr., he. Civilian. Thief."

"Only person ever to get onto Sixcrystal without permission," Alex supplied for everyone else's benefit.

"It was a dare," Marco said sheepishly. "And I only got as far as the airlock."

Alex nodded and looked at Vassily. "I am former Casphar marine. Defector. I am assigned, watch her." He nodded to Ellemarie.

Ellemarie responded with a wry smile.

"And I think we're all curious," Alex said, "as to how exactly you ended up in the Don's service."

Ellemarie screwed up her lips before answering. "I get the impression it was probably along the same lines as Marco here. My background is in computers. I'm an expert with financial systems and security."

She let that hang in the air for a minute. Alex cocked his head to the left and studied her. "You're not by any chance the person who made a large donation to a bird sanctuary with the Don's money, are you?"

Vassily answered for her. "Same."

Ellemarie pressed her lips together tightly, but the corners of her mouth were still turned up. "Let's just say I'm on probation. And it was a good cause."

"And do not let her fool you," Vassily said. "She is not frail."

"I'm eighty-two," Ellemarie said.

"Not frail," Vassily repeated.

Ellemarie's lips pursed again, but her eyes sparkled.

"Now," Alex continued, "I think it makes the most sense to travel commercial, since we're supposed to slip into Casphar territory in plain sight. That means we'll need to acquire any gear we're going to need there. That means we're going to need to have a significant bankroll that won't raise any flags in customs."

"Easiest way is to set up a company here with us as officers or executives," Ellemarie said. "Nostraspace businesses do enough business with the Casphar mines that large sums of money moving from a corporate account into a Casphar bank won't raise any red flags."

"Can you do that?" Alex asked.

Ellemarie lifted a hand off her lap, revealing an older-model DSC with a graphic of kittens on its case. "The paperwork is filed. Welcome to T.T., Inc., gentlemen. I can set up the bank account as soon as the bureaucrats give us an entity ID number."

Alex laughed, two short raspy exhalations. "Why T.T.?"

"First set of initials I found that weren't already taken. It's best to keep the company names generic. That way you can be in any line of work you decide on later."

Alex nodded and rose. "I'll arrange for us all to have bunks here. Contact anyone down on Polairmo who might miss you and tell them you're taking a business trip. Let everyone else on the team know about any embellishments you need to add to the cover story so we're all on the same page. In the meantime, I haven't had breakfast yet. Would anyone care to join me?"

Chapter 2

"Strive as our leaders might to convince us
that the 900-year peace is their doing, the
simple truth is that it is impractical to wage
war via jumpgate. Each of the multistellar
nations' jumpgates can transmit ships only to
their own jumpgates, and since the majority
of worlds are served by only a single gate,
conquest becomes impossible without massive
treason in support of the invaders. The
Suturiku Empire's annexation of Hundye ten
centuries ago is, I believe, the exception
that proves the rule, and the fact that no
nation has attempted a similar feat since only
goes to prove my thesis."
>   —Galadriel Kalama, *Government: All the
>   Ways We Imprison Ourselves*

The starliner *Anerchomeno Asteri* hung silently in
space, the crescent of Polairmo off her starboard
bow. She was an enormous tear-shaped vessel.
Unlike the plain aluminum finish that was typical of
Nostraspace ships, she was painted a vivid purple with
gold swirls along her hull that gave the impression
of feathers. Her name was embossed in large white
letters on the tallest portion of her hull in five
different alphabets.

At the top was the Hellin script of the dominant

Greekorp language, her home. Interstellar, the common language of Nostraspace and Patcorp—and the language of business in most of the other multistellar nations—came second. The blocky lettering of the Casphar language came third, with Ynos and then Suturiku logographic characters sharing one line at the bottom. The multi-alphabet redundancy made her name readable to anyone in the seven multistellar nations, though there were persistent rumors that the transliteration of her name in Suturiku meant something obscene.

A swarm of blocky aluminum-finish tenders surrounded *Anerchomeno Asteri*, each waiting its turn to dock. A new tender, larger than the others, approached the swarm. It had a red Romano family crest—an image of a horse pulling an open, two-wheeled cart flying a flag—painted on its side. This tender cut through the waiting swarm and moved toward the airlock most central on the largest portion of the bulging hull. It swung around so its windows faced away from the starliner and its airlock pointed toward it, and it slid backward until the airlocks mated.

Inside the tender, Alex, Marco, Ellemarie, and Vassily lounged on aluminum-and-velvet couches, all dressed in fine traveling clothes. Alex wore a green cape over a tan shirt and black pants. Marco still wore skin-tight blacks but had a full-wrap gray cape over it that made him look vaguely like a mushroom.

Ellemarie's cape was a more modest purple, which she wore over a green shirt and pants. Vassily had gone with a formal Nostraspace military uniform, green with pink epaulets, still absent any rank insignia. As the airlock door opened, they rose and exited the tender.

At first the airlock was compressed and narrow, but then they passed through the inner hatch into a large customs room. Decorated in Greekorp fashion with a thick green carpet on the floor, purple walls, and a long yellow customs desk, it exuded the latest high-end trendiness without crossing over into gaudiness, at least from a Greekorp perspective. Alex scowled slightly as he entered, and Ellemarie seemed to be suppressing a laugh as she took it all in.

A young woman, short and dark, stepped out of an adjoining room and stood behind the customs desk. She smiled expectantly. Her nametag, written in three different scripts, identified her as Chloe.

Alex stepped forward, grabbed his collar, and transmitted his passport and ticket information. A tablet on the customs desk came to life and displayed it.

Chloe's smile became genuine. "Welcome aboard, Sir Alexander," she said with barely a trace of an accent. "Luggage?"

"We'll be buying what we need on board," Alex responded.

Her smile broadened. "Very well, then. And your party?"

Marco took the cue and stepped forward, transmitting his passport and ticket. The young woman's smile tightened. "I trust we won't have any trouble?"

"I've never caused any trouble as long as I've lived," Marco said with such sincerity that anyone not staring at his criminal record might believe him.

"He's working for me now," Alex said. "We haven't had any trouble in years."

Her smile softened.

Ellemarie stepped up and fumbled with her collar. Alex reached over and helped her. Her passport and ticket appeared on the tablet, her photo looking extremely recent.

"First time off Polairmo?" Chloe asked.

"Yes," Ellemarie answered. "I'm not the interplanetary spacefaring type, I'm afraid."

"Well, we'll do everything we can to make your voyage a pleasant one, and hopefully it won't be your last," Chloe said with a small nod.

Vassily stepped forward and transmitted his passport and ticket. Chloe glanced at it and simply said, "You're all clear."

"Thank you," Vassily said, and he was the first one past the customs desk and through the door to the main lobby.

Anerchomeno Asteri's main lobby was cavernous. The far wall—which was at least a hundred meters away from them—and the wall behind them curved upward, following the tear shape of the outer hull. The fore and aft walls were square, though, each with a mural of stars and planets painted on it. The walls that arched in over their heads and across from them were stacked rows of balconies, sixty in all, with stateroom doors off of them and doors on either end leading to the less-grand accommodations.

In the center of the lobby a bank of glass elevators stretched to the ceiling, glass catwalks arching away from landings to each balcony, like a glowing crystal tree that moved people.

Vassily had stopped just inside the lobby, and Alex stepped around him. "This way."

As they moved across the lobby, other travelers consulted tablets and DSCs, many of them pulling suitcases behind them. Holographic signs would pop up with directions or advertisements as someone passed. Crew members mingled, always just far enough away from the guests to prevent casual conversation, but they smiled broadly whenever approached.

One of the holo-ads popped up as Alex passed. It had several photos of weathered ancient objects, and the terminal voice said in Interstellar with a crisp, clear Nostraspace accent, "Our museum deck currently has a curated collection of Old Earth artifacts. Be sure to see them during your journey."

Ellemarie snorted. "A temporary display of fakes and forgeries?"

"I don't know," Alex said. "Greekorp archaeologists are the best in the galaxy. I'd trust them to know what's real and what's not."

"None of it's real," Ellemarie said. "Old Earth is a myth."

"Then who built the jumpgates?" Alex asked.

"Seriously?" Ellemarie shuffled up beside him and matched his pace. "You seriously buy into the theory that one world built all the jumpgates? One world was the parent of hundreds of different cultures? I thought you were a linguist. You know there's no common parent language."

"There are planets with more than one language coexisting," Alex said.

"So why is there no jumpgate at this mythical Earth, then?" Ellemarie challenged.

"Jumpgates do fail," Alex said.

Ellemarie scoffed. "All seven multistellar nations lost that particular jumpgate?"

A stranger standing by the elevator chimed in. "Besides, everyone knows Patcorp built the jumpgates."

"That is lie!" Vassily roared. "Casphar built jumpgates!"

"And none of us are experts in prehistory!" Alex shouted, leaning his forehead against the elevator control console as he requested a car to their deck.

The stranger who had butted in scowled and slunk away. Ellemarie and Vassily both glared.

Marco grinned. "Can't take any of you anywhere."

. . .

Jumpgates were always located well away from the orbits of any inhabited planets. The Greekorp jumpgate at Polairmo was a three-day trip.

They occupied two four-room suites—Alex and Marco in one, Ellemarie and Vassily in the other. The bed was so soft that Alex's entire frame sunk into it every night and left him flailing to get out of it in the morning.

Their shopping took up most of their free time on the way to the first jumpgate, much of it involving Vassily and Ellemarie complaining about the various outfits being purchased for them.

On the third day, they gathered in one of the observation decks to watch their first jump. A small crowd had gathered. Jumps were popular among first-time interstellar travelers as well as those who just liked to break up the monotony of a voyage.

The observation deck's two maroon-colored bars were each staffed with a trio of bartenders, and a cannabis vendor in the corner staffed a black table with various water pipes displayed on it. Harder drugs were available, of course, but required a visit to a dispensary, where the buyer's medical clearance was checked before the sale was allowed.

Alex, Marco, Ellemarie, and Vassily assembled near the floor-to-ceiling transparent panel in the outer hull. Alex held a glass of strong mead, Marco a mixed drink, and Ellemarie and Vassily both had untouched glasses of water in front of them.

Outside, only the lights of the jumpgate were

visible in the endless night of deep space. The habitation cylinder's portholes formed a vague crescent below the brightly lit parallel bars of the jump mechanism, which stretched up from the habitation cylinder like giant posts. The lower half of each post was round, and the upper half flattened and rectangular. Each post had strips of lights running down each of its four quadrants, and powerful lights mounted to the top of the habitation cylinder shone up on them as well. The left post had a powerful yellow marker light on top of it, and the right post had blue. Ships approaching from any angle, even if their navigation systems were completely nonfunctional, could theoretically pilot through the jumpgate visually.

Anerchomeno Asteri banked toward the habitation cylinder and then rotated slowly so her keel pointed straight down toward the top of the habitation cylinder. The enormous teardrop mass then slid silently between the goalposts and came to a stop.

On the observation deck, people were milling closer to the window. Alex leaned over and said to Ellemarie, "Now watch closely."

The rows of marker lights on the goalposts glowed more brightly. Then a wave of blue light pulsed out of the flat ends of them. The wave faded, and everything went back to the way it looked before.

"What went wrong?" Ellemarie asked.

People around her laughed.

"Look closer," Alex said.

Off in the distance, a white light shone brightly on an artificial structure of some sort. The marker lights on the posts of the gate they were in didn't quite match, either—a couple of lights weren't lit, and the right post had some damage where it looked

like there had been a collision many years ago and the
dents had never been completely removed.

Ellemarie's jaw went slack with amazement as she
realized. "We're there already?"

"Well, not Reggit," Alex said, tilting his head and
pointing to the distant light of the other jumpgate.
"This is the Greekorp gate at San Jose, in DiYesu
Family space. Over there, the white light, that's the
DiYesu gate. We're going to fly over there and take
that gate to Santa Maria, which has a Casphar gate
just an hour away from it. We'll take that gate to
Reggit. We should be inbound to Reggit in less than
two hours."

"I didn't think offworlders were allowed in DiYesu
Family space," Ellemarie said.

"Not onworld," Alex said. "But they charge a toll
for ships passing through. It's their only source of
income, really. It's more expensive than using the
Node, but since all these gates are so close together,
it shaves at least a day off the transit time."

Ellemarie went silent, gawking as *Anerchomeno
Asteri* began to slide slowly forward out of the gate.

"Now," Alex said, "why don't we take a break from
shopping and go check out that Old Earth exhibit?" He
held out his arm, and Ellemarie, smiling, took it.

Marco looked expectantly at Vassily.

Vassily growled, "Do not even think."

Marco grinned and followed after Alex and
Ellemarie. Vassily stood for a moment, stone-faced,
and then followed as well. The museum deck was one
level down. They stepped out of the observation deck
into the arched main corridor, one of the restaurants
across from them, the main lobby to their left, and
the bend of the arch to their right. At the bowmost
part of the corridor, a grand carpeted ramp led down

to the museum level. They descended like royalty,
other passengers and the occasional crewmember making
a path for them as if on instinct.

The double doors to the museum stood at the bottom
of the ramp, artificial wood set in a complex, star-
shaped inlay pattern. The doors slid open as they
approached, and an attendant just inside the door
collected their drinks and set them on a small counter
behind her.

The museum spread out in front of them, carpeted in
a geometric pattern of golds, greens, and browns. The
walls were a surprisingly tasteful gray, and instead
of an evenly lit ceiling, spotlights shone down on
display cases. There were thirty-three cases: a large
one in the middle of the room, with four clusters of
eight more in the corners of the room. Alex strode up
to the main one and immediately let a single loud blat
of a laugh escape.

The other three came up behind him and studied
the large stone tablet in the display case. It was
granite, badly weathered and chipped and cracking, and
was engraved with a strange script. The info card
said, "The stone tablet presented by the King of Earth
to the colonists to mark their final departure, circa
year -3485."

"Obvious forgery?" Ellemarie asked, not able to
keep the smugness out of her voice.

"There was no King of Earth," Alex explained. "He
was a story made up in the eighth century."

Ellemarie shook her head. "I'd like your expert
opinion on the others."

They spent the next forty-five minutes circling to
case after case. Some were obvious forgeries like the
tablet, others more subtle. But Ellemarie continued
demanding explanations until one by one they fell

apart, and Alex had to concede that nothing they'd seen was evidence that Earth really existed.

Then the lighting in the room changed.

The spotlights vanished and the ceiling shifted to all-on bright mode. Background music, which had been barely noticeable before, snapped off at the same instant.

A disembodied voice filled the room, speaking Hellin. Alex tensed as he listened. The same voice then repeated in Interstellar, "May I have your attention, please. Passengers and crewmembers are asked to remain where they are. We are being boarded by Casphar military, and they would like to check everyone's identification and conduct a noninvasive survey of the ship."

Vassily and Marco tensed, too. The voice proceeded to repeat again in another language, but Ellemarie spoke over it. "I take it that's unusual?"

"Unheard of," Alex answered.

"They search me when they kill me," Vassily said.

Alex strode over to the attendant by the door. She held a forced smile on her face. "I am Sir Alexander Romano-Bennetti. I would like to know what this is about."

"I'm sorry, sir," the attendant said, her voice quavering slightly. "At this point, I don't have any more information than you do."

"Then get me some!" Alex roared. "Get the captain down here if you have to!"

"Yes, sir," the attendant said, tapping on her sleeve-com.

Alex snapped his cape and walked back over to the others. Ellemarie arched an eyebrow at him. He dropped his voice. "Guilty people behave inappropriately at checkpoints. You," he pointed at

Ellemarie, "have never been offworld before, so just act like you have no idea what's going on."

"Easy enough," Ellemarie said. "I don't have any idea what's going on."

"If I don't raise a fuss, they'll start to wonder why I'm not acting like a spoiled aristocrat. Nobody smuggled anything on board, right?"

"No," Ellemarie said instantly.

"No," Vassily said, too.

Marco said nothing.

Alex didn't move his body, but his eyes shifted in their sockets to look at him. Vassily and Ellemarie both craned their heads around to stare at him.

Marco licked his upper lip, and then bit it. He looked sheepishly up at Alex. "Just my porn collection."

Alex growled.

"It's a stupid law," Marco said.

"Is five years in prison on Reggit," Vassily said.

"Oh, come on, it's not like I'm getting laid on Reggit," Marco said. "A boy's got to have something."

Alex shook his head. "Let's hope they meant it when they said noninvasive."

The double doors opened and a small round man with olive skin scurried in. His uniform was a basic crew uniform, but his epaulets had the four bars of the captain rank. Alex choked a quick laugh, and then his face became stern.

The captain came straight to Alex and folded his hands in the Nostraspace manner. "Sir Alexander. Spiro Mamatas. Captain, he. I'm so terribly sorry. This is a new edict from Casphar."

"I am not used to being searched upon entering foreign space, Captain Mamatas," Alex said with just a tinge of anger in his voice. "Much less by an empire that doesn't even control that space. Are we still at San Jose?"

"I know, I know," Captain Mamatas said, patting the air with his hands. "And, no, we have just entered Santa Maria. The Casphar ships, they wait there. And I agree, it's entirely unreasonable. But they're not letting any ships in or out of their jumpgates without being searched."

"Out, too?" Alex roared.

"That's just a cargo sweep," the captain said. "They're verifying ID on everyone on board against the ship's manifest."

"How long has this been going on?" Alex asked.

"Six or seven weeks in Casphar space," Captain Mamatas said. "All outgoing traffic. This is the first I've encountered it at this leg of the journey."

"What are they looking for?"

The captain pursed his lips and shook his head. "Nobody knows."

Alex blew out through his lips fiercely. "Captain, first of all, I want you to know that I am not blaming you personally. However—"

The doors to the museum opened again. Six men who looked almost like Vassily stood there, each in a crisp, sleeveless tan uniform that showed a distinctive tattoo on their right shoulders—a tattoo of a two-headed raptor. All six held oversized black rifles with enormous muzzles. The one nearest the door also held a small device in his left hand. It was shaped like a box with two wands attached, and the wands pulsed with a faint blue light.

Alex arched an eyebrow at them and spoke in a loud, commanding voice. "That was quick. Did you decide to seek me out first?"

The Casphar marines didn't answer. They marched

into the room and the doors slid shut behind them. The lead one didn't approach Alex at all but instead went to the nearest display case and pointed the mysterious device at it. He waited a moment and then moved on to the next one.

Another marine stopped for the door attendant, and the other four walked over to the group. One of them spoke in clipped Hellin. The captain answered in the same language and reached for his sleeve-com. The marine took out a small tablet, looked at it, and then turned to Alex.

Alex didn't wait to be addressed. "I am Sir Alexander Romano-Bennetti of the House of Romano, thirty-second or thirty-third in the line of succession for Nostraspace. Nephew of Llewellyn Romano, Don of Nostraspace. I doubt you are high enough rank to deal with my wrath."

"I must see ID," the marine answered, mispronouncing almost every word of it.

Alex pinched his collar fiercely. The marine studied his tablet.

"Get me your commanding officer!" Alex demanded.

The marine with the funny gadget finished scanning the eight objects in the first cluster of display cases and continued around the room to the next set.

Captain Mamatas repeated Alex's request in Hellin. The marine shook his head and stepped away from Alex to Ellemarie. She transmitted her ID without being asked.

One of the other marines was checking Marco's ID. "No!" he shouted. "This is ID of twenty-seven-year-old man."

"What can I say?" Marco said, running his finger down the marine's chest. "Clean living."

Vassily growled something in Casphar. The various

marines started. Vassily stood erect, his fists clenched at his sides. He spoke again.

The marine with the gadget looked over at them, pausing his search. The one who had been with the door attendant adjusted his rifle but didn't move. The other four shifted their weight to lean in slightly toward Vassily.

"That man," Alex said firmly and loudly, motioning toward Vassily, "is a Nostraspace citizen. Anyone takes any action against him or any of us, and I will consider it an act of war."

Everyone stood motionless for at least a minute.

Finally, the marine who had been harassing Marco spoke. "We will need to see ID."

Vassily didn't move. Alex stepped away from the marine in front of him and walked behind Vassily. He gingerly reached out his hand to Vassily's collar. "Concentrate on the right file or they're going to see pictures of your goldfish." He pressed the collar.

The marine who had asked for the ID looked down at his tablet. He studied it for a moment, scrolling back and forth through both pages. He then called up another program. He spoke briefly in Casphar, and then said, "Is Nostraspace ID. Is valid."

Alex nodded slightly toward the marine who was trying to be reasonable. "Now," he said deliberately, "may I suggest that you all go away and send your commanding officer down here to explain himself?"

Nobody moved.

The marine with the gadget went back to scanning display cases.

They all stayed like that, frozen like statues until he had finished the thirty-two satellite cases and came over to check the main one. All eyes were on him as he pointed the gadget at the stone tablet. He held it in place, the faint blue light in the wands flickering. He lowered it, shook his head, and made for the door.

The other marines pivoted and followed him.

The marine who had checked Alex's ID was the last to go. He spat on Vassily's boots before he left.

Vassily stood motionless, face red, veins in his neck pulsing.

The Casphar commanding officer never did come down to speak to them.

CHAPTER 3

"The most common misconception about the
jumpgates is that there are seven 'lines.' In
fact, there are ten distinct architectural
styles, which can be divided into three broad
categories: the ring style, typified by the
Patcorp gates; the post style, commonly seen
in the Greekorp gates that operate in other
multistellar nations' space; and the obscure
petal style, only found in Suturiku space and
in Greekorp star systems. Casphar, Greekorp,
and Suturiku actually operate two lines each."
  —Leslie Wesson, *The History and
  Technology of Interstellar Travel*

The Casphar jumpgate at Santa Maria looked similar to the Greekorp jumpgate: two enormous posts and a cylindrical habitation section. However, its posts were triangular, and the habitation section was a long, slender cylinder on its side rather than a broad, flat cylinder. It was painted red and yellow, though only small patches of color were visible under its external lights, and all those patches were pocked with scratches and scrapes.

The jump procedure, however, was completely different. *Anerchomeno Asteri* pulled up in front of the jumpgate and waited. The posts pulsed as the other jumpgate had, and then blue light arced out of them. But instead of a wave transporting the ship instantly, the arcs closed around each other, and a shimmering blue frame appeared between the posts. Slowly, *Anerchomeno Asteri* began moving again. She glided into the frame, and it vanished behind her.

Meanwhile, in deep-space orbit in the Reggit system, another jumpgate glowed blue. This one looked like an enormous ring, painted red, with a shimmering blue frame lining the inner edge of the circle. *Anerchomeno Asteri* flew out of the ring, never having entered it. The blue light inside the ring went out, leaving only the light from the portholes all along the ring and four marker lights—red, white, green, and white—showing ships where the opening in the ring lay.

The space around the jumpgate was jammed with spaceships. Two wedge-shaped Casphar cruisers flanked the gate, turtle-shaped boarding pods coming and going from them like insects around a large animal.

Three lumpy merchant ships had formed a queue off to the side of the gate. They were all the same basic design, a small square vehicle in the front with a lattice behind it that was at least ten times as long as the crew module. Spherical shipping containers were strapped in the lattice, giving a loaded ship the appearance of a ribbed handle. The one at the front of the line was a typical Nostraspace aluminum finish. The next ship in line had sleek white finish with exterior lights illuminating its entire form, speaking of Suturiku origins. It towed a second lattice in drone mode, making it twice again as long. The last ship had the distinctive gaudy paint colors of Greekorp, in this case blue, orange, and green. Boarding pods were just leaving the Nostraspace hauler, and it moved into line with the ring. The ring pulsed, and then the blue window appeared inside it. The hauler crept forward, crawling into the ring, vanishing as it passed through.

Anerchomeno Asteri moved aside and took her place in a second queue, this one mostly small ships belonging to nonaligned spacers. Boarding pods from the second cruiser flew over to mate with her airlocks.

This time the inspection didn't involve the passengers, and she was underway a few hours later.

Reggit itself was on the far side of its sun, making for a five-day journey from the gate to the planet.

Alex got out of bed the first inbound day—a process that involved rocking himself back and forth in the man-eating mattress until he had enough momentum to pop out onto his feet—and wandered out into the sitting room, still naked. He pulled the complimentary tablet off the wall and pulled up the Reggit news that had been downloading since they exited the jumpgate. He sat down on the velvet-and-acrylic couch and began to read.

Most of the headlines were about a local celebrity, Austin Montierthski, who had been found in bed with ***Three Women!*** during a routine inspection of his yacht by the marines. Alex scowled as he looked over all of those. Digging a little deeper revealed articles about the current employment rates and unrest among miners in the dormitories for idle workers. Most of those managed to contain some reference to ***Three Women!***, whether it bore on the events being covered or not. Alex growled at a ***Three Women!*** reference in a piece about a drilling operation accidentally cutting a sewer line and set the search function to go back seven weeks.

Seven weeks earlier, the headlines were much more mundane. Two regional underlords had been assassinated. Miners had petitioned Emperor Habid IV for more pay and better working conditions. The jumpgate had another brief power outage but was restored within a few minutes. There was a break-in at the Casphar Imperial Museum, but nothing was taken. Suturiku government officials had protested the jumpgate fees again. Ynos had promised to find another source of rare earth minerals if prices did not come down.

Alex scanned the news thread for the assassinations. Three days later, all the headlines were about **_Reggit's Dumbest Thieves!_**, who had rented a house behind a bank, tunneled into the vault, stolen the paper scrip currency from eight different mining conglomerates, and instead of dividing the loot up had gotten into such a row back at their house that the police responded to a noise complaint. They had all been arrested, and every single item stolen from the vault had been recovered, down to the last piece of scrip. The story of the assassin's arrest was buried, and still Alex couldn't manage to get through three paragraphs without a reference to **_Reggit's Dumbest Thieves!_**

Marco emerged from his bedroom, covered only in a sheer robe, and yawned. "Are we in Casphar space?"

"Looks like it," Alex said. "Our estimated arrival time has been pushed back three hours, so I take it the inspection was slow."

"We should check to make sure Vassily didn't kill anyone," Marco said.

"I told him to stay in his suite," Alex said. He held out the tablet to Marco. "What do you think?"

Marco took the tablet, scanned the article in question, and scowled. "No physical description. Could be anyone. But that is about the time he stopped reporting."

Alex leaned back and put his feet up on the couch. "It just doesn't seem like my uncle to be carrying out assassinations."

"Could be unrelated," Marco said. "I mean, if the Casphar government was looking for a reason to pick Dale up, and they've got an unsolved assassination, the media would be none the wiser if they just pinned it on him."

"Maybe," Alex said, puckering his lips.

"So if Vassily didn't listen to you, and he did kill someone last night, do you think Ellemarie would let us know or just take advantage of the opportunity to make a break for it?"

Alex snorted and rose from the couch. "Let me get dressed and we can go next door and check."

Marco looked wounded. "Oh, don't do that!"

• • •

Vassily and Ellemarie were not in their cabin. Alex grumbled and resorted to sending Vassily a text message. Vassily responded that they were in one of the restaurants having breakfast. Alex and Marco went to join them.

The restaurant was on the same deck as the cabin but in the rear of the ship. The central elevator in the main lobby was busy shuttling passengers to various levels for their breakfasts, morning entertainment, or back to their cabins. Alex and Marco, back in their formal wear, swept along the balcony outside their cabins and through the aft doorway, marching into the restaurant like they owned it. Ellemarie spotted them from across the room and waved, chewing on a piece of a small breakfast bird.

The restaurant was carpeted in black, with red

walls that had gold bands running up them. The tables were artificial wood and seated anywhere from two to eight people. Ellemarie had already cleared off two plates of food, but Vassily's mix of cereals and fruits lay untouched in front of him. Alex sat down.

"Try the bird," Ellemarie said. "It's quite good."

Marco swept past and made for the food dispensers.

Alex studied Vassily's face. "How are you doing?"

Vassily glowered.

Alex reached out and placed a hand on Vassily's arm. "Don't worry, buddy, we're going to get you through this."

"I keep telling him to think of it as the ultimate revenge," Ellemarie said, picking her teeth with a bone. "Here he is, back in Casphar space, but with a Nostraspace passport, so no one can touch him."

Vassily leaned over to Alex and jammed a finger into the clasp of Alex's cape. "This empire corrupt. We should have no dealings."

Alex nodded and spoke quietly. "We're just here to bring our friends home."

"Big planet," Vassily said.

"Yes," Alex answered, "but there's no reason to venture much beyond the capital. That's where the spaceport is. It's the largest population center, and if for some reason they are out in the mining regions, they'll have to come back through the capital sooner or later."

"Later. That worries," Vassily said through his teeth.

Alex nodded to Vassily's plate. "Eat your fruit, you'll feel better."

"You called?" Marco said from behind Alex, setting a plate down in front of him before sweeping to the other side of the table and setting down a plate for himself. Alex's had a bird similar to Ellemarie's, which appeared to have been poached with the head still on, dead eyes looking up at Alex.

"We do this job quickly," Vassily said.

Alex nodded, picked up his fork, and stabbed the bird.

• • •

The rest of the inbound journey was uneventful. When they arrived, Alex, Marco, Ellemarie, and Vassily were escorted to the first tender, boxes of the clothing they had brought on board being rolled behind them by porters. Security pulled Marco aside briefly and checked under his cape before letting him exit.

Reggit was a vast brown planet with very few clouds and a lot of smoke in the atmosphere. The tender was a pink and gold affair, with decorative fins that poked out from each of the four corners of the hull in a sort of starburst shape. It arched down and entered the atmosphere without kicking up so much as a vapor trail before descending straight down toward the spaceport.

The city below was a perfect grid, with the spired and domed castle in the center of it. The construction here was mostly painted concrete, with small windows. Single-story buildings dominated, each set in a small dirt yard with a concrete wall around it. Where buildings were multistory, each floor was offset from the one below it to create balconies and overhangs, making the taller buildings look like they had been built by a child out of blocks.

In the newer parts of town, the concrete was fresh and unpainted. Other neighborhoods had buildings in faded reds and yellows. The streets were all compacted dirt, but concrete sidewalks ran along all of them.

The tender touched down amid a row of similar
tenders, each with its own color scheme, near the
Greekorp terminal building—a long building painted
a vivid puce. A ramp came down from the rear of
the ship, and Alex, Marco, Ellemarie, and Vassily
descended. A swarm of nonaligned spacers rushed over
to the newly arrived ship and fought with each other
over who would take the baggage in to customs. Alex
and the others didn't wait. They strode into the
building, marching past the customs counter while
transmitting their passports, and headed into the
corridor that led to the main terminal.

Once they were out of Greekorp areas, the interior
design became much more utilitarian. Terrazzo floors
had paths designated by different shades of gray,
leading to the main entrance, the shops, the other
terminals, or baggage claim. A rental agency, carved
out of the larger room by glass partitions, sat in the
corner. Alex marched in and, speaking Casphar, held
out his hand.

A broad-shouldered woman behind the desk rose,
shook his hand, then folded hers Nostraspace-fashion
and bowed. "Aaliyah Alanwar. Mrs., she. How can I
help you?"

"We're here to do some business," Alex said.
"We'll need a short-term, open-ended rental,
preferably close to the commercial districts, that can
accommodate the four of us, plus six others if our
business keeps us here more than a few weeks."

She smiled. "I have some lovely listings to show
you, then."

• • •

The house they rented was a three-story building,

recently painted white, on a narrow lot with a sizeable backyard.

After the porters had delivered their cases and made various offers for other services, Alex shooed them away, secured the door, and he and Vassily began to sweep the entire house for surveillance equipment. They checked the front-door and yard cameras, looked inside all the closets, behind doors, under furniture, and behind the ceiling panels. Then they assembled everyone in the main room.

"Until we buy some electronic countersurveillance equipment, we should assume we missed something," Alex said. "Don't discuss any business that we wouldn't be comfortable with whoever rented this house before us hearing."

Everyone nodded. Marco pulled the house tablet off the wall and placed an order for countersurveillance gear.

"Meanwhile," Alex said, "there's a bank I'm curious to check out. Would anyone care to join me?"

Vassily glowered but acted as though it hadn't been a request.

Alex, following navigation on his DSC, led them on foot about two kilometers away. The streets were crowded with miners in ragged brown clothes and the occasional merchant in pressed and tailored brown clothes. Their formal Nostraspace attire made them conspicuous. Every so often a six-wheeled mine transport would rattle by, and the curious miners inside it would stare at them as they passed.

The bank was on the edge of the commercial district, a narrow but deep building with a stone garden out front. The house behind it was in the process of being demolished by two enormous red machines, and dust wafted over with an acrid odor that filled the block. The front doors of the bank appeared to be real stainless steel.

As Alex approached, they swung open, admitting them to a small antechamber. As the doors swung shut behind them, a green scanner light passed over them, and the inner door—also stainless steel—swung open. Alex stepped inside first, with the other three close behind.

Most of the business was miners exchanging one company's scrip for another, and a line of disheveled bodies snaked away from the main counter. Glass offices lined one wall. A tall woman in her fifties with close-cropped blonde hair and a stocky build rushed out of one of the offices toward them. She wore the pressed brown unitard common to the merchant class but with a short cape behind that designated authority.

She stopped just short of Alex and folded her hands in the Nostraspace manner. "Katrina Polenski. Director, she." She bowed. She had only the faintest trace of a Casphar accent.

Alex and the others introduced themselves, and she motioned them back to her office.

"I am very honored to have you in my bank," she said as she rounded back behind her desk, which appeared to be made of concrete that used glass as the aggregate. "Please sit down. What can we do for you?"

Alex sat on the faux-wood chair closest to the desk. Ellemarie sat beside him. Marco and Vassily remained standing.

"We're planning to do some business here on Reggit," Alex said. "We're going to need a local bank that can take transfers from our bank on Polairmo and do the conversions into the appropriate local currencies."

The bank director's eyes sparkled and the corners of her mouth turned up slightly more. "We can do that for you. Our interstellar transfer system is partially automated and can dispense credits anytime, day or night, and if you need paper currency, there is never any waiting in line for business customers."

"Good, good," Alex said. "Now I do have to broach a somewhat sensitive subject. You are very conveniently located for us. However, my research shows that you had a break-in recently."

The director tensed slightly, but her voice remained calm. "That is true. However, everything was recovered, and new security systems have been put in place to ensure that similar breaches will be detected immediately."

"That is reassuring," Alex said with a slight nod and a thoughtful look. "I assume you're not free to discuss the security changes in detail."

She shook her head and held a hand out, waving it slightly. "There is no harm in discussing it with trusted customers. This bank has always maintained separate vaults. One for scrip, and another for safe deposit boxes where customers keep valuables. All is insured. Even if the scrip had been stolen, it would have been replaced the next day. The vault where your valuables will be stored has no exterior walls, and now both vaults have sensors that detect if there is motion inside or if the walls are breached."

Alex's nod became more strenuous, and he smiled. "Good. In that case, I think this bank will work well for us."

"What line of work are you in?" the director asked.

Ellemarie answered, "We make toys."

The director's eyebrow shot up. "Toys? Unusual on Reggit."

Alex continued the narrative expertly. "We're hoping to enter the market here with a new novelty item. A doll of Austin Montierthski with ___Three Women!___"

The bank director's eyes grew wide, and she clapped both hands over her mouth.

Alex continued, "Our company is Topical Toys, Inc."

The bank director dropped both hands and pressed them palms down on her desk. "It is scandalous! It... it is unprecedented! Have you still a need for investors?"

. . .

As the front doors of the bank closed behind them, Alex gave Ellemarie a sidelong look. "Toys?"

Ellemarie pulled herself up straight on her walking stick. "It had to be something where they wouldn't be alarmed that we've got no income."

"And instead we've got investors lining up. I'm making you run the business."

Ellemarie waved a hand at him. "Show me where I can get some decent sewing supplies and I'll have a prototype for you in a few hours. Who's Austin Montierthski?"

. . .

A large box was waiting for them on the doorstep when they got back to the house. Vassily dragged it inside and pried it open. He looked down and whistled.

"Nothing until the countersurveillance gear is up and working," Alex ordered.

Vassily nodded and dug deeper into the box for a smaller package of eight tiny devices, each with two sensor packages sticking off of them like oversized ears. Marco and Vassily had them set up all around the house five minutes later, and everyone huddled around the aluminum dining table.

"Why military-grade home security system?" Vassily asked.

"I like to cover all bases. Get it set up at your leisure. Any trouble coming in the next couple of days won't be anything it can handle anyway."

Vassily nodded. "Overkill."

"Okay, fine," Alex said, "real business. Any hints as to what Dale might have been doing in that bank?"

"Oh, is that what we were doing there?" Ellemarie said.

"I'm stumped," Marco said. "I mean, I know why he picked it. Even Kiera could get in and out of those vaults if they didn't have motion and perimeter sensors. But even she isn't fool enough to get in and not steal something unless they needed something on the computers."

"A bank?" Ellemarie said. "Please. I could be inside their computers from here in thirty minutes, and that's accounting for the language barrier. I don't speak a damned word of Casphar."

"But they didn't have you, and I doubt Melanie Coltrane has that sort of training. That's a real possibility. Would it also explain the museum job?"

"They broke into a museum?" Ellemarie asked.

"Somebody did," Alex said. "Break-ins where nothing is taken are particularly suspicious when you're trying to track covert ops."

"Museum is attached to palace," Vassily said.

"So if they needed information from the palace, that might make sense, too," Alex said.

Marco shook his head. "But this is all academic. We're not going to find them where they were. They're not going back to the bank or the museum, if it was them at all.”

“True,” Alex said. “Which is why we need to check out the Nostraspace safe house. Since they’re incommunicado, they probably decided the safe house isn’t safe, but there’s a chance they’ll be there. We have to assume it’s watched, though.”

“That’s no problem,” Marco said. “We just have to wait for nightfall.”

“That’s going to be a while, I’m afraid,” Alex said.

“Stupid planet with three-day days,” Vassily said.

“Please tell me it’s at least dark,” Marco said.

“They believe in exterior lighting here,” Alex said.

“Stupid planet with three-day days,” Marco said. “Send the info to my DSC. I’ll see what I can figure out.”

• • •

Alex went to the Casphar Imperial Museum by himself. Ellemarie had ordered a sewing machine and supplies and had taken over one of the bedrooms to design her doll. Marco was embroiled in planning his first heist of the mission. Vassily had no desire to step outside unless absolutely necessary and told Alex that repeatedly.

The museum stood right up against the public street off the back wall of the palace. It was painted red with a black icon of a two-headed bird reproduced on either side of the steel doors. The doors stood open, and Alex entered, transmitted payment for the entry fee, and stepped into the cavernous hall. His footsteps echoed on the terrazzo floor and off the ten-meter-tall walls. Tapestries hung down at odd intervals but did nothing to quiet the noise of the two other museum visitors shuffling past display cases.

Alex began to move around the museum, studying cases, looking around at the architecture itself.

After a while, the other two guests shuffled back out again, and he had the museum to himself.

He paused at one case in particular. Inside it sat a half-meter-tall black porcelain statue of the two-headed falcon that was the symbol of the Casphar family. He tipped his head and carefully examined the edges of the display case where the acrylic panels were joined together and where it met the plinth it sat on.

"Remarkable piece, is it not?" came a Casphar-accented voice from behind him.

A man stood in front of one of the tapestries, dressed in a long cape with gold embroidery throughout it. He held a scepter with the two-headed falcon carved into a crystal at its head. His dark features surrounded clear blue eyes set under black eyebrows so bushy that they touched each other and vanished behind his bangs. He wore a beard braided into three strands, a style forbidden for anyone but the emperor to wear.

Alex bowed. "Emperor Habid. A pleasure."

"It is nice to see you again, Sir Alexander. I think you were, what, fifteen last time you were here?"

"Nearly fifteen," Alex said.

The emperor strode toward Alex, his cape flaring behind him. "The two-headed falcon. Symbol of our power since the time of Casphar himself."

"And recently replaced, it looks like."

The emperor stopped on the other side of the case and nodded. "You have a good eye."

"The workers did a very good job, but I can see

where the case was forced recently. And the cracking around his talons indicates that he was fired before he was fully dried."

"They are all, of course, replicas." The emperor moved slowly around the case, his own eyes pointed at the statue, not at Alex. "When one ages or breaks, we simply make a new one. We use the original mold, of course. His next replacement is already in the family workshop, curing properly before firing."

"But why would anyone steal it?" Alex asked, also not looking up from the statue. "If it's easily replaced, and it's not ancient, what value would it have?"

The emperor looked up at Alex with his eyes, not tilting his head. "When I saw you in my museum, I was hoping you might answer that question for me."

Alex raised his eyebrows and shook his head.

The emperor folded his arms on top of the display case and leaned closer to Alex. He spoke quietly. "Our first thought was that it was the miners who have been causing trouble. They may not have realized the piece is replaceable and may have wanted to use it as the symbol of some sort of uprising. That is why we hurried the replacement into its place and announced that nothing had been taken. But nothing ever came of that. Then, we began to wonder who else would benefit from trying to destabilize our government. Who do you think would benefit from that, Sir Alexander?"

Alex turned slightly to look directly at the emperor. "I'm not a diplomat, Your Majesty. Is that a rhetorical question, or do you want my honest assessment?"

The emperor chuckled. "Honesty is something I rarely encounter in my position. Let us have that."

Alex looked back down at the falcon. "It would

depend on whether or not they had a plan to replace you. Just destabilizing your government only benefits the local opportunists. For the rest of us, that means interruptions to our supplies, price instability, all sorts of bad things.

"However, if someone were already waiting to be set up in your place, that's another matter altogether. You've got jumpgates serving worlds in all seven nations. You control most of the galaxy's mineral resources. You've got, by far, the best relationship with the nonaligned spacers. If someone could step in and control all that, it would make their nation much, much more powerful. So, in that case, who benefits? Pick any of the six of us."

The emperor nodded impassively. His jaw clenched, and then he spoke. "That was much my assessment, too. And then I saw you here, and I had to wonder, is Sir Alexander here for my scepter?"

Alex smiled broadly. "I wouldn't want it, Your Majesty."

"Which, of course, is what you would say if you were after it."

Alex nodded. "I'm here on business, I'm afraid."

The emperor rounded the display case again so he could look directly into Alex's eyes. "Can you tell me that the Don is not the one who stole my falcon?"

"I can tell you that I had no indication that he did," Alex said. "I don't think he would have told me if he had, though. But, to be completely frank, I can't imagine what he'd want with it. You've got gates at three of our worlds. If it was war he was after—and King of Earth knows I don't know why he would—it would be much faster to just send in the troops, seize your jumpgates there, and then send the army on here. But doing that would bring the wrath of the Suturiku and Ynos and probably Greekorp and Patcorp down on us. Wouldn't make sense politically."

"I am glad I do not need to explain that to you," the emperor said. He leaned forward again and whispered. "I need that falcon back, Sir Alexander. And you have a reputation for being able to get things done."

"Are you offering me a commission?"

The emperor smiled and tilted his head back. "Let's call it a goodwill gesture, from the Don to the Casphar."

"I couldn't possibly take on a job like that without asking the Don," Alex said. "And I'm pretty sure you don't want me sending a message through the jumpgate explaining the situation and asking."

The emperor laughed. "No, we certainly wouldn't want that. Don't you have secret codes you use?"

Alex cocked his head to the side. "None that you can't read, I imagine. And I suspect me suddenly deciding to write to my uncle would get everyone curious as to what I was really saying."

The emperor nodded, thin lipped, the muscles at the sides of his face tensing.

"But I can do this for you," Alex continued. "My work here has nothing to do with this statue. I can assure you that if I come across any information that might help you find it, I have no orders that would prevent me from sharing that information with you."

The emperor nodded and looked back down at the falcon. "I must admit, I do not understand why so many people have designs on my scepter."

Alex answered unhesitatingly. "Your jumpgate rates are usurious, the prices you charge for your ores are high, and the standard of living on your worlds is the lowest in the seven nations."

The emperor laughed through a clenched jaw. "Honesty. Yes, I suppose I asked for that."

Alex nodded, and the emperor pushed himself back off the display case. "You should consider becoming a diplomat, Sir Alexander," the emperor said, his voice clipped. "You seem to have the talent for it."

Alex watched as the emperor pivoted and moved back toward the tapestry. He paused and turned back to Alex. "Your uncle is among those who have complained about my pricing. He has invited me twice recently to visit Sixcrystal Station to discuss the matter privately."

"You should visit Sixcrystal Station," Alex said. "It's incredible. I'm particularly fond of the Morning Dome. The trees filter the sunlight beautifully, and the pools are clear and perfect."

"I am not convinced that if I were to go, the Don would not seek to take my scepter." Emperor Habid turned and strode the rest of the way to the tapestry. As he got there, two marines appeared from behind it, held it back for him, and allowed him to pass into a hidden doorway.

The marines then released the tapestry. It fluttered down and did nothing to disguise the click of the hidden doorway locking.

CHAPTER 4

"I met a foreign gentleman who told me he doesn't trust Nostraspace because we've got the Secret Services. I told him, 'Don't worry. The secret is that that's where the Don sends his useless relations so he can pay them to not work.'"
—Marianna Rees, comedian

The central steps in the house were steeper than anything on Polairmo. Ellemarie climbed them one step at a time. Walking stick first, then her left foot, then her right foot, until all three were on the same step. Repeat. In her opposite hand she held a doll of a shirtless blond man with a bedsheet wrapped around himself, with three long-haired heads sticking out of the bedsheet in various positions. Another step. Then one more to the landing.

She shuffled along the landing to the door of one of the third-floor bedrooms. Vassily was inside doing push-ups. "Can you teach me how to say, 'I don't speak Casphar' in Casphar?"

Vassily finished his set and sprang to his feet. He pronounced the phrase carefully for her. She repeated it. He tried twice more before he was happy with her pronunciation and nodded. "Why do you need to know?"

"I'm going to look at a factory, and I need to know how to respond if anyone speaks to me in Casphar."

Vassily grunted. "I shower. Go with you."

Ellemarie waved a hand at him and turned to shuffle out. "You don't need to guard me anymore. Where am I going to go on Reggit?"

"You are sneaky old lady and I keep eye on you."

Ellemarie shuffled back to the landing, and Vassily pulled off his clothes, revealing the double-headed falcon tattoo on his shoulder. He hurried through the shower and then dressed in distinctively Nostraspace attire of black pants, plain white shirt, and black vest. He caught up with Ellemarie just as she was about to head out the front door.

"Why we looking at factory?"

"Just keeping up appearances," Ellemarie said. "Our cover is we're supposed to be manufacturing and selling these." She held up the doll.

Vassily looked at it and began to chuckle. "Is very funny. Before I go, I think Austin Montierthski just spoiled rich kid. But this, this I would buy."

"Well, we just need to look at the places that are available and drag our feet a little, and no one will be any wiser that we're not really in business."

They headed out into the street. Ellemarie seemed to know where she was going. She turned left and shuffled down the street, Vassily keeping a half step behind her the whole way.

The factory was about three kilometers away, near a bus stop for the line that ran past the spaceport and down to the miners' dormitories on the edge of the city. It was tall, as tall as a two-story building but not built with the offset construction of most of them, except that there was a cantilevered section out over the main door.

The only windows were a line of clerestories on each side of the building, but otherwise it was just a mass of weather-beaten yellow concrete. Ellemarie

shuffled up the paved walkway and tried the front door.
It slid right open.

Inside, a small stone reception desk sat in an
unlighted anteroom. The door beyond it was shut, and
no other furniture was visible. The concrete floor
had an open cable channel along the wall, and just
inside the front door a line of symmetrical bolt holes
showed where an old security system had been removed.
Ellemarie left the front door open and crossed to the
inner door. It also slid open at her touch.

The factory floor stretched out in front of her.
Long rows of concrete tables lined the floor parallel
to the door, half of them equipped with sewing
machines identical to the one that had been delivered
to the house.

On the right wall, a railingless ramp began a
gradual ascent that went all the way along that wall,
along the back wall, and then up the left wall until
it landed in a doorway to offices overhead, with long
windows that looked down onto the factory floor. The
only light came from the lines of clerestory windows
left and right, but it made the otherwise barren room
surprisingly bright. On the far wall, an oversized
set of double doors stood closed.

As Ellemarie and Vassily stepped farther inside,
the office door at the top of the ramp above them slid
open. A dark round woman in her forties with close-
cropped black hair emerged and looked down at them.
She nodded curtly and spoke in hesitant and heavily
accented words. "Good day. I am Khadija Alsadat.
You are Nostraspace merchants?"

Ellemarie folded her hands and introduced herself.
Vassily remained silent.

Khadija spoke as she descended the ramp,
gesticulating over the floor. "Was clothing factory.

Very good. Warehouse through double doors below me.
Good access for shipping in rear. I was, how you
say, foreman before company closed. Too many clothes
on market. Too few miners with scrip, and we only
sell one company, and it had mines that ran low on
titanium."

"We're going to be producing these," Ellemarie said
and held up the four-headed doll.

Khadija stopped in her tracks and looked down
at the doll, her eyes growing wider. Then a little
"eep" escaped from her, and she ran down the rest
of the ramp and up to Ellemarie. She took the doll
in both hands and held it up to the light. "Austin
Montierthski! And ***Three Women!***"

"Exactly," Ellemarie said.

"Is good," Khadija said, turning the doll around
and around. "But fabric cut this way has much waste.
Can we make with different cuts?"

"This is just a prototype," Ellemarie said.

"This sell better than miners' clothing," Khadija
said. "Yes, you must rent factory. I be foreman."

"Aren't you working for the real estate broker?"
Ellemarie asked.

Khadija shook her head, handing the doll back to
Ellemarie. "I was foreman. No work since company
closed."

Ellemarie cocked her head and blinked. "Then what
are you doing here?"

Vassily answered. "In Casphar, it is expected that
employees remain with company."

Ellemarie's face began to flush. She turned to
Vassily. "Even if the company is out of business?"

"Yes," Vassily said. "Especially then. Loyal
employees should ensure that all that needs be done is
done, even if not paid."

Ellemarie's face went beyond flush and straight to
red. She turned on Khadija. "That's exploitation!"

Vassily tipped his head down to Ellemarie. "This
is why I leave."

Ellemarie jabbed a finger at Khadija. "Now you
listen here, young lady, when you work for me, there
will be none of that! If I stop paying you, you stop
doing anything at all for me! Is that clear?"

Khadija's eyes widened, and her jaw clenched with
terror. She nodded quickly.

Vassily leaned over Ellemarie and whispered to
Khadija. "Do not listen to her. She has never paid
me."

"You work for Alex's uncle!" Ellemarie shouted,
the finger pointing up at his chin now. Her focus came
back to Khadija. "And the sewers and other employees?
Are they all just sitting at home with no paycheck?"

Khadija nodded. "This is what we do when there is
no work."

Ellemarie's jaw set, and she stamped her walking
stick on the concrete floor. She shoved the doll back
into Khadija's hands. "I want them all back here!
Next shift. Figure out how to mass-produce those
and get everyone back to work. Top wages! Damn the
expenses!"

Khadija's jaw moved, but the only sounds that came
out were a few terrified clicks.

Ellemarie pivoted and marched around Vassily toward
the door. "Come on, Vassily! We've got to go sign
the lease."

"Thank you!" Khadija shouted as they vanished into
the reception area.

They emerged onto the street with Ellemarie still
moving at a furious march. Vassily trotted to keep
up with her. "I thought we only pretend to be in
business."

"The Don wants us undercover," Ellemarie fumed. "The Don can eat a few expenses!"

• • •

Sunset on Reggit lingered for four hours. Marco had gotten a full night's sleep before it had truly gotten dark. He showered and slipped into his stretchy blacks before descending to the ground floor.

Alex and Vassily were at the table eating while Ellemarie puttered in the kitchen. An electronic knock announced that someone was at the door.

"I got it," Marco said and headed up the short hallway to the front of the house. The front-yard monitor showed a furtive man in miner's attire holding a large paper-wrapped package in both arms.

Marco slid the door open. The man looked up at him. "Marco?" he asked, mispronouncing it.

Marco nodded. The man spoke a quick phrase in Casphar. Marco responded with a different phrase. The man looked up slightly, smirking as he gave the counter-counter phrase. Marco pulled a stack of yellow scrip out of a pocket in the small of his back and handed it to the man. The man grabbed it between two fingers and then passed the package to Marco. Marco lugged it inside, and the man slipped up the walk and into the darkest portion of the street.

"What's that?" Alex asked as Marco rejoined them with his package.

"This," Marco said, setting it down and pulling back the paper, "is a local treasure. Highly collectable. Local porn!"

The package fell open to reveal an enormous collection of photos of naked men engaging in various sex acts with each other.

Vassily stood up and peered down at it. "Fifteen years," he said.

Alex didn't stop chewing as he said, "Please tell me you didn't expense that."

Vassily waved a dismissive hand. "Is nothing. Ask Ellemarie what she spent Don's money on."

Alex paused, swallowed, and called, "Ellemarie?"

"It was an accident!" Ellemarie called back from the kitchen.

Vassily grinned. "Remember part about pretending to be in business?"

Alex called again, "Ellemarie?"

She appeared in the doorway to the kitchen. "I may have accidentally rented a factory, hired sixty-five women, and started mass production on the dolls."

Alex buried his face in his hand, fork sticking up like a flag of surrender.

Vassily wasn't done gloating. "She is using Don's money to shore up local economy."

"Isn't this how you got into trouble with the Don in the first place?" Alex asked through his hand.

"That was completely different." Ellemarie pulled herself up to her full height. "That was stealing. This time I'm just using his expense account for a high-risk investment without his knowledge or consent."

All the air escaped from Alex's lungs.

"It's part of the cover," Ellemarie insisted.

"King of Earth," Alex muttered. He uncovered his face and looked at the ceiling. "What do I know? With the reaction the locals have been having to the idea, it may even make money."

"See?" Marco said. "This is nothing."

Alex narrowed his eyes at him. "Don't you have a house to burgle?"

• • •

Marco left the house by the door into the backyard. He pulled the back of his collar, bringing a hood

up over his head, and then down across his face. He
slipped on a pair of black gloves, and no skin was
left showing. He put his hands on the top of the back
wall and in one silent hop was atop it in a crouch.
He went on all fours along the wall like a monkey,
crossing multiple neighbors' back walls until he came
to the end of the block, where he hopped down.

Streetlights illuminated him on the sidewalk, even
though he made no appreciable sound in his movements.
He slipped out into the middle of the dirt street
where it was darker and made off toward the older part
of town.

His path took him zigzagging through the city, once
diving into the shadow provided by a public restroom
on the corner to avoid the lights of an oncoming mine
transport. He finally stopped in front of an ordinary
one-story house in a rundown neighborhood. He checked
around, then dashed past the streetlight on the
sidewalk and up onto the property's perimeter wall.
He scampered across it and then leapt onto the roof of
the house.

Streetlights were bright enough that his silhouette
was clearly visible. He pressed himself down flat and
waited as a group of passersby went boisterously past.
Then he shimmied along the roof to the back of the
house and hung his head off.

The security shutters were all closed. No lights
were on in the backyard. He shifted his body around
and rolled off the roof, landing on his feet a meter
away from the back door.

He extracted a flat square device from the pocket
in the small of his back and pressed it against the
door. It lit up with a faint amber glow and lines
crisscrossed on its face. He manipulated the lines
with his fingers for a moment, and then the lock on the

door released. He powered off the device and tucked
it back into his pocket, slipping inside the house.

The back door opened into a long hallway lined
with doors. He shut the back door, plunging himself
back into pitch darkness. A pinspot turned on around
his neck, providing a tiny shaft of light by which he
checked his progress up the hall, pausing to inspect
each room he passed.

Finally, he stepped into the front room, and the
lights in the house came on. Marco had already taken
off the hood, and now he turned off the light around
his neck.

He first went up the short hallway to the front
door. He turned on the house security system and
brought up the history. He deleted the most recent
activity and then began reviewing the next oldest
footage. In it, a group of police officers escorted by
two marines walked down the front walkway, away from
the house.

The previous file showed three figures rushing out
of the house using both doors—a slender female figure
going over the back wall, the other two heading out
the unlighted front door into the night. All the
earlier files showed routine deliveries.

Marco switched off the system and began a
centimeter-by-centimeter search of the house,
starting in the front with the kitchen. He opened
every cabinet, pressing at the walls behind them,
checking under shelves and countertops, switching
on appliances, tapping on the floors, climbing up and
inspecting behind lighted ceiling panels, testing the
ductwork. When he was done, he repeated the procedure
in the front hallway. In the main room, he started
with a nearby chair, disassembling it piece by piece
and then reassembling it. Each piece of furniture

in the room then got the same treatment. The main
entertainment screen pulled away from the wall to
reveal a hollow cavity behind it, dusty except for
a clean rectangle pressed all the way against the
exterior concrete, the nub of a power jack extruding
from the base of the cavity in the middle of the clean
spot. Marco closed the compartment and continued with
the ceiling and ducts.

The bedrooms were empty except for a bed in each.
Closets were bare and clean. Marco checked each with
the same thoroughness as he had used on the front of
the house.

He checked the back hallway last, ending at the
back door. As he finished checking the last ceiling
tile, a foot pressed against each wall to keep himself
a meter up off the floor, he put it back together and
then dropped to the floor. He wiped his brow, looked
around, and said, "Well, shit."

· · ·

Marco reentered the house through the back door
silently. Alex called from the front room. "How did
it go?"

"How did you hear me?" Marco dumped his gloves and
emptied his pocket onto the floor.

"I'm that good," Alex called back.

Marco walked into the main room, where Alex was
seated on the couch with the house tablet on his lap.
"It's been cleaned out," Marco said. "Completely.
Police and military were there. The open-channel
message encoding device has been removed, so we should
assume that the Casphar are reading any coded messages
going through their jumpgates."

"Well, we haven't sent any," Alex said without
looking up, "and we weren't planning to."

"Yeah, but it would be nice to be able to send a coded message telling the Don that the code is compromised," Marco said, flopping down onto the floor next to his porn pile.

Alex muted the tablet screen and looked over at Marco. "Nothing that could have been a message?"

"The only dust I found was in the secret encoder compartment. Nothing that wasn't built in or basic furniture left. That clean."

"Did you check the yard, too?"

"No obvious loose dirt," Marco said. "And it's overlooked by other houses, and there's a fair bit of light even with the yard lights off, so I doubt they'd have risked that. I sure wasn't going to."

Alex grimaced. He set down the tablet on the couch beside him. "I'm out of leads. Any thoughts?"

Marco dropped onto his side, using his porn as a pillow. "I opened one of the front security shutters before I left. If they're checking the house periodically to see if anyone moves in, they'll at least see someone was there."

"Same with the Casphar," Alex said.

"Yeah, which is why we shouldn't be spending much time there."

Alex stood up and moved to the front door, activating the security system long enough to set the front door to "Sleeping Occupants" mode. He came back and looked down at Marco in a heap on the floor. "Get some sleep. We'll think of something."

• • •

Night on Reggit also lasted three days. Business continued as usual. By the following day, Alex had taken to having the four of them take regular walks together, dressed in their most distinctly Nostraspace

clothes, through the commercial districts. They ate in
fine restaurants at least one meal per day. They spent
money.

Six weeks passed.

It was early in the night cycle when Alex gathered
them again for "Operation Conspicuous."

The commercial district had no roads at the front
of the shops, only wide, brightly lit sidewalks. A
large fountain gurgled ostentatiously at the center
of the district, and there was typically a street
performer or two out playing music or performing
tricks. There was also always a large population of
out-of-work miners out asking for handouts.

Alex, Marco, Ellemarie, and Vassily snaked their
way through the crowd of panhandlers, ignoring them
all, and marched up to the front of a store. A huge
line of merchants and miners stood waiting to get into
it. A sign in the front window proclaimed in three
languages, "We have the Austin Montierthski doll!"

Ellemarie smirked as Alex shook his head.

They went on to the theater, where they took in
a show about the glorious Casphar I, who built the
jumpgates, personally colonized all the inhabited
worlds in the galaxy, saved Old Earth from starvation,
married the King of Earth, and then transcended into a
being of light.

On the way back to the house, the line at the store
had grown even longer.

They had been home about half an hour when the
electronic knock announced someone was at the door.
Marco had been in the middle of a rant about "didactic
and erroneous propaganda theatre" but stopped mid-
sentence, brow furrowing.

Alex was closest, so he made for the front door,
tapping on the screen to see who was out there.

A disheveled miner, his head down, stood there wiping his hands on his pants and shuffling his feet nervously.

Alex activated the safety catch so the door couldn't open enough to admit anyone and spoke to the miner in Casphar.

"I followed you from the commercial district," the miner whispered. "How do you want to play this?"

Alex stared.

The miner looked up, revealing a grimy face with a matted beard.

Alex's face didn't change. He inclined his chin slightly, a vague standoffish air about it.

He released the safety catch and slid the door open, then stepped back and admitted the miner.

Ellemarie and Vassily sat on the couch, looking up curiously. Marco still stood by the table where he had been pacing. Alex led the miner into the main room.

"Team, I'd like to introduce all of you to Dale Carsoni."

CHAPTER 5

"In every family, someone is ugly."
—Casphar proverb

Dale Carsoni sat on one of the chairs from the dining table with his legs crossed. "I haven't had any contact with the rest of my team," he said. "The one time I went to our prearranged drop, the undercover surveillance was so obvious that I just kept moving. I'm assuming that means at least one of them has been captured, because I don't know how they'd know to be staking it out if they hadn't caught one of us waiting there. If it's Kiera, she's most likely in the 'high value' wing of the prison, but I have no way to check that."

Ellemarie grabbed the house tablet off the wall. "I'll see what I can find."

Dale grimaced. "Melanie is Kon, so unless they know we were working together, if she's been caught she's probably in with general population or has been deported to Patcorp."

"She would have reported in if she was deported," Alex said from his seat on the couch.

Dale nodded. "And she's a damned good operative, so she's less likely to have been caught."

"Cyber security is pretty good," Ellemarie said. "This is going to take a while."

"Don't do anything traceable," Alex said.

"I never do."

Alex gave her a sidelong look.

Ellemarie grinned. "You have no idea how long it took the Don to catch me." She went back to work.

Marco had taken a chair at the table and leaned on both elbows. "If she's there, can't we just leave her?"

"Orders are to retrieve the whole team," Alex reminded him.

"And I get the distinct impression that she's the one the Don wants back," Dale said. "He resisted when I told him I wanted her on my team."

Alex looked back at Dale. "What went wrong?"

"Our mission proved a little higher profile than we were led to believe it was," Dale said. "The entire empire went on alert. Our simple exit strategy wasn't going to work. Then we caught someone tailing Kiera, and we realized the safehouse was compromised. We decided our best bet was to scatter and wait for things to cool down. They haven't."

Alex folded his arms. "I had an interesting conversation with Emperor Habid. He's looking for a statue of a two-headed falcon."

Dale's eyes moved to look at Alex, but otherwise he remained motionless. "Need-to-know," he said.

Alex shrugged one shoulder. "My orders are to retrieve you, not to finish your job for you."

"Bringing it back with me is my job," Dale said.

"And the bank?" Alex asked.

Dale's eyes flashed, and then a smile followed. "You figured out the bank was us but didn't figure out what we were doing there."

Alex arched both eyebrows and shook his head.

Dale laughed, a surprisingly high laugh. "That's where my high-value items are being stored."

Alex stared.

"Wait—" Marco said.

Ellemarie looked up from her tablet. "You broke into the bank to put something into it?"

Dale sawed the air with his hand and took a little bow.

"Is gutsy," Vassily said from his perch in the corner.

"We hired some local muscle," Dale said. "Told them the bank had some Nostraspace bullion we were after, and they could have whatever scrip we liberated."

Vassily scoffed, "Is no such thing as Nostraspace bullion."

"Exactly," Dale said. "If any of them were dumb enough to get themselves caught, the story of working for Nostraspace agents would sound totally made up. Turns out they were all dumb enough to get themselves caught."

"I wondered if you'd called the police yourself," Alex said.

Dale ignored him and went on. "We tunneled in, and Kiera and I went through. She opened the next vault and opened a vacant safe deposit box. We put the goods inside, locked it again, closed the vault, and went back to our muscle looking frustrated and upset. We told them we'd come up empty, and they could help themselves to the scrip. We were gone several hours before the police showed up."

"Well, it should be safe there," Alex said. "People aren't exactly lining up to rent safe deposit boxes there at the moment."

"Somewhat," Dale said. "It's only a matter of time until the Casphar decide to block-by-block the city, and I don't know what kind of range they can detect it at."

"Wait," Marco said, "is this detector a little box

with two blue wands?"

Dale's eyebrows went up. "That would make sense. Why?"

"They searched the ship we were on inbound." Marco stood up. "They were using it on the display cases in the ship's exhibition center. If that's what it is, the range can't be very good, because he went right up to each case."

"That'll buy us some time unless they figure out to search the bank," Dale said, "which is only a matter of time if they've actually got Kiera."

"We're not responsible for your loot," Alex reminded him.

"Your orders are to bring me home, and I'm not leaving without it."

"I believe," Alex said precisely, "that the Don's exact words were 'kicking and screaming.'"

Dale uncrossed his legs and leaned forward. "You wouldn't dare."

Alex leaned forward, too. "I outrank you."

"Only in the Secret Services," Dale said. "I outrank you in the family. I'm fifth in the line of succession."

"Are you really expecting a wartime succession? Two plans. You're 17th," Alex said.

"I thought wartime succession was just a ceremonial thing," Marco said. "I mean, like, war."

"It is," Alex said. "Keep that plan first so everyone knows you're ready and won't ever start it. Wartime succession has never happened."

"Seventeenth still outranks thirty-third!" Dale barked.

"But this isn't a family operation," Alex said coldly. "And I'm Capo on my mission."

Dale stood up and moved toward Alex. "And I'm Capo

on mine. I'll be a lot easier to remove if you work with me."

Alex cocked his head to one side. "What does the Don want with a two-headed falcon?"

Dale swatted at the air and paced off to the side. "I've got no fucking idea."

"Emperor Habid thinks its absence is destabilizing the entire empire."

Dale nodded, looking at the ceiling. "Yes, that would be why we underestimated its value. I walked into this with insufficient information."

"A lot of that going around," Ellemarie growled from behind the tablet.

Dale rounded to look directly at Alex. "I. Have. Orders."

"So. Do. I."

"And they're not incompatible," Dale said through his teeth.

The two family members glared at each other.

Marco broke the silence, sitting back down as he spoke. "May I suggest that we can't go anywhere without Kiera and Melanie anyway, so we can take some time to examine the situation and determine if we can safely rob the bank a second time?"

The cousins both backed down.

"It won't be easy," Alex said. "They learned from your first break-in and upped security significantly."

"Anything Kiera can do, I can do better," Marco said with a grin.

"No risks!" Alex said, jabbing a finger at him.

"It'll be flawless," Marco said with a dismissive wave.

"How are you going to do it?" Dale asked.

Marco winked at Dale. "No clue."

• • •

Dale returned to the miners' dormitory to sleep. Alex ordered everyone a local pocket communicator so they could stay in touch without sending messages through the deep-space network. After breakfast, Alex, Ellemarie, and Vassily went to the factory on an inspection.

There was a new receptionist, a dark-skinned woman who wore a traditional headscarf. She challenged them in Casphar as they entered.

"No, no, no!" came Khadija's voice from the factory floor. She raced into the anteroom. "These are owners. Very important people."

The new receptionist bowed her head and smiled. "Most... honored," she said, barely pronouncing the words right.

"Come!" Khadija said. "You must see! Factory cannot keep up with orders!"

She led them through, and sure enough, every table was in use, with eighty women frantically producing Austin Montierthski dolls. She laughed and waved her hands. "See! We even have orders from outside empire now. Greekorp also think doll is funny. Orders from Station Alpha. Oh, forgive." She turned and folded her hands and bowed to Alex. "Khadija Alsadat. Mrs., she."

"Alexander Romano-Bennetti. Sir Alexander, he."

Khadija's eyes narrowed slightly, and she leaned back. "Romano? Don Llewellyn Romano is relative?"

Ellemarie tensed.

Alex nodded. "My uncle."

"Ha!" Khadija exclaimed. "No wonder you have such good investment. We should make Don dolls!"

Alex smiled slightly. "He wouldn't think it was funny. And you'd need a lot more than three women."

• • •

Alex went alone to his next destination. He had scrapped Operation Conspicuous and changed into typical Casphar merchant wear.

The six main terminals each had oversized signs with the name of the empire that operated out of them, each name lighted brilliantly either with letters that glowed themselves or bright spotlights that illuminated them. Farther afield, clusters of smaller terminals, most of them rundown and older, skirted the edges. Ships of various shapes and sizes ascended and descended. Spherical cargo pods were hoisted to and from orbit by small drones. Alex jumped on one of the moving sidewalks and headed for one of the larger outlying buildings.

It was little more than a long, squat arch with massive hangar doors on one end of it. The doors were open and light streamed out of it, overpowering the moderate glow that persisted across the entirety of the landing sites.

Six small freighters sat inside, each beat up and showing signs of age in different ways. Tables stood among the ships, and wares from various worlds stood on them. Crowds of mostly merchants shuffled through the makeshift market, some bartering, some offering scrip, and others using the seven nations' currencies stored in collars, sleeves, and pocket devices. The merchants were of every ethnic stock imaginable, and some were unique mixes of different ethnicities. Their clothing came from every empire and were mixed haphazardly.

Alex spoke Casphar with the merchants. One happily showed him toys, including Austin Montierthski with ***Three Women!*** at a vastly inflated price. Another shooed him away.

Finally, a squat man at a quiet stall that sold exotic plants sized him up and switched languages. "What you ask for is expensive, Nostraboy."

Alex smiled and answered in Casphar.

"What you ask for is risky, Nostraboy," the merchant said. "Nobody here would break the law like that."

Alex switched to another language. The merchant started when he heard it.

"How many languages do you speak, Nostraboy?"

"I have a master's degree in linguistics," Alex answered, "and a second one in history."

The merchant laughed heartily. "Me? I have a degree in 'fly my damned spaceship any damn place I please!' and I like that a lot better. And I probably still speak as many languages as you do!"

"I don't doubt it," Alex said. He switched languages again, and he and the merchant spoke in hushed tones.

• • •

Ellemarie grimaced and plugged the house tablet back into the wall. She looked at Vassily. "We need to go out."

Vassily sat at the table, chewing on the end of a loaf of bread. "Problem?"

"It looks like the Casphar government has a firewall around residential addresses that I can't get through," Ellemarie said, putting on her cape and collecting her walking stick from where it stood by the kitchen. "I'm going to need to get in through a government building in order to get the information we need."

"We cannot use government building computer stations," Vassily said, taking another bite.

"Well, no, we can't legally," Ellemarie said. "But little old ladies can get away with things. Are you coming?"

Vassily grumbled, set down the last of the bread, and rose to follow her.

They headed out into the street. Sunrise was only a few hours away, and the sky had begun to glow with a purplish twilight. It was approaching shift-change time, and mine transports rattled along the street, laden with miners who had been lucky enough to get shifts.

"I am thinking," Vassily said. "It is not unusual for out-of-work miners work in house to cook and clean."

"You want a maid?" Ellemarie asked, not breaking her stride.

"I wonder if Alex want to hire Dale Carsoni."

Ellemarie slowed to a stop. Her shoulders began to tremble. She screwed up her face for a moment, but eventually couldn't hold back the laughter. She stood on the sidewalk, cackling, for a good thirty seconds.

"You have a brilliantly evil mind," she said at last. "Be sure to suggest that to Alex."

"It makes sense," Vassily said. "Keep him close without arousing suspicion."

Ellemarie started walking again. "You don't need to convince me. I just want to be there to see the Don's face when he reads the report."

Vassily grinned, and they continued down to the nearest street where they could catch a tram to the spaceport.

The tram was crowded with spaceport workers, including the woman who had rented them their house. She recognized Ellemarie and shifted back a car to sit by them. She made small talk about the neighborhoods

and the availability of domestic help the whole way
there.

The spaceport bustled with more activity than
usual. Tenders were descending like a plague of
locusts into two terminals.

Security checkpoints had been set up at the mouth
of each terminal. Marines with oversized guns stood
by impassively as police ordered every traveler to
open their bags for inspection. At each checkpoint,
someone in a blue government uniform that was neither
marine nor police stood with a small scanner like the
one they had seen used on *Anerchomeno Asteri*. It was
waved over bags and even people whose clothing had
enough room to conceal items before anyone was allowed
to pass.

Ellemarie and Vassily stood and watched the scene
at the entrance to the main Nostraspace terminal, both
with a practiced look of indifference on their faces.

Finally, Ellemarie turned away from the scene and
headed into one of the shops on the concourse between
terminals, this one selling the sort of items that
were only purchased by people who needed to prove to
suspicious spouses that they had really gone someplace
as unappealing as Reggit. Every item in it had
either a picture of the planet or the name in several
scripts.

An onslaught of passengers coming out of the
Greekorp terminal indicated that security was checking
incoming passengers as well. Ellemarie watched from
behind a line of drinking glasses as a wave of grumpy-
looking passengers went by.

Finally, pressing her collar to check the time, she
nodded to Vassily. Her movements became more frail
than before, and she shuffled carelessly toward the
real estate rental office. The woman from the tram

was organizing pictures of available properties behind the glass wall in front. Ellemarie shuffled up to the door, Vassily hanging a few feet behind her as another wave of passengers came out of the Greekorp terminal and moved between them.

Ellemarie leaned in the door. "Excuse me, I hate to trouble you, but—"

A bloodcurdling scream stopped her short.

A tall, blonde woman of no more than eighteen threw her bag down by the door to the Greekorp terminal and charged at Vassily.

Vassily had both hands up, palms outward, to defend himself before she got to him.

She ran headlong into his chest and stomped on his foot with her boot. Vassily backed up a step and placed his hands on her shoulders.

She screamed again and shouted something that may have been a sentence in Casphar or may have been incoherent ramblings. She clenched both hands into fists and started hitting his sides, using a series of exclamations that didn't require a linguist to identify as curses.

The real estate agent dashed past Ellemarie and over to the fray. Other bystanders had instinctively moved back and formed a ring around Vassily and the young woman.

Ellemarie checked all around herself, and then moved like a sprite into the office and behind the real estate agent's desk.

The young woman was now kicking as well as hitting. Vassily had extended his arms to their full length, still holding her, so the blows were all glancing.

The young woman roared and spat onto his chest.

Ellemarie tapped on the real estate agent's keyboard.

The real estate agent stood with her back to her
office, holding out both hands toward the young woman,
speaking soothingly to her.

Another roar from the young woman turned into sobs.

Ellemarie, glancing up at regular intervals, typed
with the grace and speed of a professional.

The young woman collapsed in a heap at Vassily's
feet. The real estate agent knelt beside her.

Ellemarie consulted her DSC, checked the scene
outside, then typed some more.

Vassily spoke for the first time, his tone soft.
The young woman was not placated, however. She
responded with another roar. She jerked her head
up violently, the back of her scalp connecting with
Vassily's chin. He grunted and swooned.

The young woman ripped herself out of his grip.
Pressing her advantage, she jumped up, stomped on his
foot again, and then brought a knee into his groin.

Vassily roared and crumpled.

The real estate agent grabbed at the young woman
from behind but missed.

Ellemarie typed faster.

Vassily, gasping, face red, pulled himself straight
and rose to his feet, snarling at the young woman. He
spoke three angry words.

The young woman spat again.

Two of the police officers staffing the Greekorp
terminal doorway moved toward the fracas with no sign
of urgency.

Ellemarie typed a tiny bit more, then swiped across
the screen several times.

The police officers stepped in between Vassily
and the woman, speaking to each of them with calm
detachment.

Ellemarie rose and dashed back to the doorway.

The real estate agent backed off. She stood for a few seconds, watching, and then looked back over her shoulder. Ellemarie had resumed her frail, motionless pose by the time the agent's gaze fell on her.

One of the police officers coaxed the young woman away from Vassily.

Vassily looked up from the police officer he was speaking to and said something that sounded kind to the young woman.

She charged at him again, but the police officer caught her.

The second police officer touched Vassily's elbow and motioned for the nearest exit. Vassily pivoted, taking the lead, and headed out of the concourse with the second police officer following.

The young woman was sobbing again as the first police officer led her back to her bag, which she collected.

The real estate agent returned and came directly to Ellemarie. "Apologies."

"Oh, that's quite all right," Ellemarie said. "Whatever was that about?"

"Family disagreement," the agent said. "You were about to ask?"

"Yes," Ellemarie said, her voice dropping to a whisper. "You see, one of my employees is having... marital difficulties. I was just curious if you also lease trade-class housing, just in case."

The real estate agent folded her hands in front of her mouth. "That is... difficult on Reggit," she whispered. "Difficult to get permission to rent to divorce. But... it can be done."

"Thank you," Ellemarie mouthed. She waved and excused herself with a bit less shuffle than before.

The young woman who had attacked Vassily was on

the floor again, hugging her bag, crying. The police officer stood over her, looking bored.

Ellemarie shuffled back out of the concourse and found Vassily and the second officer just finishing up. The officer took one last note on his tablet, nodded, and went back inside. Vassily's jaw clenched tightly as he looked around and spotted Ellemarie. He strode over to her.

"Family disagreement?" Ellemarie asked.

"Is nothing," Vassily said.

"Well, I'd like to thank that young woman," Ellemarie said. "That distraction was better than any excuses I could have come up with. Do you know how to get in touch with her?"

Vassily glared. "We finished?"

"Not quite," Ellemarie said, her voice going stern and flat, her posture becoming erect. "When I went to work for the Don, I swore to follow orders just like you did, and my orders are to report everything accurately and completely. Who was that?"

Vassily stared.

Ellemarie's expression didn't change.

"You are dangerous old lady," Vassily mumbled.

Ellemarie held her gaze on him.

Vassily exhaled sharply. "My daughter. She was nine when I left. I do not know how she learned I am here."

Ellemarie nodded. Then her posture shifted and she became Ellemarie again. "We'll figure out what we're going to tell Alex."

They walked home, Ellemarie pausing every few blocks to let Vassily catch up. They got home just as the first rays of sunrise crested the horizon.

• • •

Vassily sat nursing tea and eggs at the table while Ellemarie sat on the couch with the house tablet. Neither spoke.

Marco padded silently down the stairs.

Without looking up, Ellemarie spoke. "I think the bank job is probably off."

Marco looked at the bottoms of his feet. "Am I getting noisy in my old age?" Marco asked. "You and Alex can both hear me when I think I'm not making any noise."

"Consider it supernatural," Ellemarie said.

Marco slipped into the kitchen and emerged with a plate of eggs. "What's the problem with the bank job?"

"New security at the spaceport," Ellemarie said. "They're checking every bag with those scanners we saw on *Asteri*. Assuming they detect whatever it is Dale Carsoni stole, there's no way we're getting it off-planet."

"Hmm," Marco said and sat down across from Vassily. "What happened to you?"

Vassily started. "I am uninjured. How you know?"

Marco smirked. "Consider it supernatural."

Ellemarie answered for him. "Let's just say he discovered the perfect distraction, and we'll never get to use it again. There!" She pointed to the screen. "It works!"

Vassily turned. "You in?"

"Well, not in, but through the firewall," Ellemarie said. "The computer in the real estate office acts as a relay. It piggybacks whatever I'm doing on legitimate traffic that's allowed to cross the firewall, and then it does its work on the spaceport's network. It's laggy, but it's working."

The front door opened, and Alex entered carrying a

long brown package.

"Oooh, what did you get me?" Marco asked.

"All of us," Alex said, setting it down on the floor and pulling the wrapper off. An aluminum box inside was held shut with a combination lock. Alex keyed in a nine-digit code, and the top tilted up. Alex reached in and pulled out a Casphar-issue automatic assault rifle.

Vassily's eyes widened. "Where did you find?"

Alex handed him the rifle. "A good Secret Services officer can always find the black market." He came up with a slender but long handgun next, holding it out to Marco. "Your weapon of choice, I believe."

Marco smiled and took the handgun. "You know me so well!"

Alex pulled out a heavy semiautomatic weapon for himself. "We keep them in the house, hidden at all times. They're for if things go bad and we're shooting our way out, and only for if things go bad and we're shooting our way out. Is that clear?"

"Nothing for me?" Ellemarie asked.

"You're still on probation," Alex said, pulling a bundle of holsters and straps out of the case before closing it.

"You are dangerous enough with cane," Vassily said.

"So what did I miss?" Alex asked, a tinge of suspicion in his voice as he handed a shoulder strap to Vassily and a holster to Marco.

"I was just trying to get that out of them," Marco said.

Ellemarie quickly recounted the new security at the spaceport.

Alex nodded. "That settles it. Unless we can get a great price on a private yacht, there's no way we're risking it. That bird stays right where it is, and

Dale can negotiate with the Don if he's allowed to come back for it later."

Silence came over them. Ellemarie poked at the tablet. Vassily chewed. Marco examined the mechanism of his handgun.

"So what are you leaving out?" Alex asked.

"Vassily had a great idea." Ellemarie set the tablet aside and looked directly at Alex. "We need a maid."

"There is no way—" Alex began.

"On Reggit," Vassily said, "domestic work is done by out-of-work miners."

"We are not giving access to this house to any outsiders," Alex said firmly.

Vassily nodded and smiled. "Dale Carsoni is out-of-work miner."

Alex opened his mouth. He said nothing. He closed his mouth and went upstairs smiling.

Marco looked back and forth between Ellemarie and Vassily. "That was nicely played."

Ellemarie smirked and picked up her tablet. Vassily took another bite of eggs.

Marco set down the gun and folded his arms. "You're really not going to tell me, are you?"

Vassily smirked. "Need-to-know."

• • •

Dale Carsoni began reporting to the house daily, carrying cleaning supplies most days. When there were packages that needed delivering, he went out and picked them up.

On the first of the month, he accompanied Ellemarie and Vassily to the factory, carrying the box that contained the payroll.

It was late afternoon, the sunlight cutting a

slanted path across the front of the factory, shining brightly on the front door. When they opened it, their shadows stretched dramatically across the far wall.

Khadija stood by the reception desk waiting for them. She smiled broadly. "We have order from Node. One thousand units. Fad does not die, it spreads."

Ellemarie nodded approvingly. "We're going to have to keep our eyes on the news, though. ***Three Women!*** won't keep selling like this forever."

Khadija shook her head but smirked. Then she gesticulated at the ceiling. ***"Three Women!"***

Ellemarie took the cash box from Dale and handed it to Khadija. Khadija handed Ellemarie a small optical disc, which she pocketed.

"Thank you," Ellemarie said. "You're all doing amazing work."

Khadija smiled. "If all employers respected employees, all employees would do good work." She turned and headed onto the factory floor.

The receptionist handed Dale a small piece of shipping paper as they turned to leave. Dale glanced at it as he moved to the door. He jumped, expression going blank, and then stopped.

Ellemarie and Vassily exited, but Dale didn't follow. He turned back to the reception desk. The receptionist didn't look up from her work. He took her tablet and typed something onto it quickly.

Outside, Ellemarie and Vassily had stopped on the porch and were turned back, waiting for Dale. He slipped out of the factory quickly, letting the door slide shut behind him.

"Sorry," he said. "Unavoidable. Let's walk." He hurried up the path to the sidewalk.

Ellemarie and Vassily exchanged a glance and then

followed.

Dale looked both ways and then started across the street. Ellemarie and Vassily flanked him.

"I'm going to need to stay at the house a little longer than usual today," Dale said. He handed Ellemarie the piece of shipping paper.

It had a note scrawled on it: IT'S ME!

Ellemarie passed it to Vassily, whose brow screwed up as he looked at it.

Dale looked all around himself again as they got onto the sidewalk on the other side of the street. "The receptionist is Melanie Coltrane."

Chapter 6

"Not only after two or three centuries, but in a million years, life will still be as it was. Life does not change. It remains forever, following its own laws, which do not concern us, or which, at any rate, you will never find out."

    —Anonymous ancient drama from document AB9-11524, translated by Julian Zapad

Melanie Coltrane had taken off the headscarf, removed the prosthetic that changed the shape of her nose, and removed the cream that lightened her skin. She sat in the main room of the house looking exactly like her ID photo.

"I figured that the Nostraspace investors throwing money around the city were either here looking for us or would eventually attract Dale's attention, so the only logical course of action I could take was to be as close to you as I could."

Alex paced behind her. "And you've been under our noses for more than a month."

Melanie turned her head around to look up at him. "With no preestablished recognition codes, I couldn't be sure you weren't on the up and up, especially with the business doing as well as it was."

Alex stopped pacing and folded his arms. "So what went wrong?"

Melanie shook her head. "Huh-uh. I report to the Don and to him." She pointed at Dale, who sat on the couch with Ellemarie and Vassily.

Alex glared.

"You can report to all of us," Dale said.

Melanie nodded. "I was picked up for loitering at the prearranged location. They didn't have anything to hold me on, but when governments are twitchy and there's a Kon around, we get picked up. Even on Ko."

"Have you heard from Kiera at all?" Dale asked.

Melanie shook her head. "I imagine that if she did show up, she went invisible once she saw the police had me."

Alex threw his hands up. "I don't suppose there's any chance she's working for me already, too?"

Melanie let a chuckle escape. "Not unless she's a lot better at sewing than I think she is."

"She'd have herself sewn to the fabric before she made the first seam," Marco said from where he lay on the floor behind the table, both feet up on a chair.

"The disadvantage," Melanie said, "of making yourself the company that everyone on Reggit wants to work for, is that it's damned hard to get a job there. The only way I got in was by admitting I'm multilingual, and boy did that take some explaining. My daddy was a Patcorp merchant, and I decided to teach myself standard Interstellar so I could talk to him if he ever came back."

Ellemarie and Vassily tensed slightly, but either no one noticed or no one cared to comment.

"Are you out legally?" Alex asked, pausing his pacing.

"Yes," Melanie said. "They eventually packed me onto a freighter headed back to Patcorp space. That crew, as you can imagine, wasn't terribly invested in taking me back to Ko, so they were just as happy to let me walk back off again."

"Patcorp is a good sign," Alex said. "That means they couldn't break through your cover, at least."

"The Kon features and accent help," Melanie said. "And it means that once we retrieve our package, I shouldn't have any trouble getting passage as long as we're willing to risk going through Patcorp space."

"We're not retrieving the package," Alex said.

"Of course we are," Dale said.

"We're not," Alex said. "Security at the spaceport is making the Suturiku look lax. Every bag is being checked for your package."

"I can't afford another screwup on my record," Dale hissed at Alex. "It took me ten years to get over the last one."

"We. Can't. Get. It. Through. The. Spaceport," Alex said.

"So we'll book with a nonaligned spacer," Dale said.

"And which of them are you going to trust?" Alex moved over to one of the chairs and sat down, facing Dale. "Unless we've got an operative here, we'd have to assume that they'd sell us out to the highest bidder, and I'm willing to bet that's going to be Emperor Habid. What *I* should be doing is telling him exactly where he can find his package."

"That would tell him that the stories about Nostraspace operatives being behind it are all true," Dale said. "At the very least we can't leave it in the bank vault. They'll find it eventually. And when they do, they'll connect the dots, and the Don will have some explaining to do."

"True," Vassily commented.

Dale waved a finger at Alex. "And you can't afford

that, either. Half the family already thinks you're
a waste of space. You land something like that on the
Don's lap—"

Ellemarie arched an eyebrow. "I was told I have a
competent Capo."

"These two," Vassily said, "not competent."

Alex leaned toward Ellemarie. "You do."

"Alex takes orders from no one but the Don," Dale
explained. "In the family, that means you're vying
to be Don someday. But Alex also has absolutely no
ambition. Consensus is that he's just that stupid.
And if and when they find that thing in the vault,
you'll see who the family decides who the screwup is."

"So then what I should do," Alex said, "is have
Marco steal it out of that bank, then break back into
the museum and put it back where it belongs."

"Second part is easy," Marco said.

Dale flushed, looked down, and then off to the side.
"I'd rather hold off on the second part until we're
sure we can't actually get it off-planet, but yes,
even that would be preferable."

Alex shook his head. "This is beyond the scope of
my orders. My orders are to bring the three of you
home. That's it. And the fact that you're now both
working for me makes that nice and easy to do with a
simple ticket on a spaceliner."

Ellemarie looked at Vassily and then cocked her
head to look through the table at Marco. "The problem
is that the new security system knows when the vault
has been breached, right?" she asked. "The safe
deposit box is no problem?"

"Which means that even though I can probably get in
and out of the safe deposit box before the police can
get there," Marco said to the ceiling, "we're still
cutting it close for making a clean getaway."

Ellemarie looked at Vassily again. "I think I can fix that."

Dale sat up straight and turned to look at her.

Alex glared.

• • •

It was the tail end of twilight when Alex, Marco, Ellemarie, and Vassily arrived in front of the bank, Ellemarie pulling a wheeled aluminum container that was about a meter tall and half a meter wide and deep.

The bank director swept out of her glass office and up to them as soon as they entered the building. "My dear friends," she said, "it is pleasure to see you, of course. What can I do for you?"

Alex looked around. "It's a confidential matter."

She motioned them into her office. Alex and Ellemarie took the same seats they had occupied when they opened the account. Marco and Vassily hovered in the back. The director verified the door was closed, circled around behind her desk, tapped her computer screen three times, then said, "It is secure."

Alex nodded. "We've become concerned recently about corporate espionage. We didn't take many precautions because we figured in our line of work..." He shrugged.

The director smiled and nodded. "Yes, success has been unprecedented."

"Well, we've been storing sketches and prototypes in our house, but until we can improve security there, we're wondering if you've got a safe deposit box large enough to hold the contents of this." Alex tapped Ellemarie's case.

"I believe yes," the director said. She turned back to her computer, tapped the screen, and consulted it. "Yes. I will rent to you now."

"It's very important that no one be able to get visual records of these," Alex said. "I'm sure your employees are generally trustworthy, but we would prefer no one in the vault with us except you, and we're going to have to insist that any cameras in the vault be turned off while we're in there."

"In-vault camera is always off when bank open," the director said with a wave. "And, of course, I handle bank's key for you, our most important clients."

Alex nodded. "That should work very nicely for us, then."

The director nodded, tapped at the screen a few times, then rose and went out into the back room of the bank. She emerged a moment later. "Your key. Box 351."

Alex took the key and rose.

"You place in now?" the director asked.

Alex nodded, and she led the way across the bank, through an open door that had an impressive-looking ring of piston locks around it, and to the interior vault. The manager placed her hand on a black panel beside the steel vault door. The panel buzzed, and the vault door released. She stepped back and swung the vault door open.

Most of the boxes were small, the size used for documents and small collections of jewelry. Only three—351, 371, and 391—were large enough for Ellemarie's case, and they were grouped together at ground level in the far corner.

The rest of that wall had two rows lining the floor, each half the size of the three large boxes, and the entire wall held small boxes above them. A steel table stood in the center of the room.

The director walked over to Box 351 and placed the bank's key in it. Alex walked over and placed his key in the second lock. The director turned both keys, and the door opened. The box inside was also steel. She slid it out on extending rails and opened it for them. Marco took Ellemarie's case and wheeled it over. He opened it and gingerly pulled out a doll with Emperor Habid's distinctive three-braided beard but dressed as a miner.

The bank director's eyes grew wide, and she covered her mouth with both hands. "Royal family will never allow sale of that!"

Alex smiled. "The idea is to cultivate some of our new Greekorp and Patcorp vendors—"

Shouting from the main lobby of the bank interrupted him. An alarm klaxon began to blare.

"Bank is being robbed!" Vassily declared, marching out of the vault and up the hallway toward the commotion.

"Vassily, no!" Alex called after him.

In the main lobby, two figures, a man and a woman, both completely covered in black robes with full-face masks hiding their features, stood with guns drawn and pointed at the teller. They barked orders in Casphar. A half dozen miners who had been in line lay on the floor, hands outstretched.

Back in the vault, the bank director stood frozen.

"Vassily!" Alex shouted again and then went after him.

Ellemarie swooned. "My heart!"

The bank director unfroze and dashed to Ellemarie's side.

Marco popped the head off of the Emperor Habid doll and pulled out a set of lockpicks. He pulled the bank's key out of Box 351 and inserted it into one of the mid-sized boxes two columns over from it.

Ellemarie's face had gone pale, and her hands

shook. Her walking stick toppled to the floor. The bank director caught her as she crumpled.

Marco had the lockpicks in the other box and worked the lock with the speed of a jumpgate.

Ellemarie was on her knees, the bank director by her side, looking intently into her face. Ellemarie stammered, "I'll be... I'll be—" She grimaced and grabbed the bank director by the shoulder.

In the main lobby, Vassily appeared from the vaults just as the first teller was handing over a bag of scrip to the male robber.

"No!" Vassily yelled, pointing a finger at the man. "You will not rob good bank! Give back money!"

The robber loosened his grip on the money bag and pointed his gun at Vassily. The teller did not let go of the bag. The man walked toward Vassily, speaking in Casphar, leaving the gawking teller holding out a bag of money to no one.

"You will not rob bank!" Vassily shouted, closing the distance between them.

The man shook the gun for emphasis and pointed it straight at Vassily's chest.

Vassily reached out and took the gun from the robber.

The robber stood dumbfounded. Vassily pointed toward the exit.

The female robber fired her gun, missing. The shot ricocheted off one of the glass office walls and shattered a ceiling lighting panel.

Back in the vault, Ellemarie cried out and clung to the bank director as the shot echoed.

Marco had the safe deposit box open and was sliding out the inner steel case. He silently opened the lid. Inside sat a black case, slightly ajar, with a blue wand leaning into the corner of the box beside it. Marco removed the wand first, slipping it into his sleeve, and then closed the case.

In the main lobby, the male robber had returned to the teller and was trying to demand the bag of money with no gun to back up the threat. Vassily and the female robber, both armed now, were chasing each other around one of the central tables. Vassily would go left, she would go right. Then both would stop and reverse.

Marco pulled out the case and slid the safe deposit box back into place and closed the door. He popped out the bank's key and went back to Box 351.

The female robber pointed her gun over the table. Vassily brought an enormous hand down onto it, holding the gun against the table. She pulled on it twice before giving up and letting it go. He slid the second gun into his waistband, then swung a leg up on the table to come over it after her. She scurried backward.

Marco pulled two more dolls out of Ellemarie's case and slid the black case and the wand into the bottom of it. He dropped the other two dolls on top and put the bank director's key back into Box 351.

Ellemarie pulled in a deep breath and called out, "No, no, I'm fine, I'm fine."

In the lobby, the two bank robbers looked at each other and ran for the exit. They stumbled over each other, trying to get through the antechamber and outside. As they vanished into the night, a hush came over the bank, interrupted only by the still-sounding klaxon.

One of the tellers started to applaud. Alex stood at the end of the corridor, arms folded. The miners on the floor began to stand up, and they started applauding, too.

Vassily grinned. Soon the rest of the tellers were also applauding.

Alex turned and headed back to the vault. He got there just as Marco was putting the head back onto the Emperor Habid doll.

Alex bent down and helped the bank director help Ellemarie to her feet. The bank director grabbed Ellemarie's walking stick for her.

Marco stood exactly where he had been when the ruckus started, slack-jawed. The bank director glanced around, noticed him, and said, "Are you all right?"

Marco nodded quickly but didn't move.

Ellemarie grabbed hold of her walking stick and panted, "I'm... I'm so sorry. Sudden shocks make my heart palpitate. The pacemaker sometimes takes a few seconds. I'm fine now."

"We can call you hospital transport," the bank director said.

"It really does happen all the time," Alex said. "I'll take her straight to our private physician and make sure everything is okay."

"That's really not necessary," Ellemarie said. "This is all so embarrassing."

"We'll feel better if you get checked out," Alex said.

Several bank employees appeared behind Alex and were hurriedly relaying information to the bank director. She answered in Casphar and looked at Alex. "I must finish—"

"Our stuff can wait," Alex said.

Marco nodded and dropped the Emperor Habid doll back into Ellemarie's case and closed it. He slid the empty safe deposit box shut and closed it. He turned Alex's lock and removed the key. The bank director swept over and locked the bank's side, removing her key.

Marco wheeled the case over to Alex and Ellemarie. Alex led Ellemarie out of the vault, Marco just behind them with his free hand out, ready to steady her if she needed it. The bank director locked the vault behind them.

They emerged into the main lobby. Vassily was surrounded by a crowd of customers and employees, all talking at once. Alex called out to him, "We're taking Ellemarie to the doctor! We'll see you at home!"

Vassily nodded in acknowledgment.

Alex turned to the bank director. "That man is a Nostraspace citizen! If the police give him any trouble, call me and I'll come right back!"

"I will not let police molest my best customer!" the bank director called back as she swept into her office and shut off the klaxon.

Ellemarie's steps became steadier as she moved out into the night air. They crossed the street and rounded the next corner.

Alex started laughing.

Then Ellemarie started laughing, too.

"That should never have worked," Alex said. "Did you get it?"

"Oh, I got it," Marco said, smiling. "She even left me her key."

Alex's laugh turned to a cackle, and he stopped walking so he could put his hands on his knees. "She's going to swear she was staring at you the whole time, too. Ellemarie, I'm really glad you're on our side now."

• • •

The local media was already on the story by the time they got back to the house. Dale and Melanie were there, back in their disguises as miner and receptionist, seated on the couch. Dale held out the house tablet to Alex, Marco, and Ellemarie as they entered, showing a photo of Vassily smiling in the bank and a headline and news story written in Casphar.

"I'm afraid my Casphar is limited," Ellemarie said.

"Roughly translated," Dale said, "the headline says 'No-Good Defector Foils Bank Robbery' and the article proceeds to be less flattering from there. Do you have it?"

Marco opened Ellemarie's case, tossed the three dolls aside, and pulled out the black case. Dale's eyes grew wide, and he jumped up to take it from Marco, opening the case immediately. The packing material inside had been cut to the exact shape of the two-headed falcon, and it rested inside, looking regal. Marco handed over the wand next.

Dale went to take it, and then stopped. "No, actually, give that to Alex."

Marco did so.

"You turn it on at the base," Dale explained. It's got a range of about a hundred kilometers. Will chirp and blink when it's pointed at this bird, assuming it's not locked in this case."

Alex turned the wand on and tried it. As advertised, when it was pointed in the direction of the falcon, it gave a subtle alert.

"Since this bird isn't ever leaving my sight again, you can use it to find me," Dale said. "That wand is a lot more advanced than the ones Casphar has worked out, so don't let it fall into their hands."

"What's it detecting?" Alex asked.

"Need-to-know," Dale said. "And I was told I don't need to know. I just needed to use it to find this."

Alex harrumphed and headed upstairs.

• • •

Vassily returned in a foul mood several hours later. Melanie, Ellemarie, and Dale were still in the main room as he came in, switched the house to "sleep" mode, and stormed into the kitchen.

"There you are," Melanie called to him. "Wanted to congratulate you on your performance back there. I almost believed it when you almost came across the table to get me."

"And I genuinely didn't see you go for my gun," Dale said. "One second I had you covered, and then the next second, I'm disarmed. It was a thing of beauty."

Vassily came out of the kitchen with a bottle of hard liquor in his hand. "Ten years ago, would not have been almost over table. Have gotten soft in Nostraspace." He swept out of the room and slunk up the stairs, leaving a hush in the room behind him.

"Don't worry about him," Ellemarie said without looking up from the tablet. "This mission's been hard on him."

Dale nodded and headed into the kitchen. "I'm surprised the Don selected him. It's pretty predictable that he'd be catching it from all sides."

Ellemarie didn't answer, but she kept scanning the news. The Interstellar media outlets had subsequently picked up the story, and they had also noticed it was the same bank from the previous botched robbery. Their headlines were all some variation on *__Unrobbable Bank!__* and all had paragraphs implying if not outright stating that if Vassily could stop the robbery, the robbers had to be even less competent than the first set had been.

In other news, production targets in the mines had been cut again, in an effort to shore up prices given the new competition from Nostraspace asteroid mining.

The commanding officer of the jumpgate was insisting that the recent downtimes were nothing to worry about, because the jumpgate had always experienced downtimes, and spaceship captains were just twitchier than usual because of the delays being caused by the highly necessary and completely unobtrusive new security measures.

Two more formal protests had been filed about Casphar marines searching ships that were not yet in Casphar space, this time by Ynos and the Don. Most of the more recent news stories included an **_Unrobbable Bank!_** joke.

Ellemarie paused when she came across an ad. She handed the tablet to Dale. "You know Casphar culture better than I do. Is that a good price?"

Dale looked at it. "That's cheap. What's wrong with it?"

Ellemarie took the tablet back. "Only one way to find out." She opened a message window and began typing.

"What are we buying?" Melanie asked.

"Nothing yet," Ellemarie said, still typing.

"I'm assuming," Dale said to her, "that this is an 'easier to get forgiveness than permission' purchase?"

"I'm filing it under 'maintaining our cover as eccentric Nostraspace businesspeople,'" Ellemarie answered.

"What?" Melanie insisted.

Dale shook his head. "Ellemarie wants a yacht."

• • •

Alex awoke to an urgent message on his local communicator. It was addressed to all four of them, from the receptionist's station at the factory: <u>Khadija locked in her office.</u>

He pulled himself out of bed, showered, dressed, and went downstairs. The house tablet blinked that there was an urgent message. He checked, and it was identical. He leaned into the kitchen. No one else was around. Marco's bedroom door had been closed as he came downstairs, but Ellemarie's and Vassily's had been open. Fresh dishes were washing in the sink, the jets spraying them down on the final rinse.

Alex pulled out his local communicator again and sent a message to both Ellemarie and Vassily: <u>Has checking in become optional?</u>

• • •

Tri Sestry was an ugly yacht. She had probably originally been built in a Greekorp shipyard, as her rectangular main hull still had hints of pink paint, but space-hardened conduit crisscrossed over it, and two external fuel tanks, each as long as the hull itself, had been attached on both sides near the top of the hull.

The blunt-nosed cockpit on the front and the utilitarian airlock on the back were of Casphar mixed-metal design and were probably additions as well. She sat on a private pad around the backside of the spaceport, far from both the terminals and the hubbub of the nonaligned spacers' various hangars, bathed in the soft glow of countless artificial lights that kept the spaceport alive through the long Reggit nights.

Ellemarie and Vassily approached her slowly, taking in the details. Vassily's eyes became fixed as he rounded to where he could see her name painted under the port cockpit window. "We cannot buy. This is *Tri Sestry*."

They both received a message on their local communicators simultaneously, and both dismissed it without reading it.

"What's wrong with that?" Ellemarie asked.

"This is ship of Austin Montierthski. This is where he was caught with three women."

"Ah, so that explains the asking price," Ellemarie said with a smirk.

"Ms. Hayden! Welcome!" came a voluminous baritone voice from the back of the yacht. A round man descended the airlock ramp and waddled over to them. "You can see, excellent condition. Custom modifications. Very nice."

"And a bit of a reputation, I understand," Ellemarie said.

"Is factored into price," the salesman said. "And no crew, also factored into price. Is easy. Change name. New paint. New captain. New ship."

"Is less easy in Casphar," Vassily whispered to her.

"You register Nostraspace. Is easy," the salesman said, brushing off Vassily's comment. "Come inside. Very nice."

He led them up the ramp and through the airlock. It opened directly into a large stateroom that spanned the entire width of the yacht. It was clearly an upgrade, done in high-end stones and metals, with a spacious bathroom to the port side of the doorway and oversized closets to the starboard side. The bed was indeed large enough for four.

Vassily asked a question in Casphar. The salesman answered, "Original owner wanted more room for stateroom. Expanded. Sealed off original airlock. Airlocks in floor, very inefficient. This nice. Quality. Come see."

He led them out the door and up a short corridor. A common bathroom was the next door on the starboard side. Farther up the corridor, two doors stood across from one another, leading to two smaller staterooms, each about the size of the bathroom in the main stateroom. Each contained a double bed with a fold-out bunk above it and a simple retracting shelf as a closet. They looked to be original, as both had carpeted floors and walls painted blue.

The corridor ended in a combined galley and lounge that featured a low table and three couches on the port side and enough food preparation space for one person to work on the starboard side. Tucked between the food-prep area and the stateroom wall was another small sitting area with two armchairs and a small entertainment console between them. The foremost wall had a round hatch in the middle of it. There were inset panels port and starboard of it in stained glass, each depicting a bathing woman. The panels were exactly the size and shape of typical Greekorp cockpit windows.

Vassily asked another question in Casphar.

The salesman answered. "Yes, this original crew area. Cockpit, galley. When ramp for airlock removed, crew bunks moved below. Come."

He led them into the cockpit. Two steps led down to a cramped space with two seats among a sea of jet-black consoles. The salesman lifted the two steps, which folded up into the round hatch, revealing a half flight of stairs down into a small cube with four bunks in it, and a tiny combination washbasin-shower beyond them.

Ellemarie studied the layout, but Vassily wandered over and climbed into the port seat, looking out the cockpit windows onto the spaceport grounds. He nodded. "Casphar cockpit. Very difficult to fly. Alex, Dale cannot. If you buy, I fly. Vassily Cheremetov. *Captain,* he."

Ellemarie smirked.

The salesman rubbed his hands together.

• • •

Alex had the bank account open on the tablet and was comparing it to the books from the factory when the transaction went through. He grabbed his local communicator and texted: <u>SOMEONE TELL ME WHAT'S GOING ON! NOW!</u>

• • •

Ellemarie had just finished the paperwork to finalize the transfer of ownership and was beginning the paperwork to name Vassily the new captain of *Tri Sestry*, in the employ of T.T., Inc. of Polairmo, Nostraspace, when Alex stormed into the spaceport government office, Marco trailing behind.

"You bought a *what*?"

"A yacht," Ellemarie said without looking up. "We talked about this."

"We did not talk about this!"

"Sure we did," Ellemarie said. "You know me. Would I do something like this impulsively?"

Alex clenched his fists and pressed them to his temples.

Marco leaned against the wall and watched.

"Where is Vassily?" Alex asked.

"He's on board still," Ellemarie said. "He's got a lot of work to do. He's our new captain."

"Ellemarie!" Alex's fists came down from his temples and shook toward her. "You need to check with me! How the hell am I supposed to explain this expense when we get back home?"

"Simple." Ellemarie took a break from the paperwork and leveled her eyes directly at Alex. "You

look your uncle in the eye and you say, 'You sent
Ellemarie Hayden along.'"

Alex roared and smacked his fists onto the top of
his head twice.

Ellemarie signed the paperwork with a flourish
and handed it over to a nervous-looking clerk. She
shifted her weight to her walking stick and tilted her
head toward the exit. "Come, see your new yacht."

They took the moving sidewalk as far as the
nonaligned spacer hangars. They had to walk the rest
of the way to the private landing pads. Once *Tri
Sestry* was in view, Ellemarie pointed her out.

"Oh, it's pink!" Marco said. "Alex, you know I've
always wanted a pink yacht."

"And to complete the irony," Ellemarie said, "she
used to belong to Austin Montierthski."

Alex let out a whimper. "There is no way that is
going to be inconspicuous."

"When has inconspicuous ever worked for us?"
Ellemarie asked, still walking.

Alex shook his fists at the sky.

Ellemarie led them around the hull and up the ramp.
Alex was too busy seething to pay any attention, but
as soon as they were on board, Marco cocked his head,
looking at the bed.

"Wait," he said quietly.

"What?" Ellemarie asked, slowing to a stop.

Marco's fingers danced in the air, his gaze fixed on
the bed. "Close the airlock."

Ellemarie looked at him. He still concentrated
on the bed. "Yes, that's the bed where the infamous
event occurred. My understanding is the Casphar
military can open any airlock of any ship registered
Casphar, and when they docked and came on board there
they were."

"No, not that," Marco said. "Just do me a favor and close the airlock."

Alex shook his head and complied. As soon as it was sealed, Marco dropped to the floor and shimmied over to the bed on his back. He poked and prodded at it, scooting around it. Ellemarie and Alex stared.

Vassily appeared in the doorway but didn't say anything. He watched as Marco reached the head of the bed.

"Aha!" Marco stuck his finger up inside the headboard. Something clicked.

Ellemarie and Alex had to scurry to the side as the bed slid across the floor to the far side of the room, revealing the hatch to the old airlock in the floor. Marco crawled over and inspected it. The window had been painted black, but the mechanism was still in good shape. Marco triggered it, and it slid open.

Below, a bank of recording equipment sat wedged into what would have originally been the storage compartment for the airlock ramp. Marco dropped down and turned it on. Soon the screen lit up with a list of filenames, all in Casphar.

Alex peered down curiously. "Those are all women's names."

Vassily moved over to the edge of the hole to look down as well.

Marco selected the most recent file. The screen came to life with a video of Austin Montierthski himself, in the very cabin they were now standing in, having sex with three women at once.

"That dirty little pervert," Marco said appreciatively.

"This very illegal!" Vassily said.

"And more importantly," Alex said, a tinge of excitement in his voice, "apparently not discovered

when they arrested everyone on board. Good job,
Marco. Get Dale over here, now!"

. . .

Dale arrived within an hour and stood with Alex,
Marco, Ellemarie, and Vassily in the stateroom, black
case clutched to his chest awkwardly, a piece of
packing material keeping it from closing completely.

He shook his head. "This isn't ideal. If the
yacht gets inspected, they'll be inside before anyone
has a chance to get down here and close the case."

"Just store it closed," Marco said. "We all know
where it is."

Dale shook his head. "Open at all times. Orders.
Sorry. Only close the case when being searched.
Reopen it as soon as practical afterward. Those are
the orders, and if you can't follow them, I'm going to
take it and disappear, and good luck completing your
mission without me."

"Vassily is going to be staying on board," Alex
said. "The yacht has been sitting here, for sale, for
months. It's been inspected already. They're not
going to check it again until we're ready to depart,
and then there's no reason they're more likely to find
this hiding place the second time than they were the
first. If you don't want me to return it to Emperor
Habid, it goes down there. I don't like you carrying
it around the city, because eventually someone's going
to ask you about it, and if you're caught with it, I'm
never getting you home. Orders."

Dale exhaled sharply and dropped down into the
hidey-hole. He tucked the case in next to the
recording equipment. "At least let me have the wand
back so I know if it's moving."

Alex slipped the wand out of his sleeve pocket and

gave it to Dale. "Marco, this is a better storage place for your porn collection, too. As soon as we find Kiera, we're out of here, and I don't want to risk it all by you getting brought up on perversion charges."

"As long as I can rotate out a few choice pieces," Marco said.

"All of it," Alex said. "I'm sick of nobody acting like I'm in charge of this mission."

"You're only in charge of one of them," Dale said.

"Rank!" Alex barked.

"Rank!" Dale barked back.

Everyone's local communicators buzzed. It was a message from the receptionist's station again: Khadija still locked in office. Please advise. Urgent.

Ellemarie went white. "Oh, crap."

"What?" Alex asked.

"I just remembered something," Ellemarie said. "When I first met her, Vassily was being a wiseass, and I mentioned that he works for your uncle, not for me."

"So?" Alex asked.

"She figured out who your uncle is when she met you," Ellemarie said.

There was a pause as that sunk in.

Marco said it first. "And Vassily was just in the news."

All eyes fell on Alex. His voice was completely calm but slightly faster than normal. "Dale, you stay with the ship. The rest of us need to get over there, now."

Chapter 7

Alex, Marco, Ellemarie, and Vassily huddled together at the top of the railingless ramp. Below them, the factory floor was crowded with women making Austin Montierthski dolls. Ellemarie reached out and knocked on the door.

Khadija's voice responded from within with a terse phrase in Casphar.

"Go away," Alex translated.

"Khadija, dear," Ellemarie called back in a soothing voice. "It's Ellemarie. Can we talk?"

"Not yet!" Khadija yelled back.

Ellemarie looked at Alex and pursed her lips.

"Okay," Alex said, barely audible above the cacophony of the sewing machines below. "How do we want to play this?"

"She's got access to all the company books," Marco said. "Is there any way she can tie this company back to the Don?"

"Depends on how good she is," Ellemarie said. "And if she's got contacts on the other side of the jumpgate."

"That's unlikely," Alex said, "but I wouldn't want to bet the mission on it."

"It also depends on who else she's been in contact with," Marco said.

"Of all the careless..." Alex muttered and pounded on the door. He spoke sternly in Casphar.

Khadija didn't respond.

"Don't you dare threaten to fire her," Ellemarie said. "She's running this place single-handedly, and I sure don't know how to replace her."

"This business is a front," Alex hissed, the sound blending with the sewing machines.

"Remember we just bought a yacht," Ellemarie said.

Alex's nostrils flared.

Marco slipped between Ellemarie and Alex and knocked gently. "Khadija, we're just a little worried. Could you open the door and talk to us so we know you're all right?"

"You wait!" Khadija yelled back through the door. "Be here soon!"

Marco started to respond but stopped, then looked at Alex, mouth open.

Alex shook his head. "That could have come from two or three Casphar words. I have no idea which she meant."

Vassily shook his head. "We all go to prison."

"They haven't made one yet I can't get out of," Marco said.

"You have not seen maximum security of military prison," Vassily said.

"Wait," Ellemarie said, "there's a separate military prison?"

"Yes," Vassily said. "On marine base on grounds of military spaceport on far side of planet."

"You didn't—" Ellemarie silenced the angry outburst and dropped back into a whisper. "You've had me monitoring the local prison for Kiera all these months, and nobody told me about a second prison on this fortune-forsaken rock?"

"Is widely available information," Vassily said.

"In Casphar, maybe," Ellemarie growled, "which I can't read."

"Now you know," Vassily said.

"If I find she's been in there all this time," Ellemarie's voice rose again, "I'm telling her it's your fault we didn't get her out sooner!"

Vassily leaned in and whispered gravely, "If in there, no getting her out."

Khadija's voice came through the door with a sharp exclamation that might have been a cry of success or sudden, sharp pain.

Ellemarie leaned over and knocked again. "Khadija, dear, are you all right?"

"Almost!" Khadija responded from within.

Alex folded his arms and grumbled. "If we wait, we give her a chance to transmit whatever she's found to most anyone. If we break in the door and it's nothing, we're never going to allay her suspicions again."

"Is too dangerous to just break neck," Vassily said. "Local law does not like that."

"Marco," Ellemarie said, "how are you with computers?"

"Uh..." Marco said.

Ellemarie didn't pause. "Run down to the reception desk and see if you can monitor what the computer in the office is doing."

Marco ran down the ramp in an ungainly sprint.

Ellemarie looked at Alex. "If she's not using the computer, it's a lot less likely she's prying."

Just then, the door opened. Khadija stood there, eyes wide, mouth slightly agape. "Come. Come now."

Khadija backed up and let the three of them into the office. It had been taken over with fabric samples, bolts of offcuts, and spare parts for sewing machines. The computer on the desk had its monitor powered off, a strip of red fabric draped over it. A sewing machine stood next to it, threads and scraps strewn all around. An acrid scent like that created by a welding torch hung in the air.

"Stay!" Khadija motioned with both palms out. She went around behind the desk and came up with a bundle covered in black fabric. "Ready?"

The other three stared.

Khadija ripped back the sheet. Underneath it was a fabric-over-wire dollhouse representation of a building, in the same color scheme as the bank they had robbed the day before. On the right side, a lobby with a teller counter had been created out of a skillful blend of offcut fabrics from the Austin Montierthski doll. On the left side were two vaults, the leftmost one of which had a hole in its wall and a metal block inside painted to look like a pile of scrip.

Khadija held up an index finger to them. She then reached into the vault and pulled out the little pile of money. As it came out, there was a whirring sound, a spool of string wheeling out, keeping the piece of metal attached to the bank.

Khadija let go, and the pile of money snapped back into the vault with a zipping sound.

Khadija grinned and reached behind the teller counter, removing a tiny sack, also with a string attached to it. It also came out of the bank easily but snapped back into place when she let go of it.

"Eh?" Khadija smiled broadly. "Is _**Unrobbable Bank!**_"

Alex, Ellemarie, and Vassily stared at the prototype, slack-jawed.

Ellemarie started to giggle.

Vassily began to laugh, too.

"We sell this first," Khadija explained. "Then we also sell dolls of you"—she pointed at Vassily—"and robbers as add-on. We make here with same fabrics as other product except red fabric for outside. Is local. Is cheap."

Ellemarie's giggle gave way to delighted laughter. "Khadija, you are a jewel!"

Alex held out a hand and asked a question in Casphar.

Khadija nodded and handed the toy over to him. He turned and left with it.

"How long have you been working on that?" Ellemarie asked.

Khadija beamed.

Alex descended the ramp, workers occasionally glancing up curiously at the object he carried. He stepped out into the reception room.

Marco leaned over the desk and was poking at the receptionist's computer. He stopped and looked up at Alex. "I don't know how she's got that computer locked down, it's like it's not even on the networ—"

Alex held up his hand to silence Marco. Then he spoke to the receptionist in the slow, deliberate tones that one uses when speaking to a non-native speaker. "Thank you for your concern. Khadija was working on a new prototype and simply did not want to be interrupted."

Marco gaped.

Alex held up Khadija's prototype and demonstrated.

The receptionist's laugh betrayed Melanie Coltrane's real voice, but only for an instant.

"Where are you taking it?" Marco asked.

"To the bank, to see if they want to invest," Alex said. He leaned over and whispered to them, "We've robbed her twice. The least we can do is offer her a cut."

. . .

Ellemarie grabbed the house tablet as soon as she walked in the door, sitting down on the couch and getting to work. Vassily had gone back to *Tri Sestry*, and Marco had vanished along with Alex, so she had the house to herself until Dale arrived two hours later.

He didn't say anything. He went into the kitchen to get dinner started.

Alex and Marco arrived about an hour later, Alex looking smug. "No cash out of our pocket. We start production tomorrow. The profit margins look good," he said as he sat down at the table.

Dale appeared with a large plate full of steaming mice, which he had beheaded and skinned and baked in an herb sauce. He set it in the middle of the table.

"I could use the help of someone who reads Casphar," Ellemarie said.

Dale and Alex both crossed over to her.

She handed the tablet to Alex. "Got into the military prison records," she explained. "I've got one with no photo."

"Age and gender are right," Alex said.

"Date of arrest is about a week after we split up," Dale said.

"How's the height and weight?" Alex asked.

"If it's her, she's lost weight, but the height is about right," Dale said. "And look at that. Strict psychiatric observation, only Interstellar speakers to interact with her."

"I'd say not a definite," Alex said, handing the tablet back to Ellemarie, "but a good match. Definitely a Nostraspace or Patcorp national."

"And I doubt Patcorp would object to us freeing one of their operatives, worst-case scenario," Dale said.

"Are we breaking in somewhere?" Marco asked, sweeping over.

"Military prison," Alex answered.

"Tricky," Marco said. "We're going to need Vassily to help plan this."

· · ·

They all assembled in the main room of *Tri Sestry* as soon as Melanie got off work.

Ellemarie put a map of the military spaceport up on the entertainment console. Vassily stood and pointed to it. "This is spaceport, opposite side of planet from us. Airspace around here patrolled by drones and satellites. Nonmilitary ships attempting to land shot down. Popular suicide for nonaligned spacers."

"Ship-to-ship missiles or lasers?" Alex asked from one of the armchairs.

"Lasers from drones and satellites," Vassily said. "Missiles from ground. Close range, near planet, much more practical than in deep space. Never heard of ship outmaneuvering for long."

Alex nodded. "How do troops get in and out?"

"Train," Vassily said, pointing to a line on the map. "Enters here, terminal here. Identification scanned when troops board, at perimeter, and when troops exit train. Same in other direction."

"Vehicles?" Alex asked.

"Authorized military vehicles only. Road here and here. Long drive. Mostly on-base vehicles, built in plant hundred kilometer east."

Dale, in the other armchair, folded his legs. "How would they have gotten Kiera in?"

"Probably ship," Vassily said. "Most equipment, officers, high-value items come from space. Prison is over here. Four kilometer from ships, two kilometer from train terminal. Under parade ground."

"How far underground?" Alex asked.

"Do not know. Elevator access. Probably stair, but I took elevator. Told it is built to withstand orbital mass driver assault."

Dale whistled through his teeth.

"The plans I found," Ellemarie said from her position on one of the couches, switching the view over to a line drawing of the prison itself, "don't give the depth, but we can estimate. Assuming the elevator is vertical, the emergency stairs you see beside it on the lower level should form a straight line to the ones in the administrative level above ground here."

The drawing was replaced with another one, showing the floorplan of an aboveground building. It was mostly security screening checkpoints leading to the elevator, but with two large workrooms on either side.

"I'd say between twenty and twenty-two meters," she said, "depending on how steep the stairs are."

Alex pointed at the screen. "This is the aboveground portion?"

Vassily nodded. "This area, easy to penetrate once on base. Built by offworld contractor with ridiculous fondness for glass. Very large windows. General who ordered it fired later. Had shares in builder company."

"So contractors are allowed on the base?" Alex asked.

"With Emperor's permission, yes," Vassily said with

a nod and went back to the drawing. "Workers enter here and here. Prisoners enter here. Four security checkpoints before elevator for prisoners. Do not know security for workers."

Alex scratched his moustache.

Vassily continued. "Prisoners and workers use same elevator. Down here to holding area below."

Ellemarie switched to the drawing of the subterranean level.

"One more checkpoint here, then into deadly hallway." Vassily indicated a long corridor that, according to the drawing, was the only path from the elevator and stairs to the main prison complex. "Guards on both ends must hold down switches. Facial recognition is also working. Any one of three gives signal, doors close. No override from guards." Vassily mimed with a finger across his throat.

Melanie, seated beside Ellemarie, uncrossed her legs. "So a frontal assault is right out. Too many bottlenecks."

"Worse," Vassily said, indicating a large open room beyond the security checkpoint at the end of the deadly hallway. "This is general population. All loyal soldiers. Even in prison, Casphar military would defend Casphar to death. Any prisoner trying assist us would be killed by other prisoners. Then would kill us. Need an army."

"Which makes those bottlenecks even worse," Melanie said.

"When I am inside," Vassily said, "we know this door leads to high-security wing, but never inside."

"According to the records Ellemarie stole," Dale said, rising beside Vassily, "the prisoner we're hoping is Kiera is in this cell here." He indicated a tiny room all the way at the back of the complex.

"We're assuming that since these areas here are security checkpoints, these spaces over here are as well, and this looks architecturally similar to Vassily's deadly hallway, so we have to assume it's the same kind of bottleneck."

Marco, seated on Ellemarie's other side, studied the ceiling. "Where are they getting their air?"

"Recirculated," Vassily said. "Always smells like inside of spaceship. Food comes in front doors. No laundry, prisoners wash clothes in showers."

"Is water reclaimed, too?" Marco asked. "Or are there sewers?"

"Tastes like reclaimed," Vassily said.

Marco grimaced. "That's a lot of security for loyal soldiers."

"Prisoners are all told they are garrison for real dangerous criminals, in high-security wing."

"I'll give Habid credit," Dale said, "it's effective."

Alex still just scratched his moustache.

"There's another possibility we should consider," Ellemarie said. "Kiera Twight is a Nostraspace citizen. Whatever she's accused of, there should have been diplomatic notification of her arrest. You"–she nodded her nose toward Alex–"walk in there, say we know she's being held, and ask for her release. Obviously we send Dale and Melanie out of the system first."

"Disadvantage there," said Dale, "is that we're admitting the Don was behind the theft of the falcon. She wouldn't be in there if they weren't pretty sure she was involved in that. There are plenty of other facilities for whatever miscellaneous crimes she commits on a daily basis."

"Well, I don't know about Alex," Ellemarie said,

"but as a team we weren't briefed on your mission. Our orders were simply to bring you home. As far as I'm concerned, a diplomatic solution is on the table."

"I wish we could get a message through the jumpgate," Marco said. "Find out how the Don wants us to proceed."

"Light speed to the nearest Nostraspace jumpgate is only forty-seven years," Melanie said.

Marco and Ellemarie laughed.

Alex held up his right hand, index finger pointing at the ceiling. "How hard would it be," he asked, "to get an armored personnel carrier?"

Chapter 8

The sun was just coming up, but an overcast day meant the sky just grew lighter instead of the sun appearing. Alex approached the hangar where the nonaligned spacers held their market. The man he had done business with earlier was just setting up his table.

The spacer smiled as Alex approached, but the look shifted to puzzlement as Alex handed him a folded sheet of real paper. The spacer unfolded it, read it, and then started to laugh. "Expensive taste, my friend."

• • •

Melanie worked at the kitchen table with a large magnifying glass on a stand between her and a palm-sized Casphar military ID tablet. A paintbrush in her left hand, she brushed paint onto it gently as her right hand moved a fine blade in the opposite direction.

Dale, clean-shaven, came down the steps, dressed in

a crisp blue Casphar Palace Services uniform.

"Just putting the finishing touches on now," Melanie said. "Remember what I told you about your accent."

"My accent's better than yours," he said.

"My accent is plausible. Kon accents linger for generations, and though we're kind of rare on Reggit, we're all over the empire."

"My accent is fine for our purposes. If anyone asks, I'll tell them I grew up on Yllas."

She glanced over her shoulder at him with a grimace. Then she moved the magnifying glass aside and blew on the ID tablet.

• • •

Marco sat cross-legged on the deck of the galley on board *Tri Sestry*. The entertainment console screen was on, and he controlled it with the tablet in front of him. A model of Reggit hung on the screen, and dozens of multicolored lines arched around it. A new line, this one white, curved down toward the planet's surface, then deflected and turned red.

Marco grimaced and tapped on the tablet. The lines cleared, and all began forming over again.

• • •

Ellemarie came downstairs, tablet in hand. Dale and Melanie were both at the table.

"I'm ready to go," Ellemarie said, "but I still think we should have Vassily read it over once before I put it in the system. Orders never sound like they might have been written by a foreigner."

"No time," Melanie said. "We're betting that they'll be too angry to question them. Post it."

Ellemarie tapped the screen. "Good luck."

• • •

Vassily stood next to a beat-up two-person spaceship that had probably been built as a tug—oversized gravity drive on the rear, lots of paint missing, and bolts where bumpers would have been attached once. A hand-painted sign on it in both Casphar and Interstellar read, "For Sale."

Alex came up beside him. Vassily looked over at him and nodded.

• • •

Dale napped sitting up on the train, surrounded by countless Casphar marines, military office workers, and a handful of civilians. It was night on this side of the planet. Most of those who had seats napped. Those who stood looked bleary-eyed. Occasionally, someone moving fore or aft in the crowded car would catch sight of his uniform and eye it curiously, but no one spoke to him.

• • •

Melanie stepped off the moving sidewalk into the Patcorp terminal. She had forgone the makeup but was dressed in the mismatched fashion of nonaligned spacers. Security at the doors to the concourse had a crowd of people backed up almost to the doors of the terminal.

Melanie skirted around the crowd toward a row of shops that had been subdivided from the main terminal by corrugated partitions. One of them had "Consignment" painted on it in big letters. A slender man with olive skin and epicanthic folds over dark eyes sat behind a desk, tablets in front of him cycling through various items.

The man looked up as Melanie stepped into his cubicle. She stopped and leaned against the edge of

the partition and spoke without any attempt to hide
her Kon accent. "I hear you're the man to speak to
about replacing my stolen spacesuits."

• • •

The train slowed, and an announcement appeared on
the destination screens. Everyone on board stood.
Dale, massaging his knees, did the same.

Every ID tablet on the train came out of pockets
at once. Dale pulled his out and activated it. His
picture appeared on the screen, along with several
lines of Casphar text. In a wave from the front
of the car to the back, every ID tablet beeped. As
Dale's beeped, he slipped it back into his pocket.

He didn't bother to sit back down. A few minutes
later, they pulled into a terminal. Dale joined the
shuffle toward the doorway of the train car.

A ramp had extended across the deep gap between
the train and the platform. A steel security archway
stood at the end of the ramp at the edge of the
platform. Everyone in front of Dale had their ID
tablets out and were showing them to the arch, passing
through when an amber light on the top of it blinked
twice.

Dale did as the others did. The light stayed
solid. He scanned his ID again. Still solid.

A marine behind him reached forward and grabbed
Dale's hand, turned the tablet ninety degrees, then
guided it back to the sensor.

The amber light blinked twice.

Dale mumbled thanks in Casphar and stepped through
the arch.

A line of six-wheeled flatbed trucks with handrails
along the beds stood lined up under various signs.
Dale looked across the signs quickly, then hopped into

the back of one of the trucks. In a few minutes, it
was lumbering off toward the prison, himself and a
half dozen guards clinging to the handrails as the
truck bucketed them over uneven pavement.

The prison's administrative building was as Vassily
had described. Light streamed out of unusually large
windows on all sides, framed by arched concrete
mullions. The truck rumbled up in front of it, and
everyone disembarked. Dale let the guards go in first,
then followed them through the main door. He scanned
his ID tablet at the first checkpoint and was buzzed in.

A square-jawed bald man in his sixties with the
four-barred epaulets of a full colonel stood with his
arms crossed, looking directly at Dale. Dale nodded
briefly, putting on a feeble smile, and spoke.

The colonel responded curtly.

Dale stood silent, looking at the colonel
expectantly.

The colonel's face flushed, and he launched into
an angry tirade. Dale stood and listened. When the
colonel had exhausted himself, Dale held out both
palms and shrugged.

The colonel harrumphed and turned to lead Dale
through the rest of the checkpoints.

The layout was what the floor plans indicated it
should be. Multiple checkpoints. Deadly hallway.
Checkpoint. A large open area with cells surrounding
it, tables lined up perpendicular to the entryway
and bolted to the floor, laid out so the gaps between
them were narrow and not in straight lines. All the
inmates, still in their uniforms but with a black sash
printed across them, watched intently as the colonel
led Dale across to the door to the high-security wing.
Another deadly hallway, another checkpoint. Guards
observed their movement the whole time.

The high-security wing looked more like a lounge than a prison. The ceiling was low, with obvious security cameras mounted on it. Couches and tables were scattered in small conversation clusters. Higher-ranking guards and officers mingled here.

The colonel led Dale to the far side of the room and up to a steel door with a large window next to it, identical to two dozen similar doors along the perimeter of the room. The window afforded a view into the darkened cell. It was only just large enough for the bunk and the combination toilet / shower / washbasin that occupied it. The bunk was a lumpy mess with a figure curled up on it, back to the door, just a mass of tangled black hair and rumpled fabric.

Dale nodded. The colonel shook his head and said something terse. Then he unlocked the door with his ID tablet.

Dale stepped into the cell. The door shut behind him and the lock snapped into place with a melodramatic bang. Dale turned the lights on.

The mass on the bed moved.

Dale spoke with a thick Casphar accent. "I am Anton Chekhov of Palace Services. I respond to report of abuse and have orders to interview you."

The mass rolled over, revealing a hooked nose protruding from an emaciated face with high cheekbones. Eyes opened, and the figure started, jumping to a seated position.

Dale repeated his introduction.

The young woman on the bed blinked. "Yes. Yes, they are abusing me."

"Please describe," Dale said.

The young woman's back straightened. "First of all, I've been here for months, and I've never even been told what I'm being charged with. I haven't been given access to a lawyer, nor have I been allowed to contact my government. They drug me. They starve me. They interrogate me regularly using pain sticks. I'm a Nostraspace citizen and an employee of Sonic Foundry, Inc., and I would appreciate if, at the very least, you could let them know I'm here."

Dale shook his head. "This is not match for report."

The young woman sprang to her feet and thrust a finger into Dale's face. "I don't know what your plan is, but get me out of here this instant!"

Dale looked to the ceiling. "This is not my department. I am here to investigate report."

The young woman clenched both fists and beat them against Dale's chest. "Get me out of here! Get me out of here, you son of a royal whore!"

The door behind Dale slid open, and two guards pushed past him on either side. Each grabbed one of the young woman's arms. She roared and struggled against them.

Dale backed out of the cell.

The young woman's screams and curses filled the high-security wing. Dale turned to the colonel, tucked his chin, raised his eyebrows, and blew out a breath through puckered lips.

• • •

Alex, Marco, Ellemarie, and Melanie sat around the dining table, Alex occasionally glancing at his DSC.

A single-word message came through, its only authentication stamp a warning that it had been relayed from an unregistered ship in orbit. "Yes."

Alex nodded and looked at the others. "Confirmed. It's Kiera. We're on."

Ellemarie spoke. "I can still try doing the same

thing we did to get Dale inside, and insert orders for her release."

"You know as well as I do that those orders will be challenged and verified," Alex said.

"I could try to intercept that," Ellemarie said.

"And if you miss?" Alex asked.

"We're no worse off than we are now," Ellemarie said.

"Except that they'll know we know where she is and are trying to get her out," Alex said.

Ellemarie clenched her jaw. "There's just so much that can go wrong."

"And a lot will," Alex said, standing up. "That's how these operations go. Everyone has the big picture, everyone knows their part in it. When you have to improvise, improvise. Do your best to let everyone else know what we're up against when you have to. We can't start the main operation until Dale is back, so anyone who isn't heading into orbit, get some sleep."

Alex looked around the table, getting a nod of acknowledgment from everyone. Then he nodded to Melanie. She rose, and they left the house together.

• • •

Alex and Melanie walked from the shuttle stop to the nonaligned spacers' hangars. To the rear of an L-shaped cluster of buildings, a sea of old tugs had been converted to a tent city with tarps and stretches of cloth strung over and between ships. Food-prep stations had been set up at random intervals, and spacer kids prepared meals to serve to waiting groups of adults.

Alex and Melanie wended through the crowd until they found a blue tent with a wiry old lady seated cross-legged inside it. Alex nodded to her. "Did you get the payment?"

The old lady smiled. "All set."

"Wait about half an hour after you see us go to report it stolen," Alex said.

The old lady nodded. "I left the spacesuits with your other order."

Melanie's eyes grew wide.

Alex laughed. "Small network."

The old lady shrugged with only one shoulder. "We look out for each other in our community. You kids be careful now. She's a wreck."

"She doesn't need to get us far," Alex said.

They nodded farewell, and Alex and Melanie headed over to the market hangar.

Melanie started as soon as they were out of earshot of the old lady. "How the hell did she—"

Alex held up a hand to silence her. "It's all right. If they've got the network to piece together that our orders went together, but we're not in jail, they're not going to report us now. They're in it as deep as we are."

They didn't speak again.

As they approached the stall of Alex's black-market merchant with the potted plants, he rose and motioned for them to follow him. He brought them around behind his table, then up a ladder into the belly of his ship.

The cargo hold was a cluttered mess of crates, half of which were open with contents strewn all over the place. The merchant led them over to a stack of unopened boxes that had two spacesuits laid out on them, with a large bundle next to them wrapped in a dark-gray emergency thermal blanket. The merchant pulled the bundle open, revealing a small

winch; six bundles of clear, thin cable; a red box
for hardware; an orange emergency beacon; and a one-
meter-diameter boring device that looked like a dead
metal alien creature of some sort: eight narrow legs
sticking up in the air from the outer ring, a pointed
cone sticking up from the center, and four blades
connecting the cone to the ring. Alex checked each
piece over one by one and nodded.

The merchant smiled. "Pleasure doing business with
you. Do me a favor and do not mention where you got
them."

Alex chuckled. "If anyone has the chance to ask,
we'll be in no condition to answer anyway."

The merchant laughed and climbed back down the
ladder. Alex organized the items back into the
thermal blanket, wrapped them up, and then switched
on the blanket's power to activate the seal. It
contracted to hug the items inside tightly, and the
edges melted into one another until all that was left
was a lumpy gray mass with a blinking green light
embedded in the fabric. Alex pressed the light, and
the bundle powered off again.

The spacesuits were common enough, dull gray one-
size-fits-all models popular with nonaligned spacers.
Alex checked the air tanks—both status screens
read "full" and "ready." He attached them to the
neckpieces in the backs of the spacesuits and then
activated their weight reduction. Both spacesuits
then hung limply in the air, open in the front.

Melanie turned around first. She slid her legs into
the suit, then her arms. Alex closed the neckpiece
for her, and she powered it on. The opening sealed,
and the entire suit shrank to conform to her body.
She put the white helmet on, and the neckpiece sealed
to it automatically. She tapped on the right side

until the sun visor darkened to the point where her face wasn't visible. She gave Alex a thumbs-up, and they repeated the procedure for his suit. Then, Alex hoisted the emergency-blanket bundle, and they made their way gingerly down the ladder.

Nobody among the nonaligned spacers paid any attention to the pair of spacesuit-clad spacers with the large bundle crossing the tarmac to the beat-up tug with the "for sale" sign beside it.

The figure without the bundle worked the lock on the cockpit and swung the front windows upward. The figure with the bundle deposited it behind the two seats, and then both climbed inside. The cockpit windows closed again as the power came on in fits and starts. Within moments, the tiny tug was ascending away from its "for sale" sign. In the spaceport, nobody paid the least bit of attention.

Melanie, in the right seat, looked to her right as they ascended. The cockpit wasn't sealed properly, and the atmosphere from inside the cockpit escaped in a mushroom cloud of white vapor out the side of the ship. "Yeah, she's not spaceworthy," she said over the suit-to-suit communicator.

"We should have plenty of air in the suits," Alex said.

The tug rattled as they left the atmosphere, only quieting down after they were well into space and crossing over to the night side of the planet.

In the darkness, a larger ship, flying without marker lights, swept in close, obscuring the dim lights of other space traffic in higher orbit. Its forward searchlight clicked on and off twice, briefly flooding the cockpit with light.

"Right on schedule," Alex said. He reached over and opened the cockpit window. He retracted a safety line from his waist and clipped it just outside the cockpit window. Melanie pulled out a bundle of safety cord, clipping one end to her waist. She handed the other end to Alex. He clipped it to his own waist.

"Cowabunga," Melanie said over suit-to-suit before hurling herself out of the cockpit.

The gravity in the cockpit had her curling downward initially, but Alex grabbed the line connecting them with both hands and tugged. The line snapped taut, and she hurtled toward the dark ship above.

Alex let the line play out, and Melanie landed flat against the hull of the other ship. She felt around for a handhold, found one, and pulled herself along carefully until she found the rear airlock. She groped around for the clip point, found it, then pulled out the retractable safety line from her waist and clipped in. She gave the line connecting her to Alex three sharp shakes to send waves down it to him.

Alex stood up as best he could in the cramped cockpit, removed the bundle from behind the seats, and turned back to the controls with it in his hand. Flying one-handed, he turned the little tug so its nose pointed down toward the planet. The night side below had a few patches of lights marking the major mines, but otherwise it was totally dark. Alex double-checked everything, then he unclipped his safety cable from the clip outside the cockpit window. He hunkered down and stepped carefully to the edge of the window, standing on the central control panel. He checked his grip on the bundle.

Breathing deeply and steadily, Alex squatted down and engaged the autopilot.

The tug began moving immediately.

Alex jumped.

The tug passed just beneath his feet as he swung at

the end of Melanie's line. His head tipped back, and he grabbed the line with one hand, still holding the bundle with the other. He tugged on the line. He let go, then reached out and felt for it again, his hand groping in the darkness.

The line went taut, and then Melanie was reeling him in toward her. He clutched both arms around the bundle, letting her do the work.

Once she had him reeled in, they both felt around for the controls to the airlock hatch. Melanie found them first, and the hatch swung open, revealing the blinking lights of the airlock controls inside. In the dim light they cast, she swung her feet into the airlock. The artificial gravity yanked her boots to the deck as soon as they crossed through the hatch. She pulled herself upright and reeled in the line connected to Alex. He made his way in next, passing the bundle inside, where it dropped to the deck at Melanie's feet, before entering, arms first, and winding up prone on top of the bundle.

Alex stood up, stepped over to the controls, and plugged his left index finger into the ship's intercom. "We're on board."

"I see shuttle," Vassily's voice came back. "Moving to first position Marco selected."

The gravity shifted violently, and Alex, Melanie, and the bundle slammed into the side of the airlock, pinned.

"I thought you knew how to fly?" Alex said accusingly into the intercom.

"Sorry," Vassily responded.

"No, seriously," Alex said. "That mistake shouldn't be possible. Do you actually know how to fly?"

There was a pause before Vassily answered. "I took lesson!"

"What's wrong?" Melanie, who wasn't connected to the intercom, asked over suit-to-suit.

Alex shook his head. "Cadet-level gravity-drive mistake. The AI and the safeties are supposed to make it impossible. Either he's a secret hacker or Austin Montierthski was even more of a thrillseeker than we'd guessed."

"I wouldn't rule out either," Melanie responded.

Alex switched back to intercom. "Just don't cause us to lose the package prematurely. Are the drones in the airlock, or do we need to come inside?"

"In locker," Vassily answered.

Alex pointed to a small storage locker on the opposite wall. Melanie gingerly extricated herself from the wall, leaned forward, and climbed toward it.

"Do you think maybe you could fix the gravity?" Alex asked into the intercom.

A moment later, the deck was "down" again.

Melanie pulled open the locker and removed two round drones. She powered them both on and connected them to the bundle. Each one clamped down into the bundle with tiny claws. Then each began to glow with their own miniscule gravity drives. Melanie nodded.

Alex activated the intercom again. "Bundle's ready, drones are active."

"Not going to install programming until we see where tug is going down," Vassily answered.

Alex gave Melanie a thumbs-up, followed by an open-palm "wait" signal.

Meanwhile, the tug was descending steadily toward the night side of the planet. A network of low-orbit satellites came to life as it crossed. They flashed in the visible spectrum, none of them quite in sync with any of the others, so the effect was like random upper-atmosphere lightning. Then green laser beams started crisscrossing through the upper atmosphere.

Somewhere below both automated and human warnings should have been warning the tug off, but no one was on board to hear.

Tri Sestry glided to a stop with her airlock pointed down at the planet. Alex and Melanie stood in it, Melanie holding the bundle, watching the light show below.

An orange vapor trail shot up from the planet's surface, curling across the sky before fading into nothingness.

"Oh, don't tell me they can't hit it," Melanie radioed. "Could we have made it any easier to take out?"

"They'll get it," Alex replied.

Another orange vapor trail shot up, again just arching ineffectively through the atmosphere.

"Second position," Vassily reported through the intercom.

Alex instinctively grabbed on to a handrail, and Melanie did so, too. But the view through the open airlock shifted without jostling them around this time.

A third missile came up from the planet's surface. This one found its mark. First came the orange flash of the missile detonating, followed by the blinding green-white-violet flash of the gravity drive failing, detonating, and then safely imploding.

"They got it," Vassily said through the intercom. "Loading instructions to drones."

The drones both blinked red twice, then green twice. Alex nodded to Melanie, and she stepped up to the open airlock and prepared to throw it.

"They're green," Alex reported to Vassily.

"Standby," Vassily said. "Toss in three..."

Alex held up three fingers and gave Melanie Vassily's countdown visually.

"Two... One... Now!"

Alex pointed a finger, and Melanie threw. The bundle flew out of the airlock, spinning. Then it stopped as if grabbed by an invisible hand. Two seconds later, it accelerated off in the direction the explosion had come from.

Alex said into suit-to-suit, "Assuming Marco did the simulations correctly, that should pass as debris from the tug."

Melanie closed the airlock.

As soon as the airlock had cycled back to full pressure, they both powered off their spacesuits and let them drop to the floor. They stepped out of them, dropped their helmets on top of the piles, and stepped through the inner hatch into the master cabin. Once the inner hatch was closed, Alex activated the intercom. "We're clear. Space it."

Through the tiny window in the airlock hatch, they watched as the outer hatch opened again, blowing the spacesuits out into space with the escaping air.

"Clear," Alex reported. The outer hatch closed again.

Alex turned and marched directly to the cockpit. Vassily didn't look up from the controls as he entered. "We are going out to beyond first spacelane to reactivate markers and approach like not ever here."

"Good," Alex said, slipping into the other seat. "Now, let's spend a few minutes discussing gravity drive theory."

CHAPTER 9

"Secrets. Everyone has them, and yet no one seems to believe that they will be their undoing."
>   —Tyson Becca, *The Widow's Due*

Night was falling again in the capital city. Streetlights were turning on and off at various intervals as internal sensors failed to decide whether it was truly dark enough to turn on or truly light enough to turn off. A long, cylindrical building stood like a concrete drainpipe stretching the entire block, the east half lit by streetlights and the west half disappearing into shadows. Then the west half lit up, only to have the east half go dark a few seconds later. The sign that identified it lit up a moment later, Casphar script in big letters with Interstellar "Women's Migrant Worker Dormitory" in smaller letters under it.

Vassily stood on the corner, watching the door. He was dressed in a new shirt that had captain's epaulets attached to it and the name *Tri Sestry* embroidered in three alphabets on each of the crisp sleeves.

Women trickled into the dorm. Some of them walked past Vassily as if he weren't there. Some eyed him curiously, others suspiciously. None spoke to him.

Vassily stood for so long that the sky noticeably darkened. The streetlights all came on and stayed on. Still, he stood.

His daughter emerged from the dorm and headed up the sidewalk toward him. Her expression was far off, not looking in his direction at all as she moved. He moved to place himself in her path. She glanced up. Her eyes met his, and she immediately pivoted on her toes and crossed the street.

Vassily followed. "Anya!"

She didn't respond. Eyes forward, she reached the opposite sidewalk and turned to head down the street away from him.

Pressing his hand to his heart, Vassily spoke in a soft, pleading voice, trotting to keep up with her.

She marched on, ignoring him. She took a right at the next intersection, then another right at the next one. Vassily continued to speak from behind her but never attempted to overtake her.

A passerby stopped to watch the scene as they went past, but no one moved to intervene.

At the next intersection, a passing tram loaded with shoppers for the commercial district rattled by, forcing Vassily's daughter to stop.

Vassily stopped behind her. He hesitated and then spoke again.

She stooped down and scooped a handful of mud from the edge of the street. She rose, spun, and hurled it against his neck in one movement.

Vassily stood silently as she turned and crossed the street, paralleling the tram until its last car passed before cutting behind it.

• • •

Alex snored slightly in the darkness. His local communicator chirped and lit up, throwing light across the bed which cast greenish shadows across his bare form. He lifted his face out of his pillow and grabbed it. "What?"

Vassily's tense voice came through from the other end. "Customs inspector wants on board *Tri Sestry*, I said no authorization to enter Nostraspace ship. They said to call owner."

Alex sat up, muting the local communicator. He switched on the light. "Marco! Ellemarie!" he called out, grabbing clothes off the foot of his bed.

The bedroom door slid open. Marco stood there, bleary-eyed but dressed. "Trouble?"

"Customs is at *Tri Sestry*. Tell Ellemarie to get me all the pertinent legal code now." He yanked on his pants.

"I heard!" Ellemarie called from the hallway. "We need to get down there. How long can he keep them out?"

"Unmuting," Alex said, and picked up the local communicator. "Are you alone?"

"No," Vassily's voice responded. "Was away. Business. Now standing outside with marine commander, two police officers, and customs inspector. Were here when got back. Airlock is locked."

"Good," Alex said. "Tell them that surprise inspections at this hour mean they get to wait until we get there."

There were a few terse words in Casphar on Vassily's end.

"They say now," Vassily said.

"And I say we're Nostraspace citizens and we're on our way. If they're lucky, we'll show up without our lawyers." Alex disconnected the call.

• • •

The marine was tall even by Casphar marine standards, with a command-rank sash cutting down his chest. He stood erect by *Tri Sestry*'s bow, staring narrow-eyed at Vassily. Vassily stood equally erect, his jaw set. Neither moved. The police officers—one man and one woman—leaned lazily against *Tri Sestry*'s hull farther aft. The customs inspector was a wiry man with gray hair who paced, scowling, as Alex, Marco, and Ellemarie approached through the spaceport twilight.

Ellemarie's walking stick was having more trouble than usual finding stability for her elderly frame, so they approached slowly. They stopped on the port side of the cockpit.

The customs inspector stopped his pacing, pivoted, and moved up to the three of them. A relieved smile parted his lips. "Apologies for disruption," he said. "We make routine inspection of all ships gone offworld. Certain contraband."

"You're certain there's contraband on my company's ship?" Alex asked.

"No," the customs inspector said quickly, his voice beginning to quaver again. "Is routine. Look for contraband."

"What contraband do you expect to find on my company's ship?" Alex asked, pulling himself up to his full height so that he stood taller than the inspector.

"Is routine," the customs inspector said. "Must check all vessels."

"This ship was purchased by a Nostraspace corporation, and therefore any requests for inspection need to be processed through appropriate channels back on Polairmo."

The customs inspector turned and spoke to his escort. They approached as well. The female officer spoke. "Our government sent notice to Don."

"I've received no such notice," Alex said. "I need

to send a message to Polairmo to confirm that.”

“That take hours!” the customs inspector objected.

“You’re welcome to come back,” Alex said.

“We stay!” the marine barked.

“That’s fine, too,” Alex said. “As you say, it could take hours. Of course, if the agreement is on file, all our jumpgates should have it. So that’s, what, eighteen minutes to get the message to your jumpgate? If they pass it through in a timely manner to the Node, our jumpgates there are only twenty light-minutes apart. We could have an answer in less than ninety minutes.”

“You open ship now!” the marine ordered.

“Not without hearing back from my government,” Alex responded calmly.

“If you all will excuse me, I can’t stand for that long,” Ellemarie said, shuffling through the wall of Casphar officials toward the back of the ship. “I will say in passing, though, that I did the paperwork to transfer the registration myself. You should be very aware that this is now a Nostraspace ship.”

“Not relevant!” the marine yelled after her. “You open airlock now!”

“I sit on ramp now,” Ellemarie called, not looking back. She sidled up to the side of the ramp and lowered herself gingerly down into a slanted seated position.

The marine turned back to Alex. “You open, or I bring cutting instrument.”

“Do you know who I am?” Alex asked.

“You are owner of ship on Casphar spaceport!” the marine roared.

“Yes,” Alex said, his voice flat. “And I am also the nephew of Llewellyn Romano, Don of Nostraspace. If you cut into my ship, I’ll consider it an act of piracy, and since you're Casphar officials, an act of piracy is an act of war. You really, really don't want to start a war with Nostraspace."

"If you have authorization," Ellemarie called, having shifted to lying down on the ramp, "it should be no problem to produce the documentation without waiting for Sir Alexander to contact his uncle."

The marine swore again, and the four Casphar officials went into a huddle. After a moment, the male police officer was dispatched and took off toward the main terminal at a run.

"Should I put in the call?" Alex asked, taking out his DSC. "I've actually been meaning to drop my uncle a note. Business, you know."

"Wait!" the marine ordered. "We get paper."

Alex shrugged and put the DSC back in his pocket. "If you'd tell me what you're looking for, I might be able to help. Sometimes civilians see things that officials don't get a chance to."

The marine snarled. "Cargo holds are open?"

"Of course," Alex said. "We always comply with local regulations. I assumed you'd inspected them already."

"Yes," the customs inspector said. The marine glared at him, and he shrank deeper down into his collar.

"We keep perishables in the ship itself," Alex said conversationally, "and otherwise don't have any need to move cargo. She's just a pleasure yacht, you know. Used to belong to Austin Montierthski. _**Three Women!**_"

The marine squinted one eye at Alex. "Not funny."

Alex shrugged. "You're the ones who find it so scandalous. Where I come from, that wouldn't have even made the news. One of my cousins once had sex with three women and two men on the balcony of his house overlooking the crowd gathered for the Areehgab decadal regatta. Now that made the news, but mostly because Dale really was a good-looking guy when he was younger. Wanted to be a porn star, but my uncle wouldn't allow it. Insisted he work a government desk job instead."

"Not funny," the marine growled.

Alex shrugged again with a lopsided frown. "Suit yourself. We can just stand around glaring at each other until your friend gets back."

Nobody said anything.

After a moment, Alex started to brush some mud off of Vassily's epaulets. "Aren't these brand new?"

"Streets here are filthy," Vassily responded.

The male police officer came running back, huffing, holding a sheet of translucent plastic with extensive Casphar printing on it. He held it out to the marine who, holding it by the top of the page, held it up to Alex. "There is authorization. Open ship."

Alex leaned forward and read the document at a leisurely pace. "I may be missing something, my Casphar isn't the best, but I don't see anywhere on here any acknowledgment from my government. This isn't a binding agreement."

The male cop looked around and said something.

The female cop started and looked around, too. "Where is old lady?"

The marine roared and charged toward the ramp. Ellemarie was not there anymore.

The customs inspector trotted behind. Alex, Marco, and Vassily followed.

The marine ran up the ramp and yanked the airlock door open. He was already opening the inner door when the others caught up with him.

Ellemarie lay on the oversized bed in the master cabin. She picked her head up as the marine barged in. "The authorization here already?" she asked.

"No," Alex said from outside the airlock. "This is an act of war."

The marine reached into his sash and pulled out one of the blue wand devices. He turned it on and began pointing it all around the cabin.

Ellemarie put her head back down. "Wake me when it's time to go home. Or in the morning. Whichever comes first."

The customs inspector had come into the cabin, followed by the police officers. He walked up to the marine and spoke.

The marine roared and turned back to Alex, Marco, and Vassily, who were still on the ramp. "Where is?" he screamed. "Where is? Where is?"

"If I knew what you were looking for," Alex said, "I could answer that."

The marine pointed viciously and hollered, "Nostraspace spies!"

Marco slipped into the cabin and up to the marine. "Look, as long as you're in, let me give you the tour. Come on, I don't bite. Unless you're into that."

The marine glared at Alex a moment longer before letting Marco lead him to the cabin door. He continued to thrust the device in every conceivable direction as he walked.

"This, obviously, is the master cabin," Marco was saying as they exited. "The others aren't nearly as big, but they're quite nice..."

Alex and Vassily stepped into the cabin and shut the airlock behind themselves. The police officers and customs inspector stood awkwardly at the foot of the bed.

Alex leaned over to the customs inspector. "Some boss you've got there."

"Oh, not—" the inspector began but cut himself off.

"Seriously," Alex said confidentially, "what are you looking for?"

The customs inspector sighed and shook his head. "Not told."

Alex shook his own head in response. "That's the problem with totalitarian dictatorships."

Vassily smirked as the female police officer and the customs inspector both became visibly rankled.

Marco's voice came back. "We can't take credit for any of the modifications. She was just like this when we bought her. But you've got to admit, he had good taste." The cabin door opened again, and Marco swept in. The marine followed, chewing his lower lip furiously.

"Find what you're looking for?" Alex asked.

The marine stormed past him, yanked the airlock open, and marched out. The police officers exchanged a glance and then followed. The customs inspector's mouth flapped a few times before he managed "Thank" and chased after them.

Ellemarie sprang off the bed the instant the inspector was through the airlock. She had the in-room entertainment monitor on as soon as Vassily had the airlock hatch closed. The monitor was already patched into the external cameras. They watched as the group marched back toward the main terminal, the marine gesticulating broadly.

"That was too damned close," Alex said.

Ellemarie was already sliding the bed off of the hidden compartment. Vassily was down inside it as soon as it was clear. The black case stood closed. Vassily popped it open and restored it to the position Dale had secured it in.

"Nicely done, everyone," Alex said. "But I want everyone to appreciate that we got lucky. They're not likely to give up that easily if they suspect we've got the falcon. I want someone watching these monitors anytime *Tri Sestry* is on planet. Odds are good they got a weak reading through the hull."

Vassily nodded. "No reason to go away again. Will get supplies delivery."

He hopped out of the secret compartment, and Ellemarie slid the bed back into position.

Alex nodded to her. "And good call leaving the airlock unlocked. They won't believe you had time to do anything."

"I almost didn't," Ellemarie said with a laugh. If he was paying better attention, he'd'd've noticed the bed was still settling from me jumping onto it when he came in."

Alex sighed and shook his head. "Too damned close. Dale should be back at the house. Ellemarie, can you work from here?"

"I sure can."

Alex headed for the airlock. "Then you stay and support Vassily in making sure that box is closed if anyone comes back for another pass."

"Confirmed," Ellemarie said.

Vassily grunted.

Marco slipped out with Alex, closing both airlock hatches as he exited.

Alex walked briskly, but Marco soon came up and leaned into his side to speak quietly. "I'm confused."

"What?" Alex said.

"The regatta on Areehgab. I remember who was there. Dale wasn't. Did he do that, too?"

"Shush, you."

CHAPTER 10

"What are you running from, little butterfly?
Why did you wander so far from home? And when
I eat you, how will your mother know you've
died?"

  –Winifred Mondani, *The Song of the Frog*

Dale's beard had already begun to grow back. He sat in the middle of the main room on one of the chairs from the dining room table. Melanie ran a round grooming tool across his scalp, trimming his head hair to the same length as the beard, long strands of tangled hair dropping to the floor.

The front door opened, and Alex and Marco entered. "We need to add a layer of caution," Alex said as soon as Marco had the door closed and the system switched over to Sleeping Occupants mode. "*Tri Sestry* got searched, and they seemed to know we had the falcon on board."

"The sooner you get her off-planet, the better," Dale said.

"Quit moving," Melanie said.

"I'm not supposed to be pretty."

"Don't worry," Melanie said. "You're not."

"I've got Ellemarie staying there now, too," Alex said. "But we don't want to dawdle."

The front door's electronic knock sounded. Alex and Marco both turned to look at the system. "What part of 'Sleeping Occupants'..." Marco said as he went to the door. He switched the monitor over to the external view.

Three police officers stood on the front porch.

Marco flashed a hand signal to the others. Melanie and Dale made a dash for the back of the house. Alex swooped into the kitchen and emerged a second later with a hand broom and went after the hair on the floor. Marco tore off all his clothes and threw them back toward Alex.

Marco, in the nude, cracked the door open. He blinked tiredly at the officers. "Yes?"

One of the officers held out an ID tablet and showed Marco a badge that was written entirely in Casphar. He was older than the other two, with silver hair and a crisp goatee. The younger two both looked like wannabe marines, with shaved heads but nothing like the heft of a Casphar marine. The older officer spoke.

Marco shook his head. "Sorry. Interstellar."

The older officer grimaced. "We have report. Need to speak to occupants of house."

"We're sleeping," Marco objected.

"Inconvenience," the lead officer said. "Report cannot wait."

"I'm also naked."

The officer shook his head, not understanding.

"Naked. Nude. Not wearing any clothes."

The officer nodded, mouth opening with comprehension. "Ah. Is good. All men here." He leaned on the door and pushed it onto Marco's toe. Marco winced and backed up, letting the door swing open. The officers entered without waiting to be invited. "You are alone?"

"No," Marco said through his teeth, his foot in his hand. "My partner's here, too."

The lead officer walked past him into the main room.

The dining table chair had been replaced, and there was no sign of any of the hair. Alex, also nude, was just coming down the steps from upstairs. He looked quizzically at the police officer.

Marco hopped into the room, followed by the two younger officers. "Apparently there's some report that couldn't wait for a civilized hour."

"Only two of you in house?" the officer asked.

"Yes," Alex answered. "We're planning an early departure in our yacht tomorrow. The other two decided to sleep on board. We both sleep better in our own beds."

The officer nodded. "Discuss. Sit?"

Alex shrugged and motioned to the sofa. The lead officer sat down, but the other two hovered, one by the passage to the front door and the other by the passage to the back of the house. Alex and Marco both took chairs.

"We have report that resident here told daughter that protest planned."

Alex started noticeably. "Daughter? Nobody here has— Does Ellemarie have children?"

"She's never mentioned any," Marco said. "She doesn't seem the sort."

"Resident is no-good defector, Vassily Cheremetov."

Alex choked. "Vassily?"

"He's never mentioned children, either!" Marco exclaimed. "Talk about not seeming the type!"

"I'm sorry, officer," Alex said. "This is all news to us."

"Why would no-good defector," the officer continued, "tell daughter to leave city before protests?"

Alex just raised his eyebrows and shook his head, finally holding his hands out in an "I don't know" gesture.

Marco sat with his brow furrowed.

"Is no-good defector planning protests?"

"He'd better not be!" Alex blurted. "He has a job to do, and I expect him to be doing it."

"What is job?" the officer asked.

"Originally security," Alex said. "We've recently promoted him to pilot of our new yacht. We're looking for a good security person, if you know anyone."

"No-good defector has shown disloyalty before."

"Oh, come on," Marco said, rolling his eyes to the ceiling. "Everywhere we go, people spit at him. Do you really think anyone would protest with him? Can't you just see him, standing alone outside the palace with a sign that says 'Emperor Habid Unfair to Vassily'?"

"Some see violence as protest," the officer said.

Alex let out a blast of a laugh. "Oh, wouldn't that be rich? I've seen how your military responds to threats. One man with, what, a canister of his own farts against an army? No, even Vassily isn't that stupid."

The officer nodded. "You have maid?"

Alex squinted and puckered his lips. "Yes. I haven't seen him in a couple of days, now that you mention it."

"Ellemarie said he got a job in the mines," Marco said. "She likes him. Says we can do without a maid for a week."

"Name?" the officer asked.

Marco and Alex looked at each other with genuine blankness in their expressions. Marco spoke first. "I honestly have no idea."

"It's got to be in my local contacts file," Alex said, pulling out his local communicator. "Hang on."

"You do not know name of maid?" the officer asked,

tipping his head forward and raising one eyebrow slightly.

Alex shook his head. "I don't generally get close to the help. Here it is. Bruno."

The officer blinked. "Bruno?"

"Bruno," Alex repeated.

"Surname?"

Alex shrugged. "Why would he need one?"

The officer's jaw clenched. "Would no-good defector be friendly with help?"

Alex pondered for a second before answering with a drawn-out "Maybe."

"We will need to see maid when he returns."

Alex shrugged. "If you leave me your contact information, I can let you know when I see him again."

"Oh, don't be silly," Marco said with a flip of his wrist at Alex. "You never see him even when you're in the same room with him. Send the request to Khadija, our foreman at the factory. She does the payroll."

The officer nodded. "And need to interview no-good defector."

"He's on our yacht," Alex said, "though I think they may be in space right now. He said something about fuel prices being better in orbit than at the spaceport."

"And I check house for others."

Alex shrugged and stood up. "I'm happy to show you around." Marco moved to get up to, but Alex motioned for him to stay. "Kitchen's over here."

They went room to room, the officer checking every closet but not searching any more thoroughly than that. When they got to Alex's room, the officer's eyes fell on the two sets of clothes strewn all over the floor, one set clearly too small for Alex, and the rumpled bed. He scowled disapprovingly. He didn't pay any attention to the hand broom still lying over the open mouth of the trash incinerator. They finished the search and came back down the stairs to the ground floor.

One of the younger officers was typing into his local communicator as they came back. The older officer stopped, then backtracked up the hallway to the back door. He turned on the exterior light, opened the back door, and leaned out to check the backyard. A moment later, he returned. He was opening his mouth to speak when he started and pulled out his own local communicator.

The officer snapped to attention. He looked up at Alex and Marco, wide-eyed. "Which is Sir Alexander?"

"I am," Alex said. "Alexander Romano-Bennetti. Sir Alexander, he."

"Dress," the officer said. "I have orders bring you. See Emperor."

Marco giggled. "It wouldn't be Sir Alexander's first royal audience in the nude, you know."

"You shush," Alex said and turned and went upstairs. The officers were conferring quietly in Casphar as he left.

In his bedroom, he ignored the clothes on the floor and went to the closet for his formal cape. "Thank you, whoever rumpled the bed," he whispered. "Nice touch."

"Backyard is watched," Melanie's voice came down from the ceiling. "Dale's in Ellemarie's shower."

"I've got a royal summons. Get Vassily in space."

"Already done," Melanie reported.

"And get the plan in motion now." Alex's clothes powered on and conformed to his body. "Don't wait for me."

"Who goes with me?" Melanie asked.

"Marco," Alex said. "Dale's got the local rapport."

And with that, he was out of the room and heading back down the stairs.

• • •

The police had arrived on foot, so they walked the whole way to the palace. Not only was it dark, it was night, so they encountered very few people out. Nobody spoke the whole way, all three police officers moving in a trancelike daze that intensified the closer they got to the palace.

They walked past the museum and around toward the far side. They stopped at a nondescript door cut into the massive wall that surrounded the palace complex. The older officer motioned for Alex to stand in front of the door. He did so. It slid open, revealing two marines and two palace guards. The taller of the two marines surveyed the group in front of him, then stepped back to admit them.

They were in a small room with a window on one side, behind which another palace guard sat. The police officers removed their service belts and handed them over. The palace guard looked expectantly at Alex, then barked an order. Alex emptied his pockets, fingerprint-locking his DSC and local communicator before surrendering them.

A door on the far wall, invisible previously, slid open, and the marine motioned for Alex and the three policemen to enter the small metal room beyond it. They did so.

The door closed behind them, leaving them in a metal box, illumination coming from behind a metal grill overhead. The room beeped twice. The lights went out. A green scanner beam passed over them. The lights came back on and another door, also previously invisible, slid open on the opposite wall.

Two palace guards waited in the corridor outside the door. Alex stepped out first, the policemen following. The guards pivoted and flanked Alex, leading him down the corridor to an open double door. They stepped through into a large garden.

Trees, larger than anywhere else on Reggit, towered over them, creating a canopy of fragrant air. Grass grew in square planters, between which a boardwalk of real wood ran over mossy rocks. The palace guards led the way down the boardwalk, turning left at a large fountain.

Emperor Habid sat on a real-wood bench, which was one of four on a real-wood deck under the largest tree in the garden.

The three police officers simultaneously dropped to one knee and bowed their heads. The palace guards stopped.

Alex strode right up to the emperor. "It's nice to see you again, Emperor Habid."

The emperor motioned to the next bench to his left. "Please sit down, Sir Alexander."

Alex sat. Neither the guards nor the police officers moved.

The emperor got right to the point. "I must admit to you that I was extremely surprised to hear that you were being questioned in connection with reports of a planned protest on my planet. It seemed quite unlike both you and the Don to be causing civil unrest."

Alex smiled politely. "That, of course, is because I was doing no such thing. Our current theory is that our maid confided in Vassily, and he was concerned that his daughter might become caught up in it."

"He should, of course, have reported it himself," the emperor said.

Alex nodded. "Agreed. But you must admit, he has been less than welcome here."

The emperor held out both hands magnanimously. "He has, of course, made his own choices. The greater concern came when I learned that a ship, where my missing statue was suspected of being held, turned out to also belong to you."

Alex smiled and nodded, raising one eyebrow. "Is that what they were looking for? They declined to specify. Had they told me, I could have saved them a lot of time searching by simply telling them we don't have it."

"And imagine my greater shock," the emperor said, "when I learned that it's you who has been manufacturing those disgusting Austin Montierthski dolls."

Alex's smile turned genuine. "What can I say? They made us enough money to buy Austin Montierthski's yacht."

The emperor tapped a fingernail against his lip. "Sir Alexander, I do not wish to make any sort of accusation, but it seems to me that there are a lot of, shall we say, little problems cropping up around you."

Alex nodded thoughtfully, the corners of his mouth turning down. "I'd be inclined to think that your people's natural suspicion of foreigners combined with our high profile makes us logical targets for accusation and innuendo."

"It could be, it could be," the emperor said, leaning forward. "And perhaps what we need is a demonstration to our people that you are, indeed, a welcome guest on Reggit. To that end, I'd like you to remain in the palace here with me until such time as we can locate my missing statue."

Alex smiled again, the veins in his neck pulsing. "I would be honored. If I could just let my associates know."

"That will all be attended to," the emperor said with a wave.

The palace guards approached and flanked Alex.

Still smiling, Alex rose and went with them.

• • •

Melanie fussed with Ellemarie's sewing machine, cursing in Kon. A brown miner's outfit lay under a broken needle tangled in thread. Melanie's features had again changed. Her skin was lighter. She had a wispy adolescent beard and moustache growing out from around her mouth. The miner's outfit she wore reshaped her body into that of a teenaged boy.

She yanked the outfit she was altering out of the machine and brought up its menu to access the instructions on changing a needle.

Marco entered. He, too, was altered. A beard, thicker than Melanie's but also adolescent in texture, covered his lower jaw, and he had developed thick eyebrows and a brow ridge that made his eyes vanish beneath them. He held two yellow cards. "Forgery's not my forte. How do these look?"

Melanie glanced over at them. "Fine. No one's going to look too closely. The photos are secure?"

Marco nodded.

"That's the most important thing. They do look to make sure the photo on the card is the one that was originally there. Prevents people from killing someone for their work card."

Marco shook his head. "Stealing is a much more honest way of life."

"How about sewing?" Melanie asked. "Do you know how to use this damned thing?"

"No."

"Screw it, we don't have time." She threw the half-altered miner's outfit to him. "Get dressed. If anyone asks, it's your dad's."

"And how am I supposed to know what they're asking?" Marco asked.

Melanie sighed. "We don't have time for that, either. Let's go."

· · ·

Marco's miner's outfit didn't fit at all. The pants legs didn't come down far enough, and the sleeves were only long enough because the top was too loose all around. He wore the whole outfit cinched tight with a belt around his waist, and he walked with a shuffle and one hand on his hip. Melanie's outfit fit better, and with the hood up and her head down, she looked the part of a young miner heading out on his first job.

They arrived at a corner, where fifty other miners were waiting, and slipped into the crowd. The streetlight only illuminated half the crowd, and Marco and Melanie stuck to the shadows.

More miners arrived until the crowd swelled to about a hundred. It was still ten minutes after the last one arrived before the mine transport rattled toward them. It was a long metal tram, two cars with three axles each, open on all sides with the driver riding atop the front car in an open cage. It rumbled to a stop, and two marines stepped off, one from each car. The one in front barked out orders, and the miners formed two jagged lines, all with yellow work cards out.

Marco and Melanie fell into the line for the back car, Marco in front. As he got to the front of the line, he handed his forged work card over to the marine, who looked remarkably like a young Vassily. The marine pressed his thumb against the photo on the card and tried to slide it. Then he glanced at

Marco's face before handing the card back to him.
Marco climbed on board.

Melanie handed her work card over next. The marine paused, looking at the photo, his thumb hovering above it. He looked at Melanie and spoke gruffly.

Melanie shot a short exclamation out through her teeth and snarling upper lip.

The marine laughed and handed the work card back to her. She elbowed past him and onto the tram.

Marco looked at her questioningly, but she shook her head and pointed him toward two empty seats all the way in the back. She took the seat in the back corner of the tram, a spot with nothing except the seat back to lean on or hold on to. He took the seat next to her.

They settled back for the journey.

• • •

Vassily was napping in *Tri Sestry*'s pilot seat, Ellemarie in the seat next to him with a tablet connected to the communications system by a physical cable. In her pocket, her local communicator buzzed, and the tablet screen flipped over to its interface. A message, blinking red, had appeared.

"What does this mean?" Ellemarie asked.

Vassily opened his eyes and leaned over. "Security system in house. Police can signal emergency if no answer at door. Security system sends message. Answer and say no emergency."

Ellemarie pressed a small icon in the lower corner of the screen. The house's exterior camera view filled the screen, revealing three policemen on the porch.

"Hello," Ellemarie said in a strong, clear voice. "Can I help you, gentlemen?"

There was a lag of a few seconds before one of the

officers perked up like he had heard and responded.
"We have report of emergency."

"No emergency there," Ellemarie said. "We're all in orbit in our yacht. Our security system shows no one is in the house."

Again there was a lag. The policeman grimaced. "Open door. We check."

"Sorry," Ellemarie said. "No emergency. False report. Have a nice day." She disconnected from the house system.

A few seconds later the emergency entry request was blinking on her screen again.

"Must answer every time," Vassily said. "If no answer, door unlocks. Safety feature."

"This is going to be a long couple of days," Ellemarie muttered, answering the call again.

• • •

Dale stopped at the front desk of a long, cylindrical building. He stamped his thumbprint against a reader and then took a stylus and signed something in Casphar script underneath it.

The system blinked for a moment, then displayed a series of questions. Dale typed a response to each of them.

The system blinked again, a little longer this time. Then it blinked green and printed out a blue card with Dale's picture on it. Dale took the card, read it, and proceeded to an elevator to the second floor.

The second floor was nothing but bank after bank of bunk beds, three tall, lined up in tight rows with narrow lockers standing between them. Dale walked down the central aisle, alternately glancing at the blue card and the number hanging over each row of bunks.

Finally, halfway down the length of the building, he turned right and moved down the row. Most of the other bunks had figures asleep on them. A few other miners were awake and moving around quietly.

Dale reached a stack of bunks, checked the card against the letters on the bunks, and then collapsed onto the bottom bunk.

From two banks over, someone spoke in a strong but hushed voice. Dale sat up, rolled onto his belly, and looked.

Another miner looked back and forth around himself and then pulled a handwritten sign out from under his mattress. He showed it to Dale.

Dale smiled and nodded approvingly.

• • •

On the front porch of the house, a half dozen marines had arrived and stood behind the police officers. The security system buzzed insistently. A moment later, the doorbell lit up yellow, and Ellemarie's voice came out of it. "Sorry, boys, still no emergency." The system went dark and silent.

One of the marines said something, and the police moved back. The six marines moved up to the front door. The two in front pressed their hands against the door, their fingers right next to the jamb. One of them nodded, and the other four hurled their body weight against the door. As they did so, the door bowed inward, and the two in front stuck their fingers between the jamb and the door and pulled.

The door inched open a crack. The two next-closest marines shoved their fingers into the crack as well and pulled, too.

With a resounding crack, the door slid open, jumping out of its track along the bottom.

A klaxon sounded, and every light in the house

began to strobe. The marines all pulled themselves up
and straight. One of the marines in front shrugged
his head toward the inside of the house. The other
five charged in, and he followed.

The main room was empty and dark except for the
strobing light.

A mechanical but firm voice spoke first in Casphar,
then in Interstellar. "Intruder alert! Enter
override code or defensive measures will begin in
fifteen seconds!"

One of the policemen ran into the house and
turned on the security system's interface. He typed
frantically.

Two of the marines charged into the kitchen and two
more ran back to the stairs. The remaining policemen
remained outside, peering in with concern.

The policeman at the security console swore.

The klaxon went silent. The strobing light
stopped. Everything went black inside.

A hissing sound came from the ventilation system.

One of the marines started barking orders in the
darkness, but his voice gave way to wracking coughs.

Upstairs, a gun fired. Another boom followed
immediately.

The windows on the second floor blew out. Flames
rolled out of the frames.

CHAPTER 11

"It is well established that governments gain
their power through either consent or fear.
Critics of a government always ascribe the
source to fear, while advocates ascribe it
to consent. Our challenge is to determine
empirically which citizens are ruled by consent
and which citizens are ruled by fear."
    —Xiaolin Chang, *Matters and Procedures
    for the Betterment of ALL*, translated by
    James Pyle

Across the street from the house, a small crowd had gathered, watching. The concrete walls and roof still stood, albeit charred. A military cordon had been set up around the property, including soldiers on the roofs of the two houses next door. Large floodlights had been set up on extending poles in the backyard.

Two body bags lay unceremoniously in a pile in one corner of the front yard. A large van sat in the street two doors down, and technicians in black overalls carried charred property out of the house to a table that had been set up on the front walk, where each item was documented and then placed in a fabric bag and sealed.

Another group of technicians in gray overalls were transporting the steady stream of sealed bags to the van, where they were checked in by technicians in white overalls. In the artificial light, the whole scene moved in and out of shadow like some sort of abstract painting.

Khadija stood among the onlookers across the street, a ledger tucked firmly under her left arm.

One of the soldiers on perimeter duty stepped forward and stopped a technician who was emerging from the house with the charred remnants of Alex's gun. They spoke over it briefly, the soldier rubbing his hands together. Finally, the soldier nodded and carried the blackened gun over to the processing table.

Khadija turned, her head bowing a little, and walked away.

She didn't speak to anyone as she wound through the streets to the factory. It was morning, so people were arriving at work in various offices and factories, but Khadija moved with such intent that people got out of her way as their paths were in danger of intersecting. She was at a full march as she burst through the front doors of the factory.

One of the sewers was working the reception desk. Khadija slammed the ledger down on the desk. The bang reverberated like a gunshot, and the woman at the desk jumped.

Khadija launched into a tirade.

The sewer at the reception desk listened politely at first, her expression growing more and more concerned as Khadija went on. After a moment, wild-eyed, she pulled out her local communicator and started sending a message while Khadija continued ranting.

The inner door to the factory floor slid open. Two more women stood there, looking into the reception area with quizzical expressions.

Khadija turned to them and started her rant over again.

Neither of the two new women waited as long as the temporary receptionist before looking alarmed and pulling out local communicators. One of them was still sending a message as she backed out of the door, repeating Khadija's rant, even as Khadija continued.

Work came to a halt on the factory floor. The rant passed from woman to woman. Fists were raised. Nearly everyone sent messages out on their local communicators.

And soon all voices were raised at the same time, a cacophony of angry women replacing the cacophony of machinery.

• • •

Alex reclined on a real-wood couch in one of the palace's sitting rooms. The walls were entirely real-wood paneling, and the floor planked with a contrasting real wood. Even the palace tablet Alex was reading was set in a real-wood frame.

Two palace guards flanked the door, keeping their gazes respectfully off in space. They were clearly accustomed to long hours standing at attention.

The wood-panel doors slid open, and a slender woman with black hair folded into a flattened swoosh on top of her head entered. Her cape and slacks were bejeweled and of fine fabric, in contrast to her blouse, which held to her curvy form supportively and functionally at the expense of being fashionable.

She smiled, fine lines at the edges of her eyes wrinkling into tiny crow's feet as she did so. "Sir Alexander," she said. "I heard you were visiting."

Alex rose. "Princess Aiez," he said, tucking the tablet under his arm and moving to her with a hand extended. "It's lovely to see you again."

She took his hand and curtseyed formally. Then she glanced at both palace guards wryly. With a smirk, she threw her arms around him and kissed him on both cheeks. He laughed. "You're going to cause a scandal!"

"I do not care!" She pulled herself off of him and wrapped an arm around his free arm. "Come, walk with me. How have you been?"

"Fine," Alex said, "except for hearing in the media that your father decided to burn down my house."

She laughed. "The media does not care for Father. It was your own security system that burned it down."

Alex's voice was exasperated, but he spoke with a smile nonetheless. "Nothing in my security system protocol was set to light the house on fire!"

She waved a dismissive hand at him as she led him out into the corridor, the two guards following at a respectful distance. "It was set up to maximize confusion, and you had to know a typical marine would fire a gun when surprised. Your choice of gas proves the case against you."

"I wasn't expecting marines to trip the system."

"So you say, so you say," she said, laughing again. "I do hope you did not lose anything of value."

"It was a rental," Alex said.

"See, then? No harm," Princess Aiez said, guiding him out a set of double doors and into one of the courtyards. "Did I ever tell you of the time my father had my boyfriend disemboweled in this courtyard while my sister and I watched? Boyfriends are much harder to replace than houses."

Alex leaned over and spoke quietly into her ear. "Especially once your father gets the reputation for disemboweling them."

She howled with laughter and waved her hand at him again.

"It really is a nice palace you have here," Alex said. "I'd never seen anything except the formal ballroom before last night."

"Did I not smuggle you up last time you were here?" Princess Aiez asked. "How foolish of me."

"I suspect my mother was watching you the whole time," Alex said.

"She was," Aiez answered. "A formidable woman, your mother."

"Second in the line of succession under the wartime plan," Alex said.

"I imagine the Suturiku would think twice about doing anything that would put her in charge," Aiez said, looking up at one of the trees they were passing.

Alex spoke plainly. "They're not the only empire the Don is willing to go to war against."

"Oh, do not be a bore," Aiez said. "You know I have no part in politics. Except that I think my father hoped your uncle would marry me at one point."

"I suspect that you would have murdered him in his sleep if you had," Alex said.

Aiez smiled broadly but with closed lips, stopping to look at him. "Very likely. Very likely. Come, how are you liking the palace? Not too confining, I hope. I know you are used to a much freer range than I am. I so rarely get to leave."

"Oh, it's not confining at all," Alex said, turning her and starting to walk again. "It's very spacious. Much more comfortable than the house your father just burned down. Plus, I never feel confined when I'm choosing to remain somewhere."

"I am so glad," Aiez said. Her head tilted

slightly, and her eyes turned toward the top of the perimeter wall. "The walls often feel like prison walls to me."

Alex shrugged. "Then walk outside past them."

She laughed ruefully.

"I'm serious. Walk outside. You'd be amazed what you would encounter moving among your subjects."

"I am quite certain I would be killed."

"I doubt it," Alex said. "Your father is so worried about insurgencies and disloyalty that he's locked you away from reality. And the reality is that people want a leader they feel is listening to them and cares about them. I bet that if you walked outside today and just listened to your subjects for a few hours, you could completely avert whatever protest your father thinks I'm guilty of stirring up."

She stopped moving again. She withdrew her arm from his. She dropped her hands down to his hands, and she clasped both of them gently. Her smile turned sad, and her voice grew quiet. "I do not doubt your logic. And in Nostraspace, it would be good advice. But we are not Nostraspace, Sir Alexander. Our ways are different, older. We trust in the loyalty of our people. You pander to yours as if you were their servants."

Alex leaned forward slightly and whispered, "I am their servant."

Aiez sighed slightly and looked back toward the palace wall beyond the trees.

"Why don't we get breakfast?" Alex asked.

She wrapped her arm in his again, and they began moving toward the opposite end of the courtyard.

"I do not think you are," Aiez said suddenly.

"What?" Alex asked.

"Their servant," Aiez said. "The Nostraspace

people. You do not serve them. You follow orders."

"The Don's orders are always what is best for the people," Alex said.

She cast him a sidelong glance. "Then why are you here? What does the Don gain by sending you here?"

Alex raised one eyebrow at her. They crossed back indoors, and she hugged closer to him in the narrow corridor. The guards stayed two paces behind.

"Do not claim the Don did not send you," Aiez said.

"I'm afraid he didn't," Alex said. "I saw a business opportunity. In my family, it's outcompete everyone else or end up stuck at a low-end government job making people feel like they've got the ear of the Don because one of his no-good relatives has no choice but to put up with you."

"Now you contradict yourself," she said.

"Not really, no," Alex said. "By coming here and making money, I acquire wealth. That wealth gets spent here, yes, but also back home, where it helps improve the standard of living for my people, and your people. I'm happier. I'm more comfortable when I'm rich instead of a civil servant, but either way, I'm still helping my people. And here I'm also helping your people."

She laughed and shook her head. "You are as scandalous as your Austin Montierthski dolls." She checked over her shoulder and leaned over to him before she continued. "I have three of them."

Alex laughed. "Don't let your father find out!"

They crossed into a dining room. Like the rest of the palace, it featured a lot of real wood. Thirty small round tables were scattered around the room. Servants sat at some of them, eating. They all sprang to their feet as Princess Aiez entered. She motioned for them to sit down and spoke with a commanding voice in Casphar. The dining servants hesitated but eventually began to sit down again after Aiez and Alex had selected seats at an unoccupied table in the corner.

Large plates full of eggs and fruit appeared in front of them almost immediately, the servants who had delivered them vanishing as quickly as they came.

Aiez leaned forward, her mask of formality falling and revealing a woman with a hard, low voice. "Alex, it is wrong that you are being held here. I will speak to Father if you wish."

Alex raised an eyebrow. "Held here? I'm a guest. I can leave at any time."

Aiez's expression fell, chin tipping down, eyes turning up to keep looking at him.

"I'll prove it," Alex said. "Go tell those two guards not to let me out of their sight under any circumstances. Promise to have them disemboweled if they fail."

Aiez let a small laugh escape through her nose. She set down her utensils and rose. She swept over to the guards, once again the picture of royalty and command. She spoke to the two guards in low, firm tones. They nodded obediently.

When she turned around, Alex was gone.

The two palace guards jumped.

Princess Aiez roared and screamed at everyone in the room. Servants appeared from the kitchen, staring blankly. The servants who were eating blinked, uncomprehending. Aiez roared again.

Meals were abandoned. People sprang to their feet. Servants scattered in every direction. The palace guards split up, one heading up the corridor they had come in through, the other running into the kitchen.

Aiez stood alone in the dining room. Her voice

remained strong, but it took on a plaintive quality.
"Sir Alexander?" She looked around. "Are you still
in here?"

In the kitchen, the palace guard turned around
three times, then pointed at one of the cooks and
shouted. The cook shook his head. The guard then
ran out of the kitchen through a door on the far wall.
As the door slid shut behind him, he looked left and
right in a corridor, trying to decide which way to go.
The cooks watched him go, then went back to work.

Alex, his cape removed and wrapped around his arm,
stepped out of the walk-in freezer, tying an apron
over his clothes. No one even looked as he moved
over to one of the counters, took a plate, and began
loading it with food. A moment later, he was out the
same door the palace guard had exited.

The guard was all the way down the corridor to
the left. Alex turned right and walked, the plate
outstretched, right past a cluster of huddled palace
guards deep in conference.

The corridor turned to the right and then dumped
out into a much larger, more formal corridor. The
ceiling in this one was double height, and the wood
paneling was a complex inlay of four different woods
in a herringbone pattern. To the right lay a large
archway with the formal ballroom beyond.

Alex turned left and headed toward a set of double
doors flanked by four palace guards. None of them even
glanced in Alex's direction as he walked past them.
The double doors slid open automatically, and Alex
vanished into the darkened space beyond.

Setting the plate down on a small table just inside
the door, Alex took off the apron and put his cape
back on. He folded the apron, picked the plate back
up, and set the apron under it, and then moved farther

into the room. He spoke a firm word in Casphar.

The lights turned on, revealing an ornate throne room, decorated in woods of dozens of different species and colored with stains in every color of the rainbow. The throne itself was hand carved with figures of two-headed falcons. Smaller wooden chairs flanked it. Alex selected one of these and sat down, eating the food on his plate with his fingers.

Emperor Habid's voice came from behind the throne. "Perhaps you might care to explain, Sir Alexander, how it is that I am supposed to be disemboweling my palace guards?"

Alex looked up.

The emperor appeared from the hidden passage behind the throne, and the throne slid back into position.

Alex smirked and held out his plate. "Would you like a kebab?"

• • •

The sun was beginning to set on the mountain range that surrounded the planet's abyssal valley. A reddish cloud-swept sky cast deep shadows in the passes as a heavy freight train rattled down a mountainside.

One flatbed car was occupied by the mine tram. Marco and Melanie still sat together in the back row, leaning into each other, eyes closed. All around both cars, miners shivered in the freezing air, huddling together for warmth, some sleeping.

Melanie cracked one eye open. She sat motionless for a moment, then poked Marco. He grunted. She poked him again, and he opened his eyes. He began to shiver convulsively as soon as he was awake.

Silently, Melanie slipped out of her seat and dropped to the narrow strip of flatbed railcar between

the tram and the plunge to the track below. She
inched along the side and slipped back behind the
tram. Marco followed, sticking the landing and moving
along the narrow strip with the grace of a cat.

As Marco rounded the back of the tram, Melanie
already had her beard off and was pulling off her
miner's outfit. Underneath it, a crisp green military
uniform looked like it had been cut specifically for
her figure. She pulled a small bag out of the inner
pocket of the miner's outfit, then shoved the outfit and
her discarded prosthetics into it.

Marco was out of his miner's outfit a moment later,
revealing a sloppily tailored green uniform.

"I wish we'd had time to alter that," Melanie
said. "Just remember that Casphar regard people with
developmental differences as inferior, so act like
you've got cognition issues."

Marco nodded, taking the bag from Melanie and
shoving his outfit into it.

"Beard," Melanie reminded him.

Marco's hand flew to his face. He touched the false
beard, felt along it a bit until he found an edge, and
pulled it off. He shoved it into the bag, too.

Melanie gestured toward the back of the train, and
they started walking. They hopped the gap between the
flatbed car they were on and a tiny service platform on
the empty ore car behind them. Melanie pulled herself
up onto the top of the car's sidewall, then reached
down to give Marco a hand up. With her help, he made
it to the top effortlessly.

The wind tore at their hair and clothes as they
stood up and walked along the sidewall of the ore car.
When they got to the end of the car, Melanie squared
her shoulders, leaned forward, and leapt to the next
one. She hit the sidewall and kept going, sliding

down inside the empty ore chute.

Marco tipped sideways, struggling to balance on the moving car in the wind. He righted himself and leapt. He came down in a squat on the top of the next car's sidewall, reaching out and grabbing the corner with his hand to steady his landing. He reached down with his other hand and helped Melanie scramble back up.

"Thank you," Melanie said.

"Always one for the team," Marco replied.

They then repeated the walk along the sidewall with Marco in the lead.

The next car was a passenger car. The wind blew Marco sideways again. He recovered and leapt, coming down on the roof of the passenger car less gracefully than usual, but still upright. He turned around and held a hand out for Melanie. She squared her shoulders against the wind and leapt. He grabbed her hand as she came down. She wrapped her arms around him, and he spread his legs to balance her weight as she came down. She nodded, and they both let go and moved toward the back of the passenger car.

The car to the rear was shaped like a passenger car, but this one had a series of vents with smoke coming out of them along one side. The two cars were connected by a flexible tube. Marco reached down and pulled the tube back from the passenger car at the top. He held it open, and Melanie lowered herself down through the gap. Marco followed.

They landed on a small bridge between the cars. Melanie picked Marco up by the waist, and he shoved the tube back into position. She set him down and opened the door to the rear car.

A galley stretched the length of the car, cooking surfaces on one side, tables and chairs on the other. A counter separated the two, staffed by a single attendant who alternately took orders and dashed to

the various parts of the car. There were one or two
other people in uniform in the car, but the rest of
the patrons were dressed in business attire, mostly
women.

Melanie stepped up to the counter, waited for
the attendant to get to her, placed an order, then
pointed to an empty table. Marco sat down obediently.
Melanie waited for the food.

• • •

Tri Sestry drifted along outside the main orbital
sphere of influence, still only a few light-seconds
away from the planet. Reggit hung like a great brown
ball, half lit, off the port bow.

Vassily napped in the pilot's seat. Ellemarie
paced on the other side of the hatch by the galley.
"I don't like the silence," she said.

Vassily didn't open his eyes. "Is plan. Nothing
to do until Melanie and Marco in position."

"And I don't like sending Marco in. He doesn't
speak a word of Casphar. What happens if someone
gives him an instruction?"

"We hope they believe him stupid."

Ellemarie grumbled.

• • •

Dale walked through the second floor of the dorm,
carrying a bundle of discarded packing material. At
the far end of the building, three men stood side
by side in the aisle like military guards. All was
quiet behind them except for an occasional murmur of
conversation.

As Dale approached, one of the men smiled and
spoke slightly louder than would be natural for their
proximity. "Bruno!"

The men parted to let Dale pass. Beyond them,

several dozen miners were crouched on the floor and lying across bunks with paintbrushes in their hands, carefully lettering messages onto paper, packing material, thin sheets of metal, and whatever else might be conscripted into being a sign. Three young men hustled over to Dale and took the packing material from him. They distributed it to people who did not have a sign to work on.

An older miner gestured for Dale to come over. Dale went along a series of bunks to where the old miner had several signs leaning against a bunk, with blanks next to each one. The old miner pointed to the first one. Dale looked at it and then spoke with a thick Casphar accent. "Low wages kill miners."

The old miner handed a pencil to Dale. He sketched the words onto the first blank.

A dark-skinned young miner, clearly of Kon descent, sidled up to Dale. "You speak Interstellar?"

Dale nodded and answered in Casphar.

The old miner looked surprised and pointed to the next sign in line. Dale glanced over at it and translated, "Unkind work conditions."

The young Kon shook his head and said, "Unfair."

Dale nodded. "Unfair."

The old man scrounged for a second pencil and set the Kon to work sketching the letters on the next one.

"Thank you," Dale said, still speaking with the thick Casphar accent. "Is good have more help."

The young Kon answered, "It is an important protest. When do we start?"

Dale said, "Media see more in daylight."

The young Kon nodded. "Daylight soon."

Dale finished the sign he was working on and circled past the young Kon to the next sign. "Also, must be safe. More miners in city than military. Patient." He cocked his head at the sign. "Good work now?"

The young Kon looked over. "Safe. Safe work now."

Dale started lettering the blank next to it. The old miner began painting in the letters Dale had sketched on the first sign.

The young Kon leaned closer to Dale. "Protest starts soon? Yes?"

"Patient," Dale said. "Yes, soon."

Chapter 12

*"The risk with giving orders is that your
soldiers will follow them."*
    *—Nostraspace Infantry Officer's Training
Manual*

On the only patch of level ground in a deep valley, a low, wide factory building sat—a shock of gray among green. The road to it was paved but looked as if it hadn't been maintained for decades.

Downslope from the factory, several paved lots sat in terraces, each lot filled with a different sort of military vehicle: long armored personnel carriers, wide-bodied tanks with spiked treads, trams, two-person vehicles, and even landscaping equipment.

A cylindrical hire car climbed the road to the factory. It pulled up out front, and the rear door slid open. Melanie, still dressed in her Casphar uniform but with the last vestiges of her makeup removed, slid out heels first. As she pulled herself upright, Marco's head appeared, and he stepped out behind her. Melanie closed the door, and the car drove off again. Melanie pulled her Casphar ID tablet and a small green card out of an inner pocket and strode purposefully up to the door. Marco shuffled along behind her, keeping his head down.

On the front porch, Melanie pressed the knocker button. The door slid open in front of her just as Marco arrived behind her. They stepped into a small dark reception area. Melanie nodded curtly at the young man in a green uniform behind the desk, showed her ID tablet, and placed the green card in front of him.

He picked the card up, gave it a quick read, and nodded. He fed it into a slot.

Melanie's face betrayed nothing as she waited. Marco shuffled slightly and put his hands into his pockets.

A moment later, the card emerged from the slot, and the young man took it again. He rose, studying it, and stepped through a door behind his desk.

Marco moved around to where Melanie could see him. He tipped his head up slightly and raised his eyebrows.

Melanie's jaw tightened slightly. Her head twitched to one side. Marco looked back down to the floor and held his position.

A few minutes later, the young man came back with a tablet and a stylus. He handed them to Melanie, pointing and giving some instructions. Melanie nodded and signed the forms.

The young man took the tablet back, gestured down the hill, and gave some more instructions.

Melanie nodded, barked an order at Marco, and marched out the door. Marco trotted behind her.

A flight of concrete steps led down to a gate in the top parking lot. Melanie stopped just to the side of the gate. They waited.

After a while, the gate rattled open, and an armored personnel carrier roared out of the stacks toward them. It had a large mesh-covered window in the front but otherwise looked like a solid mass, wheels covered by a metal skirt that cleared the ground by less than a centimeter, retracting slightly whenever it came to an imperfection in the paving.

The APC came to a stop halfway out the gate. The engine shut off. A hatch on the side just in front of Melanie slid open. A middle-aged Kon woman in civilian attire stood there. She smiled broadly at Melanie.

Melanie smiled back, her eyes gleaming, and extended a hand.

The driver took her hand in both of hers and jumped down to the pavement. They exchanged a few words.

Melanie turned and spoke curtly to Marco, pointing to the hatch. He climbed up into the APC and left Melanie and the driver talking.

The inside was simply a long cabin with benches running the whole length, hand straps above the center aisle. A hatch matching the one Marco had come through stood exactly opposite, a fold-down section of bench in the upright position on it. Marco turned into the cockpit and took the right seat. He studied the console for a moment and then pressed and held a gray button. The engine roared to life.

Melanie entered the APC and shut the hatch.

She walked up to the cockpit and took the left seat. She turned on the screens in front of her, navigated through a few menus, and made a quick adjustment. "There. That should be safe now. Internal microphones are disabled."

"I can't believe that actually worked," Marco said.

Melanie half shrugged. "It's all about knowing the culture. Casphar don't question orders. If it's something that looks fishy, they verify them, but otherwise, if they've got orders, they follow them. Vassily wrote the orders. Ellemarie inserted them into their system. They're expecting us, so nothing looks out of the ordinary, even as we drive off in their APC. Hang on. These things have no shock absorption except in the seats." She put the APC in gear and maneuvered it out of the gate.

The Kon woman waved to them as they turned onto the road and headed back down the mountain. She went back into the yard as the gate began to close automatically.

Marco had extricated his DSC from his shoe. He typed a message to Alex, Vassily, and Ellemarie: <u>Has my package arrived?</u>

Seconds later, a yellow dot appeared on the map on the APC's control screen. "There's our locator beacon," Melanie said. "It's only about five kilometers off from the target. Nice job."

Marco smiled. "I just ran the simulations. You executed the drop."

A response came back from Ellemarie: <u>Don't know. The government burned down our house, and Alex has been incommunicado since they arrested him.</u>

Marco read it. "That's not one of the standard responses."

Melanie slammed on the brakes. Marco slid into the front console. He righted himself and showed his DSC to Melanie. "But they activated the locator beacon. It's got to be them, or they wouldn't know."

"Could they have gotten it out of Alex somehow?" Marco asked.

Melanie looked at him. "You've known him longer than I have. Can you imagine him breaking under interrogation?"

"He never broke under anything I've ever done to him," Marco said.

"Is it possible they actually burned down our house, and Ellemarie thought that answering not in code would be less suspicious?"

"How do you burn down a concrete house?"

Melanie shook her head. "Okay, I'm ranking here, but this is your mission. What do you think? Does that mean abort?"

Marco examined the ceiling of the APC. "King of Earth, I don't know. I haven't known Ellemarie much longer than you have."

Melanie put the APC back in gear, and they started rolling again. "Do you want to risk code?"

Marco nodded, then ran his tongue across his teeth and shook his head. He typed a response, only to Ellemarie: <u>Burned down our house?!</u>

Melanie drummed her finger on the center console as they waited for the response.

It came two minutes later: <u>Read the news. Yes, burned down our house. No word from Alex. Hope you and the girlfriend are having fun.</u>

Marco showed it to Melanie. She grunted. "Don't download the Interstellar feeds. They monitor those, and they might wonder why they're coming down to an APC. Here, let me get the Casphar services up. You ready to drive?"

"Not really," Marco said.

"Tough, try it," Melanie said, sending control over to the right seat. Marco tensed as the map and directional controls appeared in front of him. "You're supposed to be my driver. They're going to wonder if you can't drive."

"And they're not going to wonder that you're a Kon," Marco said.

"There are Kon in the military," Melanie said. "It's tougher, of course. You need to be the best to even have a chance of being regarded as equal, and you'll never get a commission, but the Kon who get in are heroes to the other Casphar Kon. Here it is. For the love of jumptech, they really did burn down our house!"

"That screws up all our codes," Marco said, not taking his eyes off the twisting road.

"We don't have any way to exchange new codes," Melanie said. "Your call. Abort?"

Marco screwed up his face but still refused to look away from the road. "Dale's been doing all that work to organize the workers' protest. Without the distraction, this plan doesn't work, right?"

"Right," Melanie said. "Protests on Casphar attract the full attention of the military. If they're not looking away, there's no way we pull this off."

"You know Dale," Marco said. "Can he get the miners to be patient for another week?"

"From what he told me," Melanie said, "I think he's worried they're going to start marching before we're ready."

"Then we keep going," Marco said. "I mean, what the hell, it's not like anyone's marrying me out of this life anyway, right?"

Melanie smiled. "You and me both, kid."

"Answer Ellemarie for me," Marco said. "Tell her, 'She's fine. Going hiking. Wish we had a home to bring her home to.'"

Melanie laughed and typed the message.

CHAPTER 13

"Never look where the magician tells you to
look."
          —Christopher Delmonico, magician

Dale's local communicator buzzed. He lay on his bunk
in the dorm, right arm over his eyes. He rolled
over, uncovered his eyes, and pulled the communicator
out. It was a message from Marco: <u>What's for dinner?</u>

Dale sat up on the bunk and typed back: <u>Cabbage
soup. Have you rented new house yet?</u>

Vassily responded with a thumbs-up.

Ellemarie responded with a thumbs-up.

Marco responded with a thumbs-up.

Alex didn't respond.

Dale stood up, stretched, and pulled back his
mattress. Underneath it was a sign written in Casphar
and Interstellar: MINERS WANT WORK! He pulled out
the sign and let the mattress drop back into place.

Several other miners were looking at him
quizzically. He nodded and spoke.

The floor erupted with activity. Miners sprang from
bunks. Protest signs appeared from under mattresses,
in lockers, and inside clothes. Men sent messages on
their local communicators and noisily headed for the
elevator.

• • •

The APC roared down the road across the abyssal wasteland. The mountains lay behind, vanishing in the fading light. Running lights sliced through the darkness, revealing nothing ahead, aside, or to the rear.

Inside, Marco had strapped himself to one of the benches in the back and was inventorying items he was taking out of a singed thermal blanket. The drones beside it were burned and cracked, but the items inside it looked as fresh as when Alex and Melanie had first wrapped them. They bounced and jostled with every imperfection in the road, even as Marco struggled to secure them into lockers under the bench.

The cockpit display panel blinked twice and switched to an amber color.

"We just went on alert!" Melanie yelled back. "The protest must be starting!"

Marco attached the boring device to a seatbelt and, leaving the blanket and drones on the floor, unbuckled his seatbelt and rose. He grabbed the overhead hand straps and with wide, deliberate steps, pulled himself hand over hand up to the cockpit. "Do we have our orders yet?"

"Not yet," Melanie answered, "but give Ellemarie a little time. Too much chatter and they might connect the dots."

Marco pulled his feet up off the floor, hands still in the straps, and swung himself into the seat next to Melanie. He tied into the live newsfeeds and observed images of miners lining up in the streets with protest signs of all shapes and sizes.

"Whoa," he said. "It's big."

Melanie glanced over. "As long as it stays peaceful, the bigger the better."

Marco shook his head. "This whole mission has been

about things getting out of control."

Melanie nodded. "You and Alex usually work alone?"

"Not always, but Vassily and Ellemarie are new."

Melanie switched on some of the autopilot features and looked at the newsfeed a little longer. "Ellemarie has good instincts," she said at last, "but this is no line of work for her."

"No line of work for any of us," Marco muttered. "How did you get into it?"

"The usual," she said, not looking up. "Got into trouble on Ko. The officer who busted me thought I had potential. Turns out he was a Nostraspace operative. I figured it's better to work for the Don than a local crime syndicate. No independence either way, but this way at least I'm not counting the days to prison. And I think having to play the part of a respectable Kon did more for making me a respectable Kon than anything else ever did. Used to think it was a sign of weakness. Thought I was selling out my people. Now, I get to be an ambassador by day and a troublemaker by night."

Marco smiled. He pointed to the feed. "There's Dale."

"Blending in nicely, good," Melanie said. "What about you?"

"Family business," Marco said. "Thought I was going to go independent, but it turns out I was signed up since I was a baby. Mom worked for the previous Don. Ended up married to one of Alex's uncles for a while. She's retired on the alimony now. She taught us kids everything she knew, including how to marry your way out of the lifestyle. Never worked for me. It was always 'almost' with me. Almost the right man. Almost the right time. Problem is, my prime man-trapping years and my prime thieving years are pretty much one and the same, and I'm a better thief than a man trap."

A sad smile pulled at Melanie's features. "And there's no retirement home for the unacknowledged agents. Never wore a uniform?"

Marco shook his head.

Melanie let a long exhale out. "I don't know Alex well, but he seems like the type who's going to do right by you."

Marco half shrugged and looked ahead into the darkness.

• • •

Alex was reclining on a wooden couch in a sitting room when the doors slid open and two more palace guards joined the ones already keeping an eye on him. The emperor strode in a moment later. Alex sat up.

"Sir Alexander," the emperor said. "It seems our protests have materialized after all."

"Really?" Alex said. "I haven't read the news since this morning."

The emperor swept over and took a seat next to Alex. He leaned forward and looked directly into Alex's eyes. "And you had nothing to do with this?"

Alex held out both hands. "You've got all my communicators. Unless I set it up weeks ago."

The emperor tapped his finger against his lips. "This I would not put past you, Sir Alexander."

"With all due respect, Your Majesty," Alex said, "how do protests benefit me? It's the miners, I assume?"

Emperor Habid's eyes narrowed. "Yes..."

"Since Vassily knew about it, I figured it had to have come from Bruno," Alex said. "And since he doesn't have any family I know of, it's most likely miners. Plus, I can analyze news as well as anyone. Would you like my advice?"

The emperor laughed bitterly. "Your advice, no doubt, advances the Don's plans."

"I have no instructions to act against you," Alex said, the corners of his mouth pulling down but his eyebrows moving up. "As far as I'm concerned, a stable Casphar Empire is good for Nostraspace. We rely on your mines and your jumpgates. So, yes, helping you keep the peace is in the Don's best interests."

"Then what is this advice?"

"Go out and talk to them," Alex said.

The emperor reared up, back straight, looking down his nose at Alex. "Negotiate? You expect me to negotiate with protesters?"

It was Alex's turn to laugh. "Oh, I would never suggest such a thing. But protests happen because people want those in power to listen. That's all you need to do. If they think you've listened and they think you're aware of their concerns as you make your decisions, they'll be a lot happier accepting them."

Emperor Habid IV blew a raspberry.

Alex blinked, then shrugged. "Or, you could sit here behind these walls and be angry about it. The anger is just going to foment in that case."

"Or I could send in the troops," the emperor said menacingly.

Alex shrugged again. "Again, I'm not a diplomat, but as far as I'm concerned, the Don has no position. If you'd like to check with our embassy, I'm sure my cousin there could advise you where we officially stand."

The emperor rose. "If this is, in fact, a Nostraspace plot, both you and your cousin the ambassador will find yourselves wishing I had disemboweled you both."

Alex looked bemused. "In that case, I hope your investigations are truth-based."

The emperor snapped his cape and swept back out of the sitting room, two of the palace guards following him.

Alex reclined back onto the couch again.

• • •

Ellemarie and Vassily had the feed from the planet surface on all the monitors. Ellemarie was seated in one of the armchairs while Vassily paced from the hatch to the cockpit and the corridor to the staterooms.

"We can't wait much longer," Ellemarie said. "If they get to the base without orders, they'll be told to park the APC and then get sent off to whatever tasks need doing."

"Is not good," Vassily said. "Why has Habid not deployed troops? Not usual. Not usual."

"The military must be spread very thin at the moment," Ellemarie said. "Searching every ship coming in and out of the system."

"And probably other systems," Vassily said. "Still not good."

"You know," Ellemarie said, "if it helps, I can also listen with the pipe I'm using to insert orders."

"Yes." Vassily stopped pacing and moved over behind her. "Show me chatter."

Ellemarie tapped on the tablet in front of her, sending the signal to the larger entertainment console. There was a several-second delay, and memos started flashing across the screen. Vassily stared at the screen, Casphar text projecting subtly across his features.

"Good," he said at last. "Military is on alert.
Orders to stand by. Is good time. Transmit."

• • •

In the cockpit of the APC, the newsfeed vanished,
and text appeared in front of both seats, with a
blinking amber title across the top of the screen.

Melanie smiled. "We've been ordered to position
the APC on the parade grounds to provide protection to
the prison. We are to remain in position and may not
leave the vehicle. One of us is to remain awake at
all times."

"It's about time," Marco said.

In front of them, the thin line of lights that
marked the base perimeter had already appeared on the
horizon and drew steadily closer.

"You'd better take over driving again," Melanie
said. "With orders like that, it's not inconceivable
that they'll send out an escort for us."

Marco grumbled and transferred the driving controls
to his seat. Relying mostly on autopilot, he checked
the map and the speed. Melanie got up and, using the
handholds, moved toward the tiny restroom in the back
of the cabin. By the time she returned, they were
rolling slowly and clumsily up to the gates.

The weather had turned windy and misty. The
running lights caught wisps of haze and dust that
swirled around the APC.

A small guard shack stood in the middle of the
street—four concrete walls with a solar panel roof.
The APC lurched as it came up and stopped to the left
of it. The hatch closest to it slid open, and Melanie
stood there.

The guard emerged from the shack, clutching his
coat close around his throat. He shouted a question

to Melanie. She nodded in return. He waved them on, and the outer gate began to slide open ahead of them. Melanie gave a clumsy salute and pulled the hatch shut again.

"They have our orders," she confirmed to Marco as he put the APC in gear, and it lurched forward. Melanie caught herself against the side of the cabin. "Good news is, nobody is going to doubt that you're too stupid to speak."

"Do you want to drive?" Marco yelled back at her.

Staggering as the APC lurched, Melanie put herself in the cockpit seat and took control of the APC. It smoothed out almost immediately.

Marco looked over sheepishly. "In my defense, nobody taught me."

Melanie shook her head and steered the APC through the inner gate and turned right toward the parade ground.

The base was darker than it had been on Dale's visit. The base perimeter lights were burning at full, but on base, the exterior lighting had been dimmed or extinguished altogether, and most of the buildings were completely dark. Even the prison's administrative center had its formidable windows darkened with blinds.

Periodically, a searchlight would sweep across the base from the perimeter, but otherwise all was quiet and dark as the APC rattled up to a spot in the grass directly above the underground facility.

Melanie and Marco both studied the map on the console, Marco comparing it to a tiny tablet in his hand. "Right here!" he cried.

Melanie stopped the APC and turned off its engine. She switched menus on the screen in front of her. The interior lights came on, burning deep red, and a blast shield came down over the front windows. Outside, the running lights turned up to full, casting beams in all directions through the mist and dust.

Marco was out of his seat first, gathering up the discarded thermal blanket. Melanie came in behind him and released a catch in the floor. A hatch dropped downward, stopping as it hit grass below, forming a short slide. She put hands on either side of it and lowered herself through, standing at an awkward angle.

"Shovel," she said.

Marco scanned labels on the various lockers and cubbyholes around the APC.

"The first and third characters are the one that looks like a Suturiku shrine entrance."

Marco focused on a narrow locker labeled as described. He pulled it open and took out a small spade. He handed it to Melanie. She examined it briefly. "That'll work." She vanished under the APC.

Marco began unpacking the boring device.

Under the APC, Melanie grunted and muttered in Kon.

"Do you need help?" Marco said down to her.

"There's really only room for one down here. The sod is just particularly dense. The soil on this planet must be worse than I thought. I have no idea how they got the grass to grow at all."

Marco set the boring device next to the trap door and attached a clip to the central section. He then started opening under-bench lockers until he found one near the hatch on the right side of the cabin that had a line spooled under it. He grabbed the end, pulled it over, and set it into a clip by the hatch and then clipped it to the device.

The spade came out of the hatch handle first. Marco took it and set it on the bench. He then tipped the boring device at an angle so it could go through the hatch diagonally and lowered it down to Melanie.

A moment later, clumps of dirt clattered against the underside of the APC, fragments popping up through the hatch.

Melanie reappeared. "I've got it set to stop when it hits strata with different densities, so we're going to have to keep an eye on it. Is the clip set to feed?"

Marco nodded.

"Good." Melanie hopped back up into the cabin. "Now, we wait."

• • •

The march of the miners moved inexorably toward the palace. It had more than tripled in size since they took to the streets—far more participants than any one dorm could supply, a good quarter of them women. Signs appeared to have been painted in a hurry, some of them with pigments still running, many of them painted on dorm-issue bedsheets.

Media drones buzzed overhead, circling like falcons ready to swoop.

Dale stayed in the middle of the crowd, allowing young agitators to move out in front of him, shouting.

No troops were visible yet. No vehicles were attempting to use the streets they were marching on, either. Crowds of onlookers gathered at various intersections, mostly businesspeople. The handful of miners in the various crowds generally started following along with the march on the sidewalks.

At the front door of the museum, a group of women were setting up a portable stage. The march was still several blocks away, but it moved itself toward the stage like an amoeba driven by a primitive instinct.

An amplification system had just been installed

on the stage when the march arrived in front of the museum.

Khadija took the stage, microphone in hand.

• • •

"No, no, no, no, no," Vassily said, grabbing the monitor with both hands. "This is not plan."

The feed had stabilized on an image of Khadija on the stage, an arch of women in both business and worker attire behind her. She spoke into the microphone in a modulated, inviting voice.

"What's she saying?" Ellemarie asked, leaning forward in the armchair.

Vassily knelt beside the monitor. "She says emperor is deliberately keeping people down. Burns houses of those who come to help. Says women stand with miners. Demands arrest of Habid."

"Isn't that good?" Ellemarie asked.

"No," Vassily said. "Protest, all eyes on protest. Riot, all eyes everywhere. We need protest, not riot."

"Khadija's not the sort to incite a riot."

"She demands emperor come speak to people."

"And the miners are likely to riot if he doesn't?"

Vassily turned to look at her. "Miners likely to riot if he does."

• • •

Alex had taken one of the wall tablets and was seated under a tree in one of the courtyards. His palace guard escort had taken to standing a little closer to him since his last conversation with the emperor, and they flanked him just over each shoulder. One of them snapped to attention. Then he spoke to Alex in Casphar.

Alex arched an eyebrow and stood up. The guards stepped around the bench and began leading him. Alex tucked the tablet under his arm and followed closely enough that they could still keep an eye on him with only a quick backward glance.

They led him to a ramp that led down underneath the palace. The ornate wooden decor gave way immediately to utilitarian concrete and metal. The ramp was steep but not unmanageable.

A steel door halfway down opened with the hiss of an airlock as they approached, a second door beyond it doing the same. The ramp leveled out and turned into an extruded steel mesh. Then railings appeared, and it carried them out over an enormous chasm in which an enormous globe hovered.

Then the bridge widened into a ring-shaped balcony wrapping around the equator of the globe. The exposed portion of the globe glowed slightly, a tiny-scale replica of the capital city right in the center, most of the buildings glowing white but with various intersections pockmarked with red, yellow, and green dots so densely packed that they gave the impression of paint splatters.

Emperor Habid IV came around from the far side of the globe, three men in generals' uniforms from three branches of the military flanking him.

"You asked to see me?" Alex said with a small smile and nod.

Habid smiled thinly. "You are the first foreigner to ever see my planetary situation room."

"I'm honored," Alex said. "I understand the Suturiku have something similar on each of their planets. Theirs are bigger and more brightly lit, of course."

The emperor didn't take the bait. However, he

pursed his lips slightly before continuing. "My generals are also skeptical that you are not responsible for these protests." He waved at the splatters of color around the model of the city.

"I'd be curious to learn how I managed that," Alex said. "That's quite a lot of unrest to sow without much contact with the locals."

The emperor tapped on the railing beside the globe. A holographic screen illuminated over the globe, playing an image of Khadija speaking at the rally. "Yours, I believe?" the emperor said.

"My foreman, yes," Alex said. "I haven't interacted with her much myself, but she's loyal and hardworking, all I really ask."

"She is inciting the crowd in your name," the emperor said.

Alex cocked his head and listened to the rhetoric for a few minutes, wandering slowly around the globe. Another bridge and ramp descended to the ring from the opposite side as well, and Princess Aiez was padding down that ramp to join them.

"Casphar isn't my best language," Alex said at last, "but it sounds to me like she's asking for you to hear the workers' grievances."

"I do not negotiate with people who do not know how to behave in a civilized manner!" Emperor Habid roared.

Alex shrugged. "Then I don't know what I can do for you."

The emperor crinkled his nose. "You are going to address the crowd."

• • •

Marco lay on the bench of the APC, napping. Melanie sat on the floor, her legs through the hatch, eating unidentifiable canned meat with her fingers.

A steady hum from under the vehicle stopped. Marco sat up the instant it went quiet. Melanie set her can aside and dropped down underneath. A moment later, her head popped back up. "This is it. We've hit concrete."

"Ready when you are," Marco said.

"Give us about fifteen centimeters of line and then lock off the feed. We don't want it dropping through the ceiling."

Melanie vanished back under the APC, and Marco went to the clip with the line through it and adjusted it. From below the APC, the hum resumed, but at a lower pitch.

"Fifteen more!" Melanie called up from below. Marco let more line out.

Then, all at once, the hum stopped and the line went taut.

Marco stuck his head down under the APC.

The line fed down into a perfectly round hole, the exact diameter of the boring machine, which had sides of earth compacted to the density of steel. The sod was folded back beyond the hole, roots sticking up like insectoid hairs. Melanie knelt beside the hole, looking down it. "It's dark, but I think we're through," she said.

Marco slid through the hatch and crawled over next to her. The edges of the bore hole were cool at the top but still steamed slightly down below. The end of the hole wasn't visible in the darkness. "How long before it's cool?"

"Half an hour," Melanie said. "Help me reel the borer up."

It took half that time to get the borer lined up with the bottom of the hole correctly to allow it to move at all. Then hauling it up was a tedious task that involved moving it in tiny increments and then jiggling the line so it stayed lined up properly to slide back up the hole it had made.

As soon as they pulled it from the hole and set it aside, Marco disconnected the line from it and attached it to his own waist.

Melanie handed him an earpiece. "It's set so sensitive I'll be able to hear you breathing. I won't be able to answer unless you mute it. A whisper is plenty."

Marco stuck the earpiece in his ear and swung his legs into the hole. With each foot pressed against opposite sides, he began to shimmy down. The hole wasn't much wider than he was. He used his upper arms to secure his upper body, spreading them slightly akimbo to create a wedge.

It was a six-story descent. As he approached the bottom, he turned on a small light attached to his belt, which cast a shadowy glow down on his feet. The compacted earth gave way to a ring of compacted concrete, with open space below. Marco twisted and shone the light down. There was a gap of half a meter, then a ceiling made of lighting panels below.

"I'm down," Marco whispered. "Tension on the line, then lower me slowly."

The line on his waist went taut. Marco released his arms, then his feet. He swung backward and bounced off the edge of the hole behind him. The line jerked, and he dropped a tiny bit, then descended gently. "Stop," he whispered as his legs cleared the hole. He kicked in every direction before whispering, "Nope. Can't find a foothold. Take me down some more."

Marco dropped again at first, then descended even

more slowly. As soon as his waist was out of the
hole, he folded his legs into a pike. He used his
arms to push his waist away from the hole, arching his
back until his head came free.

He planted his feet against a wall. With the rest
of the line Melanie played out, Marco turned himself
around to face downward, feet against a concrete
partition that went all the way to the concrete roof
of the bunker. He held on to the edge of the hole
with his left hand while his right groped around on
his belt. He removed a tiny silver device with two
prongs coming from it. "Okay, I'm going to have to
swing."

He let go, instantly spinning back to face up as
he swung away from the wall and descended. He curled
into a ball and turned over before stretching out
again, his belt now reversed, the light shining up
on the concrete roof. He swung back and forth like
a pendulum. At the bottom of each swing, he barely
cleared the backside of the lighting panels below him.

A small box and an antenna jutted up from the
joint of four different lighting panels—the mechanical
end of a security camera. On one swing past, Marco
attached his device to the back of it. "It's on."

Melanie reeled him up a little but let him keep
swinging.

Marco worked a hand up to his earpiece. "Tell me
what you see," he panted.

Melanie's voice came back in low, hushed tones.
"Cell's empty."

"Shit," Marco said. He curled back into a ball,
pointed his head downward, and then extended his
legs up into the hole. He spread his legs to anchor
himself, arching his back so he could look down at the
ceiling below him. "Can you get into the system?"

He held his finger on his earpiece for a long time. "No," Melanie finally responded. "Looks like they built it right. The cameras only transmit. Can't access any of the others by being attached to this one. Plus, the transmitter is stamping metadata into it, so we're going to have to plug directly into the chip."

Marco reached out toward the camera. "It's just a hand length out of reach."

He dropped again, and he yanked his hand back just before it would have gone through the ceiling. He jerked to a stop and hung for a few seconds before reorienting himself. He extracted a packet of tiny tools from a pocket inside his sleeve and took the case off the camera. He then moved the device to attach it directly behind the lens. He touched his earpiece again. "It's on."

"I see it," Melanie answered. "I'm recording empty cell now."

"This is going to be tricky," Marco whispered with a growl in his voice. "These cells aren't exactly private. Any idea if we're in the right spot or how far off we are?"

"We should be close," Melanie answered. "Can you tell if you're in a corner cell?"

Marco twisted so the light shone on all four walls. "Cell is also built right. Concrete all the way to the top of the bunker. But one wall is a different texture than the other three, so it's probably the only exterior wall."

"In that case," Melanie said, "she's probably in the next cell north, and our estimates of the layout were off by a couple of meters."

"Unless they've moved her," Marco said.

"If that's the case, we're not finding her anywhere.

Do you want to come up, move the APC, and try another hole?"

"I don't think we can trust Dale to keep the protest up that long," Marco said. "Let me know when you're looping empty cell to the transmitter, and I'll open the ceiling."

"We should have enough now."

Marco let go of the earpiece and reached down to the lighting panel immediately below the hole. With a bit of working on the corner with one of his tools, it popped upward. He slid it out and laid it diagonally across four other tiles. The cell below was dark, except for a bright stream of light coming through the large window. "Cell's dark," he reported, switching off the light on his belt. "Lower me."

He dropped a bit again, then descended smoothly headfirst into the cell. His hands reached the floor first, and he walked them forward so he came down into a pushup position. As the line continued to play out, he crawled across to the window. He pulled his hood out of the neck of his outfit, securing it over his head, then pulled the collar up over his mouth so only his eyes and nose showed. He reared up enough to peek out the window quickly, then went back for a longer, more detailed look. "Common room is empty at the moment. I'm unhooking. Send down the borer."

The line zipped up almost as soon as he had it disconnected. Marco pressed himself against the steel door and waited. A few minutes later, the borer drifted down into view. Marco caught it before it hit the ground. "Got it."

He climbed on top of the bed and leaned the borer against the wall. Leaning back and looking away, he turned it on.

With a roar of shattering concrete, the pointed

bit at the center of it grabbed hold of the wall, sending a shower of concrete dust and rock fragments everywhere. Marco let go, and it pulled itself into the wall. The outer ring began glowing blue. The dust and fragments subsided as the ring came to rest against the wall. The roar gave way to the low-frequency hum. Detritus from the boring instead moved along the channels that connected the ring to the central cone. The concrete glowed like lava and compacted until no more rubble was being ejected.

Marco climbed off the bed and crawled over to the window again, checking. Two guards moved across the room, but neither looked toward the cells, both instead focused on a tablet they shared between them.

The hum stopped. The borer dropped out of the hole on the other side of the wall. The edges of the hole still glowed slightly, steaming.

Marco jumped up on the bed again and peered through.

Keira stood on her washbasin on the far side of the room. She looked into his eyes, staring for a second, blinking. "Marco?"

"The edge is hot. Your camera isn't disabled. Do you think you can get through without touching?"

She waved him aside. He hopped off the bed. A moment later, she dove through the hole, landing on the bed in a forward roll that carried her right off the foot of it and onto the floor. Marco dashed over and helped her up.

She looked directly at him. "Does Mom know you're here?"

"Does Mom know *you're* here?" he asked back at her with a sourpuss scrunch of his eyebrows. "Up!"

He clipped the line to his belt again and hoisted her by her upper legs into the ceiling. Lighting

panels cascaded down around him as she used her arms
to haul herself farther up. He released one leg, and
she kicked until her foot found his shoulder. She
stepped up, and he released her other leg so she could
stand on both shoulders. "Ready?" he asked.

"Ready," she answered.

"Hoist," he said into the mic.

Nothing happened.

. . .

The main doors of the museum opened, and Alex
strode out, followed by two palace guards and a
translator in a green military uniform. A woman who
had been speaking on the temporary platform stopped
and turned. The crowd's attention fixed on Alex as the
museum doors shut behind him.

Khadija recognized him and appeared out of the
group of women at the back of the stage. She scurried
over to him and clasped him by the hand. She led
him to the stage. People onstage scrambled to find a
second microphone, handing the one that had been in
use to Alex and bringing out a small one of the sort
used for dictating voice memos into a communicator for
the translator.

Alex took the stage and looked out at the crowd.

Dale stood in the middle of the crowd, looking
straight at him, a wide-eyed, tight-lipped expression
on his face.

Alex spoke one sentence at a time, pausing to let
the translator finish each sentence before proceeding.
"The emperor has asked me to speak to you. My name is
Alexander Romano-Bennetti. Sir Alexander, he."

The translator rendered the name as "Sir Alexander
Romano-Nostraspace."

"The emperor," Alex continued, "wanted me to assure

you that he burned down my house accidentally, and no one should protest on my behalf."

Dale's expression became strained, his lips pursing more tightly.

"And truthfully," Alex said, "I'm rich and can afford to replace everything I lost. I come from Nostraspace and can go back there at any time. I am a free man, and I do not need your protests. So, do not protest for me."

Dale's face screwed up, eyes closing, his shoulders trembling silently.

"I have suggested to the emperor," Alex went on, "that he meet with some representatives to ensure that he understands your grievances. He wanted me to pass on that he will not meet with anyone who is protesting, and he expects you to return to your homes and wait patiently for him to decide on his own to fix whatever problems you're experiencing."

The translator went silent.

"He didn't give me a timetable for when he might get around to that."

The crowd surged forward before the edge of the stage caught them. Dale lost his footing briefly but then looked up and glared at Alex warningly.

"But don't worry," Alex went on, "the emperor is quite certain that you should trust him."

The crowd roared and surged again. Dale vanished behind several taller men.

• • •

Marco still stood with Kiera on his shoulders. He yanked his hood down and touched his earpiece. "Melanie?"

"Winch is jammed," Melanie reported back. "My guess is the two of you together were too much weight."

"Even together, we weigh nothing," Marco whispered fiercely.

Kiera muttered in the exact same tone that Marco always used. She wrapped the line around both of her hands above her head and then pulled. She hoisted herself up enough to pull her feet up so that her toes pressed against the edge of the hole. She then pulled hand over hand until she had her back into the hole, at which point she pressed with her legs to secure herself. She dropped the line and shimmied upward until there was enough room below her for Marco. She tugged the line twice.

Marco wrapped the line around his right arm, grabbed it with his left hand above, and pulled. As his right arm reached his left, he unwrapped it and reached with his right hand above. As he grabbed with his right hand, he wrapped his left and repeated.

Kiera tugged on the line as he climbed. As he passed through the ceiling, he kicked his feet up until he inverted and placed his feet against the hole. He climbed hand over hand until he was able to fold himself into the hole the same way Kiera had. Once he was wedged in, he stopped, panting. "I need to breathe. Go."

Kiera pulled herself to a standing position, feet and hands pressed against opposite sides of the tube. She inched up it.

Marco fed the line through the clip on his belt but did not lock it off. Once his breathing returned to normal, he also began to shimmy up using the same technique as Kiera.

Climbing six stories with that technique took some time. Melanie waited at the top of the hole with a hand outstretched. Kiera grabbed it, and Melanie hoisted her out of the hole.

"Nice to see you, partner," Melanie said to the panting Kiera. Kiera smiled and scampered up through the hatch into the APC.

Melanie held out her hand for Marco next, and he caught it a minute later. She hoisted him up, too.

He settled into a sitting position on the edge of the hole, cut the line, and let it drop. "We left it a mess down there. We should move out now."

"Then get your ass up there," Melanie said, motioning with her thumb over her shoulder at the APC.

Marco rolled onto his knees and clambered up through the hatch. Melanie went around to the other side of the hole and unrolled the sod back over the hole. She didn't take the time to make it pretty. The APC engine roared to life around her, and she scrambled up the hatch, closing it behind her. "Roll!"

The running lights on the APC went out, and it lurched forward. It rumbled forward ten meters and then started a lazy turn back toward the perimeter of the base.

The little light escaping from the shuttered windows of the prison's administrative building switched to blinking amber. A klaxon pierced the night air, and every exterior light on the base turned up to full power.

Melanie settled into the left seat of the cockpit and brought up a screen with a flashing amber header on the top and Casphar text scrolling by at a furious pace. "They've noticed," she said.

"Do you want to drive?" Marco asked from the right seat.

"Yes," Melanie said. "You and Kiera stand on that thermal blanket. Secure any gear you truly can't survive without."

Marco switched the controls over to her and hopped out of his seat, holding the hand straps as he moved into the back. Melanie turned the APC toward the fence and accelerated.

Six guards came out of the administrative building and ran toward the APC, rifles pointed. Two of them stopped and started firing. Bullets pinged off the armored hull. The other four continued running until one stepped on the patch of disturbed sod. The sod collapsed, and he vanished down the hole.

The two nearest guards turned their attention to their vanished comrade. The other three gave chase on foot.

The inner fence was straight in front of the APC. The perimeter lights were all trained on the vehicle.

Melanie didn't slow. "Hang on!" she yelled.

The APC intersected with the fence, which arced with blue light, bolts of electricity jumping from the fence to the APC and then from the APC to the ground. The engine hiccoughed, but the enormous machine kept rolling.

"One down, one to go!" Melanie yelled.

Marco and Kiera stood on the thermal blanket, each holding a corner of it close to their chests with one hand and a hand strap with the other.

Higher-caliber guns were now firing at the APC as it headed for the outer fence. The first round kicked up a crater behind it. A second round took out a chunk of the outer fence, denting the armor as it passed. The outer fence went dark seconds before the APC impacted it. No electricity sparked. The fence tore like paper, and the APC was through.

Melanie's controls were blinking and flashing, but the APC was still moving. "Marco," she yelled, "get up here and see if you can get autopilot running.

Kiera, fold up that thermal blanket. We're going to need it!"

Another shot from the big-caliber gun hit the APC's tail, sending it sliding. Melanie recovered and kept charging across the barren landscape toward the road.

Marco landed in the right seat and lost no time powering down everything. With the shield still down and all the lights out, Melanie drove the APC forward blindly. Less than a minute later, the lights came back on, and the system rebooted. He brought up the autopilot system. "It's up. We overshot the road."

"Good." Melanie stopped the APC. "You two, out. Take the thermal blanket."

Kiera had the right hatch open immediately. Marco was out of his seat and moving for it, asking on the way, "What's the plan?"

"That's a spaceport. We're going to have air cover on us any minute now," Melanie answered, switching the autopilot over to her station. She programmed in a destination and started the APC moving again.

Marco had just jumped down when the vehicle rolled off. He and Kiera backed away as it turned back toward the road. Melanie appeared in the hatch. She reached out and took the hatch with one hand. Then she jumped, yanking the hatch shut behind her in one motion. She hit the ground and rolled.

Kiera was off running for her instantly, dropping the thermal blanket. Marco scooped it up and ran after her.

The APC turned onto the road and picked up speed, running lights on again.

Kiera arrived beside Melanie and dropped to her knees.

"I'm alive," Melanie said. "Honestly, the electricity was worse. I want both of you over here and on the ground, under the thermal blanket."

Marco arrived. "What are we doing?"

"Thermal blanket," Melanie explained. "No heat goes through, so the thermal infrared can't see us through it. We're going to lie here in a pile with it over us until the air cover has decided we're not here. It's going to get hot. Don't, under any circumstances, give in to the temptation to let some cool air in. That's what'll make us visible."

Kiera lay down next to Melanie. Marco flipped the thermal blanket out and lay down next to Kiera as it came down over them like a parachute. It barely covered the three of them, Kiera having to curl her feet up to keep them under it. Melanie and Marco held it down on the edges. It bunched up where their fists gripped it underneath.

A two-man military craft, all cockpit and armament, swooped overhead, searchlight trained on the retreating APC.

It fired a missile.

The APC shot ten meters into the air in an orange fireball. It crashed back down, nose first, crumpling like a melting candle, blackened and folding.

Marco, Melanie, and Kiera stayed huddled under the blanket, unmoving as the shock wave rolled over them.

• • •

Ellemarie and Vassily watched on the large entertainment monitor aboard *Tri Sestry* as the museum doors opened again and Princess Aiez exited, flanked by four palace guards. She marched to the stage fearlessly.

Vassily whistled through his teeth.

"Who is that?" Ellemarie asked.

"Princess Aiez, second daughter of Habid," Vassily

said. "Looks good!"

Aiez climbed onto the stage, crossed to Alex, and took his microphone without asking. She turned, face stern, and addressed the crowd.

Vassily snorted.

"What?" Ellemarie asked.

"She said she will meet three representatives," Vassily said. "Hear grievances."

"Isn't that good?" Ellemarie asked.

"How will mob select three?" Vassily asked.

Sure enough, the crowd of miners was surging again.

Khadija stepped forward and took the translator's microphone. She began to speak.

"Ah, good," Vassily said. "Khadija says she represents women. Suggests one miner step forward and one businessperson. Ah, now says if not back in two hours, assume arrested, and burn palace to ground."

Princess Aiez shot Khadija a fierce look but pressed a smile onto her face.

Alex moved to the side of the stage and hopped off, staying there.

The crowd surged again, and the old miner who Dale had helped translate was hoisted onto the stage. He blinked, bewildered, then nodded and bowed to Aiez.

Aiez's eyebrow arched, revealing surprise, but she smiled close-mouthed and beckoned for him to rise.

From the sidewalk in front of the palace, a group of two dozen men and women in business attire approached. They stopped beside the stage, and one woman stepped forward. She knelt down on one knee and spoke.

The crowd roared.

Aiez opened her mouth to speak, but then cocked her head and closed it again. She handed the microphone over to a nearby woman and moved back toward the museum. Khadija, the old miner, and the businesswoman followed, flanked by the palace guards who had come out with Aiez. The group vanished into the museum, and the doors closed behind them.

Two more palace guards waited by the stage, but Alex was no longer anywhere to be seen.

• • •

Melanie pulled the thermal blanket back and checked. The air was clear. The APC still burned down the road, and a group of soldiers were running along the road toward it. "We have to move, now."

Marco also released his side of the thermal blanket and rose to a crouch. Keira crumpled the blanket to her chest.

Melanie winced as she stood up.

"You're hurt," Kiera said.

"It's not bad," Melanie said. "We have to move."

Kiera stood.

Melanie started moving in the direction of the base.

"Wait," Kiera said.

"It's a two-hundred-kilometer walk in the other direction," Melanie said. "It's back in or nothing. First sign of air traffic, everyone under the thermal blanket."

Kiera muttered.

They began moving slowly, all hunched, Melanie limping. The search lights from the intact portions of the fence were trained on the burning APC and the troops heading for it. They crossed the road at a dark spot and followed the tracks the APC left, back toward the dark portion of the perimeter fence.

The outer fence was unguarded. The inner fence had two of the guards who had been chasing them posted on either side of the hole they had made, belt lights slicing through the darkness. Both looked inward toward where a winch had been set up over the hole the guard had fallen down.

Melanie grabbed Marco and Kiera and pulled them both close to her. She touched each of their cheeks in turn with a series of hand signals. Each nodded and moved silently away, vanishing into the night.

Melanie limped closer to the fence. She dragged her feet slightly, stopping when her toe found an obstruction. She bent down, rising again with a stone in her hand. She threw it.

The stone skittered into the fence, causing it to ring then spark once. Both guards jumped and turned to look in the direction of the sound. Melanie slipped behind both of them and arched to a position between them and the winch. She began walking back toward them from inside the base. She spoke.

The guard nearest to her jumped. He turned and looked at her.

Melanie spoke again.

The guard shook himself out of it and began gesturing to the damaged fence and speaking. Melanie surveyed the damage, nodding, occasionally asking a question. She periodically clicked her own belt light on to examine a bit of damage more closely.

The guard followed her as she moved the length of the damage. She nodded to the second guard, who grunted. With a dramatic grimace, she clicked off her belt light and nodded to both guards. She pivoted and marched back in the direction of the spaceport. The darkness swallowed her in moments, and the guards went back to their stations.

Soon two more figures were beside her, moving silently.

They drew nearer to the spaceport. A munitions sled was parked at the very edge of the tarmac, only half in the light. A group of women in green uniforms pulled cylindrical bombs off of it and carried them one by one over to a nearby gunship. A hand reached over and touched Melanie's breastbone to stop her. Melanie reached the other direction and stopped Marco. Kiera vanished silently into the night.

The women were working in two lines. A single woman stood on the munitions sled, handing cylinders left, then right. A woman would take each and then walk to the gunship, returning empty-handed. There was a good fifteen to twenty seconds in which the woman on the sled was alone, picking up the next cylinder carefully, before the next person arrived to take it from her.

She handed a cylinder right, then stepped into the gloom at the back of the sled for her next cylinder. In the darkness, she slipped, something catching her.

Then her neck snapped.

When the next woman arrived left, she looked up and found no one waiting for her in the back of the sled. She called out. When she got no answer, she climbed up onto the sled and grabbed a cylinder out of the gloomy back. By then, another woman had arrived right, so she handed the cylinder down and went back for another.

Kiera dragged the dead soldier, a cylinder across her legs, on the thermal blanket a hundred meters back from the tarmac. She shifted the body to place the cylinder underneath it, then removed the uniform. She stripped off her own prison uniform and dropped it over the body. She then wrapped the thermal blanket over the body. She reached into the bundle, fumbled for a minute, then yanked her hand out and powered the blanket on so it constricted and wrapped closely around the body and munition.

She dressed in the dead soldier's uniform carefully in the darkness, wrapping her hair around itself into a disheveled bun, and then she returned to where she had left Melanie and Marco.

Melanie sized her up in the weak light from the spaceport. "Did you get her ID tablet, too?" she whispered.

Kiera pulled the tablet out of a pocket.

"Marco, tools," Melanie whispered, taking the tablet.

Marco handed over a tiny tool, and Melanie opened the ID tablet's case. She fussed inside it, muttering in Kon and shifting the angle of the case to catch what little light she could, until a tiny piece of metal came loose. She discarded it.

Kiera held out a finger. Melanie pressed the innards of the ID tablet against it. It beeped once and blinked. Melanie closed its case. "Let's hope you look a little like her," she whispered.

They began moving again, but no longer toward the spaceport. They moved silently until they came to a lighted pedestrian path.

"Move like you have orders," Melanie said under her breath.

They started encountering people again, most of them scurrying or outright running somewhere. Nobody questioned them. The train station lay ahead of them. The train was already boarding, full of marines and a handful of soldiers.

Melanie approached the security arch and placed her ID tablet in it. It thought for a second and then cleared her through. Marco followed. It cleared him, too. Kiera went last.

The system blinked, confused.

Kiera stepped through the arch anyway.

Nobody challenged them. They all boarded the train and waited for the doors to close.

Chapter 14

"'But how did you know I was your sister?'

'Nobody else would have gotten so upset about
my underwear.'"

—Maria and Elizabeth, *Disguised*, script
by Mona Caroli, directed by Joan Jonas

Tri Sestry set down at the spaceport just long enough
for the airlock to open, the ramp to descend, and
for Alex and Dale to emerge from a nearby cluster of
nonaligned spacers and dash on board. She was moving
again as soon as the ramp began to retract and before
the airlock was even closed.

Alex and Dale moved through the master cabin, up
the corridor, and into the open galley / lounge area.
Ellemarie was in one of the armchairs, monitoring the
protests on the main entertainment console.

"Any word?" Alex asked.

Ellemarie shook her head.

"Melanie's good," Dale said. "If they're in
trouble, I'm sure she's going to get them out of it."

Ellemarie switched the console over to a stream of
memos. "This is what's coming out of that base where
the prison is. Computer translator is making a hash
out of most of them. Vassily has been translating as

much as he's had time for, but we're baffled."

Alex crinkled his brow. "What the—"

"Body burst into flames?" Dale said, reading the stream.

"Or maybe consumed by ordnance?" Alex said. "That makes no sense."

"That's what Vassily said, too," Ellemarie said. "But it references Kiera's prisoner ID number."

"This says thirty-six casualties from the burning body. How does a burning body kill thirty-six people?" Dale asked.

Alex scratched his head. "Did Kiera keep pockets of toxic gasses under her skin?"

"It would have to be ordnance," Dale said. "This says an explosion. But how does a body have live ordnance in it?"

Alex furrowed his brow. "Same word in Casphar for an outrush of gas. Maybe an explosive gas?"

"Here it says 'working to identify,'" Dale said. "So they're not sure if it's her or not."

"Even if it's not, that means things didn't go well," Alex said.

"There's also this," Ellemarie said, switching documents again. "Vassily says this doesn't look like normal activity."

Alex and Dale read. "No," said Alex, "scrambling spacecraft to operate just outside the perimeter fence isn't normal. And closing that road is definitely not normal."

Dale nodded. "That implies that the full reports aren't going through the system and are being sent directly to the palace."

"Not surprising," Alex said. "But it also means we're not going to get more than snippets this way. How is Aiez's peace conference going?"

Ellemarie switched the monitor back to the protests. "They all came out a few minutes ahead of the deadline for riots. Vassily was flying at that point, but the Interstellar media reported that the businesswoman addressed the crowd, saying that the conversation was being very productive, praised the princess, and said they were going back for four more hours."

"Oh, I hope she doesn't defuse the situation too much," Dale said. "We need these protests, or we'll never get through the jumpgate." He turned to Alex. "I only met her the once, and she was sixteen. How good a diplomat is she?"

Alex scoffed. "She's got social skills like she did when she was sixteen."

"Khadija doesn't seem the type to confuse social skills with diplomacy," Ellemarie said.

"No," Dale said, "but the business class might."

"She's there to derail the talks," Alex said. "The women's movement and the miners' protests ran the risk of finding common ground. The business class had to jump in to protect their own interests. If their representative is liking what Aiez is doing, odds are good they're not moving terribly far on the workers' demands."

"Let's hope not," Dale said.

"Let's hope not?" Ellemarie roared. "Do you have any idea what life is like for these people?"

"Okay," Dale said, holding up both hands placatingly. "Let's hope it takes until after we're safely out of the system for everyone to find a way to live happily ever after. How far are we from the jumpgate currently?"

Alex ran his tongue across his teeth before answering. "*Tri Sestry*'s faster than most liners, and Reggit is pretty close to its closest pass to the jumpgate, so we can be there comfortably in two days, a day and a half if we don't mind looking like we're making a break for it."

"Plus the holdup of ships waiting to be searched," Dale said glumly. "I wish we knew what happened down there."

• • •

The train sped out of the base. Marco, Melanie, and Kiera had found a spot against the side of one of the cars, surrounded by oversized marines. The jostling of the crowd continually risked pushing them to the floor to be trampled.

The door at the front of the car opened, and two marines entered with ID tablet readers. They barked out an order, and everyone around them pulled out ID tablets.

Kiera slid down the wall. Marco and Melanie exchanged a glance, Marco biting his upper lip. They pulled out their ID tablets.

The marines worked their way methodically through the car, scanning a tablet, checking the readout, then ordering the owner to step behind them. The crowd shifted continually, keeping a visible gap between those who had been checked and those who had not.

Melanie was farther forward. The group around her thinned until a marine with a scanner stood directly in front of her. She handed over the ID tablet. He scanned it. He grimaced and scanned it again.

He spoke curtly.

Melanie furrowed her brow and cocked her head. She reached into her pocket and pulled out a green card, showing it to the marine.

The marine craned his neck to read the card, then

scanned her ID once more. He shook his head.

Meanwhile, the second marine reached Marco. Marco held out his tablet, and the marine scanned it. That marine shook his head and spoke.

Melanie split her attention between the two marines, speaking to the one in front of Marco and pointing at her ear. She then looked at Marco, held up her green card, and gestured.

Marco reached into a pocket and came up with a similar card. The first marine stepped over and examined it.

All eyes in the car were on them now, side conversations having fallen silent.

The car shook as the train passed through a junction. The door at the front rattled, sliding open slightly before sliding itself shut again. The scrape and thump of it overpowered the whine of the train's engine.

Melanie spoke again.

The marine grimaced. He took both green cards and gestured toward the front of the car, giving a curt command.

Melanie leaned into Marco's field of vision and gave a hand signal. He nodded.

The second marine resumed scanning ID tablets behind Marco. The first marine started walking toward the front of the train, the crowd parting for him. Melanie conversed casually as they walked. As they entered the next car forward, the marine relaxed slightly and began holding up his end of the conversation. Melanie and Marco followed him obediently to the front of the train.

An amber sign on the door at the front of the forwardmost car sported bold Casphar lettering. The door itself had a simple keypad lock on the handle.

The marine typed in a six-digit code and slid the door open. The car in front was darker than the rest of the train. He held the door open and motioned Melanie and Marco inside. They stepped through the door.

The body of a woman in a green military uniform lay sprawled on the floor behind the driver's seat of the train.

Marco and Melanie parted to either side of the door as they entered.

The marine stepped into the cockpit car. He stopped in his tracks, looking down at the body.

Melanie leapt. She had both of the marine's wrists secured before he could react.

Marco sprang on the door and slid it shut.

Kiera flew over the back of the driver's seat. She landed on the marine's chest. Both crumpled to the floor.

Melanie lost her grip in the struggle. She took two steps back, then moved back toward the door. The marine rose, throwing Kiera off. Melanie came at him from behind and got an arm around his throat.

Marco slipped in and removed the marine's sidearm.

The marine roared.

Kiera sunk a knee into the marine's stomach. Her knee stopped dead. The marine didn't flinch. He tossed his head sideways, sending Melanie into the wall.

Marco fired. Blood and brain matter exploded across the cockpit.

The marine crumpled on top of the body of the driver.

Kiera knelt on the floor in front of both bodies, panting.

Melanie, covered in gore, dragged herself to her feet, grimacing with each careful move. "Well, I guess that's one solution. I'm getting too old for this shit."

Marco stood, gun now pointed at nothing, shaking.

Melanie wiped her face with a bloody sleeve. "Nicely done, Kiera. I swear you can turn invisible. If the door to the car hadn't opened on its own, I'd've sworn you were still back there."

Kiera nodded but looked at Marco. "Are you okay, little brother?"

Marco just trembled.

Melanie grabbed the back of the driver's seat and steadied herself, fixing her gaze directly at Kiera and Marco. "Someone get ahold of *Tri Sestry*."

• • •

Ellemarie jumped as an alert came through on the entertainment console. "I think that's a video call request. It looks military."

Dale slipped into a stateroom. Alex stepped over and accepted the call.

Kiera sat in the driver's seat of the train cockpit, ill-fitting uniform still splattered with blood and brains. "Kiera Twight. Miss, she."

Alex folded his hands. "Alexander Romano-Bennetti. Sir Alexander—just Alex when working—he. It's nice to finally meet you."

Melanie appeared in the frame over the back of the seat. "So, we, uh, sort of hijacked a train full of Casphar marines."

"I suppose that means you're at least well guarded," Alex said.

"Yeah, about that," Melanie said. "We took out one, but it took all three of us, and I'm not sure Marco is handling it well. We'd sort of love an extraction, if one can be arranged."

"Are you in the vacuum tube yet?" Alex asked.

Kiera replied, "Yes. We transitioned to vacuum about ten minutes ago."

Melanie picked up from there. "And if I remember right from Dale's mission, we don't emerge again until about fifteen kilometers from the terminus. I can't imagine they're not going to realize something's up before then."

"In a vacuum tube..." Alex said. "That's not as easy as you might think."

"Dead marine. Dead pilot," Melanie said. "And there's no way to lock the door so the marines on duty can't open it."

Vassily's voice came from the cockpit, crying first in Casphar, then, "No! No! Turn on live newsfeed now!"

"Hold on, Melanie," Alex said.

Ellemarie's fingers danced over the tablet, and the monitor switched to live drone footage of the palace. Emperor Habid IV stood on one of the palace balconies overlooking the protesters. Princess Aiez stood beside him, trembling and crying.

Habid held a gun to her head.

He spoke in sonorous tones, his voice echoing, amplified throughout the city.

Alex turned white.

Dale rushed out of the cabin he had hidden himself in. He blanched, too. "No... Oh no..."

"What is it?" Ellemarie asked.

Nobody answered for a moment. Finally, Dale said, "He's saying that Aiez has attempted to usurp the throne, negotiating with... protesters, I guess... against his wishes and orders. He says all power lies with him, and judgment has been passed."

Emperor Habid IV fired the gun.

Aiez winced momentarily, then her face went blank.

Her body rocked forward over the railing, plunging into the crowd below.

The crowd surged forward.

Gunshots came from the palace. Miners in the crowd began to drop. Weapons appeared in the crowd. Miners started firing back.

The drone footage banked suddenly to the left, then went dark.

Alex, Dale, and Ellemarie stared at the blank screen for a moment before Ellemarie switched back to the call.

"Melanie," Alex said, "it looks like all hell just broke loose in the capital. Stop the train. We're on our way."

• • •

The vacuum tunnel stretched through a pass between steep granite cliffs, tiny patches of snow dotting the mountains around it. *Tri Sestry* came in low, through the mountains, wending slowly between peaks.

Alex had joined Vassily in the cockpit and was doing the flying himself, with Vassily walking him through the specifics of Casphar cockpit design.

"All right," Alex said, "this should be the place."

Vassily brought up the communications screen in front of both of them. A video call connected a few seconds later. Melanie was now in the driver's seat.

"How is everything down there?" Alex asked.

"The passengers are starting to ask questions," Melanie said. "Luckily my commanding voice is keeping everyone out for the moment, but that's not going to last."

"Okay," Alex said. "I want the three of you as secure as you can possibly make yourselves. This is

about to get very, very rough. When you get out, head
back along the path of the tunnel. We'll pick you up
a few kilometers downslope."

"What are you going to do?" Melanie asked.

"Show Vassily what's wrong with his flying," Alex
said.

Melanie winced. "Oh sh—"

Alex cut off the call. Vassily looked at him
questioningly.

"Remember when I told you that letting the gravity
drive get out of balance could cause all sorts of
damage?" Alex asked.

Vassily's eyes narrowed. "Yes?"

"This is what can happen." Alex moved the controls
precipitously.

Tri Sestry, hovering above the vacuum tunnel,
banked sharply to the left, stopping just before
slamming into the cliff. A wave of distorted light
radiated from her gravity drive and crossed the vacuum
tunnel.

The vacuum tunnel exploded.

A shower of concrete dust and rubble blasted
through the ravine. Rocks toppled off the cliffs.
As the shock wave passed, the train lay broken and
twisted on the floor of the ravine.

Casphar marines clambered out of the wreckage,
pointing guns up at *Tri Sestry*, but she was off and
arching toward the sky before they could get any shots
off.

The cockpit car hadn't dropped as far as the rest
of the train—it was still hanging from the edge of the
shattered tunnel. The emergency hatch popped, and
Melanie climbed out. Dozens of marines were running
up and down the train, pulling survivors out. One
came up and took Melanie's arm, yanking her free.

Melanie pointed in the direction *Tri Sestry* had

gone and shouted.

The marine turned back and repeated Melanie's words in a booming voice.

Marines readied their weapons, and soon they were climbing up the wrecked train past Melanie. Four of them began rearranging rubble until they had created a path to the top of the tunnel ahead. Marines climbed single file onto the top of the tunnel and followed it deeper into the mountains.

Soon the exterior of the train was clear. Moans of the injured and dying came from the inside, but the able-bodied were all off in pursuit of *Tri Sestry*.

Melanie reached down through the emergency hatch and helped Kiera out. Kiera turned around and helped Marco out. Marco was sporting a head wound bound with strips from his shirt.

They made their way down the wreckage, ignoring a hand that reached out from one of the lower cars imploringly.

• • •

Tri Sestry sat lopsided in an open patch of alluvium about two kilometers from the tunnel. Marco, Melanie, and Kiera moved like the walking dead toward her.

Alex and Dale waited on the ramp. As the three wounded arrived, they ushered them up the steps, Dale checking Melanie's injuries and Alex checking Marco's.

Vassily and Ellemarie waited in the master cabin. Alex and Dale led Marco, Melanie, and Kiera into the ship. Alex closed the airlock. As soon as it sealed, he said, "Head for the jumpgate."

Vassily didn't move right away. He squinted, finally saying, "Ellemarie explains."

Vassily turned and marched up the corridor toward the cockpit.

The others turned and watched him go. Alex then looked at Ellemarie quizzically.

Ellemarie pulled herself to her full height on her walking stick. "The thing is," she said, "that the situation in the capital has gotten worse. It's an all-out civil war. Most of the city is on fire."

"So?" Alex said.

"So Vassily's daughter is there," Ellemarie said. "And he's not willing to leave her."

Alex looked at the ceiling. "We don't have time for this!"

"And, under Nostraspace law," Ellemarie said, "Nostraspace employees are entitled to evacuation in the event of civil unrest. I've sent a message to Khadija to have everyone meet us at or near the factory."

Alex marched toward the front of the ship. "We're not here in any official capacity. We have no obligation to evacuate anyone who isn't already on this ship. I'll fly if I have to."

"About that," Ellemarie said to his back. "Vassily and I figured out how to seal and lock the cockpit. You can't get in."

Alex stopped short and pivoted back, his face flushed and his nostrils flaring.

"You can feel free to arrest me," Ellemarie said. "This is probably a probation violation."

Marco had sunk down onto the bed. He spoke weakly. "I hate to take sides, but I think they're right."

Alex looked at Dale.

Dale shook his head. "No. My mission is to get that bird out. Fetching these two"—he tipped his head toward Melanie and Kiera—"was optional according to my orders."

A silence hung in the air.

Finally, Melanie spoke. "There's going to be mass confusion. My sense of Casphar culture is we're not at any greater risk flying into the city than we are heading straight out, and when we get searched on the way out, having a ship full of refugees may actually be less suspicious."

Alex looked at Kiera. She rubbed her shoulder, grimacing. "I'm just a passenger."

"She agrees with me," Marco said.

"Oh, I do not!" Kiera yelled at him, her voice lilting like a petulant teenager's. "You have never known what I'm thinking!"

Marco looked over at Alex and nodded. "That means she agrees with me."

"I should have throttled you when you were born!" Kiera roared.

"You were two!"

"I could still have throttled you!"

Alex shook his head and turned around. He walked out of the cabin, shouting back, "If this gets us killed, I'm spending the next seven lifetimes making sure you all think Habid was gentle!"

• • •

Tri Sestry took a low-altitude arc over the planet's north pole to return to the capital. Melanie, Marco, and Kiera sat on the couch in the lounge, reporting to Alex and Dale, who paced in perpendicular paths that had them repeatedly stepping around each other. Ellemarie sat in the armchair, monitoring footage of a burning city on the entertainment console.

"So how did the body end up exploding?" Dale asked.

Kiera shifted over the arm of the sofa, letting her head tip sideways. "My guess is that the habit that

Casphar marines have of shooting when they're startled literally blew up in their faces."

"What did you do?" Dale asked.

"I figured that if the body was easy to identify, they'd know whose uniform and ID tablet they were looking for," Kiera said. "So I put one of the munitions in the thermal blanket with her, and I opened the case before I sealed it up. That sort of round uses blanchiate, which is caustic, and would disfigure the body, if not dissolve it altogether, depending on how long it took them to find it. It's a munition, though. It's very explosive."

Dale nodded.

"That's probably how they burned the house down, too," Alex said. "The faster-acting knockout gasses are also the more flammable ones."

"Think of it as training the next generation of Casphar marines to be less trigger happy," Kiera said.

"The good news," Melanie said, "is that it's going to be a while before they're sure it's not you in that blanket. They're going to be assuming it's not, but if they think you're high value, it's possible we pulled you out to execute you and keep you from talking."

Alex changed the subject. "Did you leave anything in the APC that can be traced to us?"

Melanie shook her head. "Assuming you did a good job buying the gear we used, the missile should've done a pretty good job eliminating the biological traces. We used the APC's own equipment as much as possible, as per the plan. But it's not going to take them long to figure out there are no bodies in it."

"The bigger issue is the field of view of the security cameras in the prison," Kiera said. "I won't swear that the one in my cell didn't see Marco, and

if I could recognize him, facial recognition will
eventually, too."

Marco had the middle of the sofa, head tipped back
onto the backrest. "It shouldn't have, but things
were happening fast, and I was more worried about
being spotted through the window. Plus, I don't
have a criminal record here, so it's only if they're
actively monitoring us."

"Which they probably are," Alex said.

Vassily's voice came over the ship-wide sound
system. "Approaching city."

Alex stopped pacing and turned to the three on the
sofa. "You." He pointed at Kiera. "In the hidey-
hole under the bed. Keep an eye on things with the
surveillance system down there."

"First sign we're being boarded," Dale said, "close
the case."

"We're all here!" Alex roared. "Close it and leave
it closed!"

"Doesn't work that way," Dale said. "My mission,
my rules."

Alex growled.

"I'll show you," Marco said to Kiera, pulling
himself up off the sofa.

"I'm probably best served hiding in plain sight,"
Melanie said. "Did a makeup kit make it over here
before the house burned?"

"Cabin on the right," Alex said.

Melanie got up and limped down the corridor after
Kiera and Marco.

Alex turned to Dale. "I'm blaming you for all of
this."

• • •

The capital city lay burning. It wasn't a

complete conflagration, but at least ten percent of the buildings smoldered or flamed, plume after plume of black smoke rising into the atmosphere. In the commercial district, charred boxes stood where businesses had been. The residential districts were less severely impacted, but even there, nearly every block had a burning house on it. The palace still stood, apparently undamaged, in the distance. *Tri Sestry* came in low from the north, skirting the edge of the city.

The buildings on both sides of the factory had been torn open and looted. A white line had been painted on the sidewalk in front of the factory, with awkward lettering in both Casphar and Interstellar: NOSTRASPACE OWNED! A cordon of a dozen armed miners stood on the sidewalk in front of the factory, standing guard. In the streets, looters—mostly miners but also some women and businesspeople—scampered in and out of other buildings. Two buildings farther down the road also burned, but no one crossed the line painted and protected by the miners.

Tri Sestry banked and came over the factory from the rear. She hovered over the roof and descended gently. Her landing gear extended, and she touched down, bending the ventilation pipes as she did so.

Several women came out the back of the warehouse, into the yard, and looked up. They rushed back inside and returned a moment later with two ladders. The first they set up to the roof of the warehouse. They climbed it with the second ladder and then set that ladder up from the warehouse roof to the factory roof. The first of them was just reaching the top when *Tri Sestry*'s ramp finished lowering, and the airlock door opened.

Vassily stepped out onto the ramp, looking fierce

against a backdrop of smoke and flame. He barked something at the woman at the top of the ladder. She hustled up onto the roof and ran up to him. He spoke again.

She shook her head and answered in a quavering voice. He motioned for her to get on board. She ran past him, and he strode into the ship after her.

Alex and Ellemarie stood by the bed. Marco and Melanie, with Melanie again made up as the receptionist, lay on it. Both had additional bandages covering their features.

"Anya is not here," Vassily said. "Women say only workers here. Did not get message."

Khadija appeared on the ramp behind Vassily. "Local communication down after I get message. Only got through thirty women. Have others running to houses now."

"I go find Anya," Vassily said. "If not back, you leave me."

Vassily ran down the ramp before anyone else could speak.

"We gathered supplies," Khadija said. "Bringing up now."

"Make it quick!" Alex ordered.

Khadija nodded and scurried down the ramp as well.

Alex turned to Ellemarie. "You'd better show me how to lock the cockpit hatch, just in case."

"It doesn't lock," Ellemarie said. "This is a private yacht."

"You said—" Alex's face went blank with understanding. Then a wave of annoyance came over it. "Ten!" he yelled. "I will hunt you across ten lifetimes!"

• • •

Smoke curled through the streets and hung in certain districts like an acrid fog. Most everyone in the streets carried a weapon of some sort, mostly improvised clubs, but also a fair selection of illegal firearms. Every so often gunfire would sound, causing everyone in the street to scatter.

Vassily ran in the middle of the street, boots covered in grime, toward the women's dorm.

The yard in front of the dorm burned, a makeshift bonfire made up of parts of a tram and prisoners' and workers' uniforms.

A group of sixty women stood arm in arm, blocking the road, staring down an enormous military tank.

"Anya!" Vassily called out in the chaos.

The tank rattled forward, its turret turning so the gun was pointing menacingly at the two women at the center of the line. The line took half a step backward but held together.

A miner dashed up beside the tank. He shoved something into the treads and then retreated. A moment later, an explosion derailed the tread from the armored wheel. The tank turned several degrees around the now-stationary tread before stopping, the barrel of the gun swinging past the line of women, just missing them.

A cheer came up from various other people on the street.

The turret pivoted back toward the line.

Six women from the center of the line charged forward and leapt onto the turret, some hanging from it with their arms, some with their arms and legs. The gun tilted up and down. One woman dropped off, but the other five held on.

Two more miners charged forward from the sidelines and mounted the tank itself. They began pulling at the hatch on top of the turret.

The turret continued rotating until it pointed at the side of the women's dorm.

All at once, the gun recoiled, knocking the women off to the dirt below, sending the miners toppling backward from the top of the tank.

The side of the women's dorm shattered, leaving a hole that exposed all three floors inside the cylinder.

Vassily ran past the protest, toward the smoking and dusty hole, crying out Anya's name.

There had not been very many women inside the dorm, but those who were inside came rushing toward the hole. Several women were buried under rubble.

Vassily arrived at the edge of the hole and found a broad-shouldered, dark-haired woman pinned under a slab of concrete. He squatted down and lifted. Two women rushed over from inside and pulled her free. Vassily dropped the slab. The two women knelt beside the injured one and applied pressure to her legs. Vassily yelled over the din, "Anya Cheremetova?"

One of the women shook her head. Vassily patted the injured woman on the shoulder and spoke briefly in a reassuring tone. He ran past them into the dorm.

It was laid out much like the men's dorms, but with privacy curtains on each bunk. Vassily called his daughter's name repeatedly as he ran down the aisle. As he reached the elevators, he stopped. The first-aid kit hung between the two shafts. He pulled it from the wall and ran back to the injured woman, unpacking it. He had a spiderlike first-aid drone unwrapped by the time he got there, and he dropped it on her.

"Papa?" came a voice from above. Vassily looked up.

Anya stood on the edge of the third floor, holding the side of the hole in the concrete with one hand, looking down at the scene below.

"Anya!" Vassily yelled. He held up both hands and motioned for her to stay.

She vanished back into the building.

Vassily quickly checked that the first-aid drone was working and ran back into the building himself.

Anya burst out of the stairwell by the elevators just as Vassily got there.

She hurled herself into his arms.

• • •

Another group of ten women, two of them clutching babies, ran up the street and crossed the line around the factory. They vanished through the front door and moments later were in the rear yard climbing the ladders.

Khadija met them at the bottom of *Tri Sestry*'s ramp and hurried them on board. "One more runner!" she yelled inside.

Up the street, a column of marines marched toward them.

Alex appeared in the airlock, leaning out and looking in that direction. He scurried down the ramp and to the edge of the roof. Khadija appeared beside him. "We may not have time."

Khadija shook her head. "Miners not let them past."

"This isn't a warship," Alex said. "If they decide to open fire, they won't need to cross the line."

A streetlight fell in the road in front of the column of marines. Several of them opened fire. People scattered, but two miners fell, bleeding on the ground in front of the marines.

From the other direction, two more women sprinted toward the factory. Khadija spotted them. "There!"

The two women ran into the factory. Alex moved back up the ramp and was inside the ship before the women made it to the roof. Khadija spoke with one of the women briefly as she got to the top of the ladder, then sent her into the ship with the other. She stood at the bottom of the ramp.

Ellemarie appeared in the airlock, leaning on her walking stick.

"That is all who wish to go," Khadija reported.

"Then get on board!" Ellemarie called back.

Khadija shook her head. "No, I start this. I stay here. Finish it."

"Khadija," Ellemarie yelled, "don't be crazy. This isn't ending well for anyone!"

Khadija reared up. "I make end well! Good luck, good friend. I fight for future you showed."

Khadija snapped her heels together and gave a Casphar salute.

Ellemarie returned it.

Khadija stepped onto the ladder and began to descend.

Up the street, the column of marines had picked up the light pole, and with a single heave, cast it aside. They formed up again and resumed marching, walking right over the bleeding bodies of the two miners they had shot.

Ellemarie turned and called back into the ship. "That's all the employees who are willing to go. Still missing Vassily."

Halfway up the corridor, Marco relayed the message. A moment later, he relayed back, "Bring up the ramp but leave the airlock open."

Ellemarie flipped a switch, and the ramp began to retract. As soon as it was in motion, so was *Tri Sestry*, lifting off gracefully from the roof.

The column of marines halted. The marines at the front of the line leveled guns at *Tri Sestry*. A few shots were fired, but they were still at a distance. *Tri Sestry* turned away from them and moved slowly over the streets between the factory and the women's dorm.

Vassily and Anya were about a kilometer away, running.

Tri Sestry flew ten meters above the road, coming around a corner in front of them. Vassily saw the ship and stopped. He grabbed Anya around the waist with his right arm and waved his left arm over his head broadly.

Alex and Dale sat in the cockpit, Alex at the controls, Dale finessing the gravity drive. Alex looked back over his shoulder. "Get everyone as far forward as possible!"

The lounge and corridor were packed with women. Marco made his way through the crowd and opened the doors to the cabins, indicating for women to move into them. Many did. He made his way to the back, repeating, "Move forward!"

Melanie, who sat cross-legged on the bed surrounded by other women, repeated in Casphar.

Women moved forward. Ellemarie hung back as the group moved out of the master cabin, leaving Marco and Melanie behind.

"What's he doing?" Ellemarie asked.

Down on the street, Vassily moved Anya to the dead center of the road. He shouted warnings to people around him.

Tri Sestry moved directly over his head.

Then the ship's nose pulled up, tipping upright to a ninety-degree angle with the ground, her open airlock pointed straight down. Then she began to back down toward the road.

Vassily guided Anya so they were directly underneath the open airlock.

The ship descended until their heads vanished inside the airlock. Then their chests.

Vassily wrapped his other arm around Anya and jumped. She shrieked briefly as the ship's gravity took over and they slammed to the floor of the airlock.

Ellemarie peered down at them from the master cabin. "They're in!" she yelled. Marco ran up the corridor, repeating.

Tri Sestry shot straight up like a missile.

CHAPTER 15

Vassily left Anya in the master cabin. She sat on the edge of the bed next to Ellemarie. Marco and Melanie had both collapsed face down across the bed and were asleep. The crowd of women had spilled back into the cabin after the airlock closed, but it parted for Vassily as he made his way to the cockpit.

Alex and Dale were still in the pilot seats, each leaning over the center console so intently their heads were almost touching.

"It looks like the starboard reserve tank took damage," Alex said without looking up as Vassily climbed down the steps into the cockpit. "Assuming you filled it with the other one."

"Did," Vassily said.

"It's dry now," Alex said. "We burned through everything onboard, and we're most of the way through the port tank now. Low-altitude flying and all those stunts to pull off rescue missions."

"Fuel stations in orbit," Vassily said.

"Are all closed down," Alex finished. He stood up, sliding the seat back and stepping around it. He tipped his head back to look directly into Vassily's eyes. "I don't want to sound like I don't understand

what you did, but you endangered this mission. You
endangered this mission seriously. Your daughter did
exactly what a Casphar citizen would be expected to do
and told the authorities that you'd told her about the
planned protests. And you running back after her has
put our escape seriously at risk. That will all be
reported."

Vassily nodded. "Would not respect you if not."

Alex exhaled sharply through his teeth. "Okay.
Now that that's clear, we could use your local
knowledge. State of emergency, Habid is trying
to stop any traffic he can without sparking an
international incident. No fuel stations. Right
now, the best Dale and I can come up with is that
Anerchomeno Asteri happens to be outbound at the
moment. We see if we can book passage on her for
everyone and have them haul *Tri Sestry* out of the
system."

Vassily nodded. "Would complicate—"

Dale interrupted. "We got company. Looks like
we're about to be boarded."

Alex dashed past Vassily, up the steps, and ran
down the corridor and into the master cabin. "We're
getting boarded. Thump twice if you understand."

Without opening their eyes, Marco and Melanie both
knocked twice on the headboard. Ellemarie drummed her
walking stick twice. The floor answered with two slow,
deliberate knocks from below.

Alex turned to Anya. He spoke a brief phrase
in Casphar. She answered. He nodded and turned to
Ellemarie. "Ellemarie, I'd like you to meet our new
manager of product placement. Could you get her on
the payroll in the next five minutes?"

Ellemarie nodded and gestured for Anya to follow
her up the corridor.

Melanie spoke into the bedspread. "They're going to give you hell about the babies."

"I doubt even Casphar marines could get them away from their mothers," Alex said.

Outside, a slender Casphar cruiser shaped like a mixed-metal spear point moved across *Tri Sestry*'s bow. A single breaching pod ejected from the starboard aft, a device that was little more than a semicircle of metal with a hatch and an enormous O-ring on the flat end, glowing pulse engines firing around the widest diameter of the circle.

Tri Sestry stopped and rotated to bring her airlock around. The breaching pod altered course for it. It slid around to *Tri Sestry*'s stern, and the O-ring extended to seal around the outer hatch.

Alex worked the controls from inside the master cabin, opening the outer airlock hatch. The O-ring pulsed briefly with the pressure change. The breaching pod hatch opened, and four weightless Casphar marines jumped across into the airlock. As the ship's gravity took them, they dropped to the deck with heavy thuds. Each carried a rifle over his shoulder, and one held one of the two-wanded devices used to search for the falcon.

Alex closed the outer hatch behind them, then opened the inner one. "Good morning," he said brightly. "Alexander Romano-Bennetti. Sir Alexander, he."

"We search ship," the lead marine said.

Alex tipped his head up. "We are Nostraspace citizens in a private vessel, transporting ourselves and our employees to safety in light of civil unrest on the planet below. May I ask what we're accused of transporting illegally?"

"We search ship," the lead marine said, pushing past Alex.

Alex stepped aside and let the other three enter as well.

The lead marine was already sweeping the ship with the two-wanded device when the second one pulled a tablet out of his pocket and barked an order.

Melanie, without taking her face off the bed, held up an ID tablet. The marine with the tablet walked over and scanned it, grimacing at the readout.

"IDs?" Alex asked. "Is that what you're doing? Checking IDs?" He squeezed his collar, and his own ID replaced Melanie's on the marine's screen. Marco, also without moving from the bed, did the same.

The lead marine was already out of the master cabin, running his sweep. The marine with the tablet asked a question. Melanie answered weakly.

"They were injured in the riot. Streetlight fell. Is that what he's asking?"

Melanie answered in broken Interstellar with a Casphar accent. "Wants doctor information."

"We're treating them here," Alex said. "Marco is a Nostraspace citizen. The young lady is our receptionist. That should all be there."

The marine spoke again. Melanie translated, "He says to remove bandages."

"Are you a doctor?" Alex asked.

The marine turned to him. "Check ID."

Alex reared himself up to his full height. "Look at my ID and ask yourself if you really want to be accusing me of smuggling people on stolen credentials. Everyone on this ship is who their ID says they are. We didn't hire anyone who didn't have proper ID."

The other two marines rolled their eyes and pulled out tablets, heading out of the master cabin.

"We check ID," the remaining marine repeated.

"These two people were injured on your planet,"

Alex said. "We're leaving without a fuss. Do you really want my embassy involved in this?"

"Orders!" the marine insisted. "We check."

Marco rolled over. "Look at my damned face already!"

"Do you really think his forehead being uncovered is going to make the rest of his face suddenly not look like his photo?" Alex asked.

"Nostraspace ID good," the marine said. "Casphar ID. Remove bandages."

Melanie rolled stiffly onto her side, then, placing an arm behind herself, lowered herself onto her back. She reached up and gingerly peeled back the bandages on her face, teeth clenched, grunting and hissing as she did so. Her makeup stayed in place underneath.

The marine held his tablet beside her face, then grimaced with disappointment.

"This is the part where I admit that the babies up front aren't actually on the payroll," Alex said, "but I understand that even Casphar aren't barbaric enough to separate children from parents who are fleeing violence."

The marine growled at Alex.

The other three marines returned briskly. The lead one motioned for the airlock. Alex moved over to the controls. "Have a lovely day," he said with an artificial smile.

The lead marine closed the inner hatch before Alex could. They opened the outer hatch and jumped for their pod. Alex closed the outer hatch as soon as they were through it.

"I'll tell everyone when their ship is gone," Alex said in a strong, clear voice.

The floor thumped twice in acknowledgment.

"Do you have enough air?" Alex asked.

The floor thumped once.

Alex nodded. He closed the cabin door as he left, leaving only Marco and Melanie in the room.

As he walked through the ship, his employees kept stepping into his path to thank him. He smiled at each of them. Anya and Ellemarie were in the armchairs. Ellemarie looked up as he passed. "Hired with almost two minutes to spare."

"Good job." Alex turned to Anya and spoke in Casphar. She looked chagrined in response. Alex smiled sincerely and headed for the cockpit.

Vassily had taken the other pilot's seat.

Dale looked up as Alex entered. "We're on with *Anerchomeno Asteri*. They're not thrilled with the plan, but money talks. We're all going to be in two cabins. All they've got."

"We don't need luxury in an evacuation," Alex said, stooping and leaning forward to look out the front window.

The screen in front of Vassily lit up with messages. He turned, scanning them, and then cursed.

"What is it?" Alex asked.

Vassily cursed again. "Ships in queue angry. Casphar have disabled jumpgate."

• • •

Even though it only took five minutes for the breaching pod to return to the Casphar ship, it was a full hour before another ship rising from the planet's surface prompted the Casphar to veer off and leave *Tri Sestry* to proceed without escort. Alex headed back to the master cabin once it was off their proximity alert screens.

Anya had taken charge of the galley. The throng of passengers had made space for her and three assistants, who were already working together like they cooked together all the time. Food was coming off the prep surfaces at steady intervals and being distributed through the crowd. As Alex passed, a bowl of ghormeh sabzi was placed in his hand.

The corridor was harder to navigate than earlier, with less room for people to make a path for him. He opened the door of the master cabin, and three women spilled into it with him before they made their way back into the corridor and the queue for food. Marco, Ellemarie, and Melanie were all sleeping on the bed. Alex shut the cabin door and released the catch on the bed without waking them. The bed slid, and the cover to the hidden compartment opened.

Kiera lay across a long crate beside the surveillance gear, which was still powered on. Her eyes were closed. Sweat covered her face, and the green uniform she still wore was drenched.

Alex lay down on the deck and reached down to prod Kiera.

Her eyes opened, and she gasped dramatically. Her face remained fixed with wide eyes and an open mouth for a few seconds before she began breathing deeply. Eventually she rubbed her head and sat up. "I don't think I'm going to make it three days down there without an oxygen tank," she said weakly.

"Change of plans anyway," Alex said. "We don't have enough fuel, so we're hitching a ride commercial. Unless we can come up with a good ID tablet to match your current persona, we're going to need to work out a way to smuggle you on board."

Kiera stood up stiffly and picked up the black case with the falcon in it. "That's not hard if you're offloading all these people. I can vanish in a crowd." She clicked the latches open on the case and set it back in place, slightly ajar.

Alex looked down at the crate she had been lying on. "Is that Marco's porn collection?"

She shrugged. "It's somebody's porn collection. Marco's taste is usually a bit less brutish than that."

Alex shook his head and held a hand down to her. "Actually, let's take the falcon out of there. With this many passengers, it'll be less conspicuous just in the closet than having us trying to keep everyone out of here so we can get in and out of the compartment. Odds are good we're going to be searched at least once more."

Kiera nodded and handed up the case. Alex set it aside and helped her up, too. He slid the bed back into place. "Get cleaned up. I'll see if Marco has another set of clothes on board."

"Even if he doesn't, I don't care at this point," she said as she began peeling the sticky uniform off her skin.

Just then, the cabin door opened. A woman came in with three bowls of food. She let out a small yelp and vanished again, leaving the door open. Kiera, half undressed, stared.

The woman returned, now carrying four bowls of food. She deposited three on the bed next to the sleeping forms of Marco, Ellemarie, and Melanie and held the fourth out for Kiera.

Kiera took it. "Thank you."

The woman gestured at the uniform.

Kiera stared for a moment, then set the bowl aside and finished undressing. The woman took the uniform and scurried back out of the cabin.

Kiera looked at Alex, who shrugged. Kiera picked up the bowl of food and took it with her into the shower.

Alex ate as well, then checked the master cabin closet. He found an extra stretchy black outfit of Marco's and hung it in the door of the bathroom. He closed the case with the falcon and picked it up by the handle. He made his way through the crowd, returned his bowl to one of Anya's assistants, and entered the cockpit. Vassily sat in the pilot's seat, Dale in the co-pilot's.

Alex descended the steps and set the case down.

"Jumpgate back up ten minutes ago," Vassily reported. "Casphar claiming routine downtime. Captains in queue say ship almost spliced. Not routine."

Dale turned and saw the case. His eyes widened slightly, and he pushed the seat back and quickly unlatched it.

Alex looked down at the case, then at Dale, then at Vassily.

"How many light-minutes are we from the jumpgate right now?"

"Twelve," Vassily said.

Alex ran his tongue over his teeth. "Let me know if the jumpgate goes back down in about ten minutes, okay?"

"There's no need," Dale said. "It will." He stood up and raised the steps to reveal the access to the crew berths. He picked up the case with the falcon in it and headed down. "It should be back up about two minutes after that."

Alex whistled through his teeth. "King of Earth. There's no way they're letting us through the jumpgate with that thing."

"We close case when go through jumpgate," Vassily said.

"Except we can't," Alex said. "Can we, Dale?"

Dale came back up from the berths and lowered the steps again. "That's need-to-know."

"Dale," Alex said, "I think we need to know."

Vassily turned to look at them.

Dale shifted uncomfortably. "Close the hatch," he said at last.

Alex climbed the steps and pulled the cockpit hatch closed. "That's not just a symbol of the Casphar authority. It's actually controlling the jumpgate somehow. When the scanners can't pick it up, the jumpgates don't operate. What the fuck is Uncle Lew thinking?"

"It's not my job to ask him what he's thinking," Dale said. "My orders were to get it. He didn't tell me what it was, either. I figured it out when we kept accidentally shutting down the jumpgate while trying to keep it hidden in the capital."

"But why?" Alex started to pace, but the tiny space meant he could only take a half step and then turn. "Taking it is bound to cause an international incident. What's his game?"

"I. Don't. Know!" Dale sat down on the steps.

Vassily looked at them both. "Do not understand."

"We're twelve light-minutes out from the jumpgate," Alex explained. "The jumpgate went down just about twelve minutes after Kiera closed the case because we were about to be boarded. Only it wasn't twelve minutes after. It *takes* twelve minutes for those messages to reach us, which means it went down the instant she closed it. She reopened it just about twelve minutes before you got word that the jumpgate was back up. I closed it to carry it through the ship so I wouldn't spill it with the crowds out there. So, twelve minutes after that, you should get word that it went down again."

"But message from it should take time to get to jumpgate," Vassily said.

Dale shook his head. "Jumpgates are faster-than-light technology. Whatever this thing is, it works like a jumpgate. Instantaneous."

"Is it all the Casphar jumpgates or just this one?" Alex asked.

"For obvious reasons," Dale answered, "I haven't made inquiries. But what good is seizing control of only one?"

Alex stopped pacing and stared at the ceiling. "And there's only one time in recorded history when a single world has changed alliance, and that was the Node. Just about every line present. Not since the Suturiku conquered Hundye has any nation gotten control of another line. And that's as much legend as history."

Vassily shook his head. "Still does not make sense."

Alex waved it off. "Historian talk. The point is, the Don threw us all in far, far deeper over our heads than any of us were told."

"Makes sense," Dale said. "If we're caught, if we genuinely have no idea what we've got, it would be a lot harder to get anything useful out of us."

"Except it doesn't make sense," Alex said. "Stealing something like this? That's a major operation. That's not something you're capable of."

Dale started to protest, "I'm—"

"I'm not either!" Alex interrupted. "This should have been years of planning. One team gets the falcon, hands it off to another team that doesn't know what they're carrying. They hand it off to a third team that doesn't know the first team. This is way above either of us."

"I'm sitting here with it," Dale said.

"By luck more than anything else," Alex said. "And the hard part is still ahead of us. They're going to be watching for this thing. We can't hide it *and* use the jumpgate. The nearest non-Casphar jumpgate is, what, 200 years away by gravity drive? Uncle Lew sent us both in with no realistic way to get out again."

"Hundred twenty-five years," Vassily supplied. "Assuming fast ship and unlimited fuel."

"But *why*?" Alex asked again.

Dale threw his hands aside. "Can't help you! The question is, now that you know, what are you going to do about it? My orders are to bring it home. Your orders are to bring me home."

"And we both know," Alex said into his moustache, "that when the Don gives you an order..."

"Exactly." Dale snarled and hissed through his teeth. "Can you imagine if I hadn't figured out what it was and just tried to go through the jumpgate with it?"

"How *were* you planning to get it out?" Alex asked.

"Put it in a suitcase and leave with it," Dale said. "We. Had. No. Idea. What we were stealing. I don't know what Uncle Lew thought we'd do."

"Get caught, probably," Alex said.

"Seems like it," Dale said.

"No, seriously." Alex's voice grew quiet and thoughtful. "The only possible outcome for us, you not knowing what you're carrying, me not knowing your mission, is for us to walk straight into Casphar custody. What does that get Uncle Lew?"

"But Habid had you and Kiera," Dale said.

"But he had nothing on either of us. So neither of us were ever officially in custody. I was a 'guest.' Kiera was an anonymous prisoner number. If he'd been able to prove we were involved in something...”

“He’d’ve had to contact the embassy,” Dale finished for him.

“Which means,” Alex said, “that we were an excuse to invite Habid to Sixcrystal Station for that quiet little summit he’s refused twice.”

Dale nodded, rubbing his tongue over his teeth. “Give Habid an ace he can hold—namely us—and he’s no longer afraid. Out of all the people in the Secret Services, we’re the Don’s closest relations. Not just random distant cousins. We’re actually his nephews. High-value prisoners. Habid walks in thinking he’s in control of the situation because of that. That makes a kind of perverse sense.”

“And you two,” Vassily said, swinging a finger back and forth to point at both of them, “can be counted on to screw up.”

Dale glared.

Alex started laughing. “We do have that reputation, don’t we?”

After a moment, Dale started laughing, too. “And we go and screw up his plans dramatically by being competent.”

“You two,” Vassily said, “not competent.”

Dale and Alex both laughed so hard they doubled over.

Alex stood upright first, wiping his eyes with his forefinger. “So, do we mess up Uncle Lew’s plans even worse by figuring out how the hell to get this thing out of Casphar territory, or do we call up Emperor Habid and tell him we found his missing toy?”

Dale laughed harder at that suggestion. “Oh, my orders were not to volunteer to get caught. I say we make Habid work for it. I like the idea of showing up at Sixcrystal Station having pulled off the missions we were supposed to botch.”

"Yeah, me, too," Alex said. "Dump it in Uncle Lew's lap and let him deal with the fact that we destabilized an empire getting it."

Dale cackled.

"Is not funny," Vassily said.

"Actually, it is," Alex said, breaking up again himself. "Because Uncle Lew is probably going to have to call up Habid and apologize, and then hand us both over to him for disembowelment."

The cousins doubled over laughing again, Vassily glaring down at them.

"You could... You could..." Dale gasped, "claim you had no idea what I had stolen."

Alex screamed laughing.

"Not helpful," Vassily growled.

Dale rolled to his knees and gasped for air. "Which brings us back to the idea of contacting Habid ourselves and ratting out Uncle Lew. He might even play along and go to Sixcrystal Station."

"Oh, no," Alex said. "He'll disembowel us."

Dale dropped into a sitting position on the step. "The problem is, they're going to search whatever ship we're on. Once they realize that every time they search our ship, the jumpgate goes down, they'll figure it out and take the ship apart plate by plate. The only reason they haven't figured it out yet is because most people forget about light-speed lag unless they're trying to have a real-time conversation. And when we get searched at the gate, there won't be lag. We're not getting through that jumpgate."

Alex rolled to a seated position on the deck. "We'd need a military escort."

"Even then," Dale said. "Plate by plate. Unless there was a general standing there with ironclad orders. Anything less, they'd challenge every step of the way, and even Ellemarie couldn't intercept all that."

"And marines waiting on other side of the jumpgate," Vassily reminded them.

Alex's expression had gone vacant. "Military escort... General..."

Dale lowered his chin and looked at Alex. "Oh, you are not—"

"No," Alex interrupted. "Think about it. We're supposed to get caught. That's actually the plan."

Dale shook his head. "Don't even—"

"This is empowering!" Alex shouted. "Seriously. How many brilliant but risky ideas have you rejected because the most likely outcome was you in custody?"

Dale stared for a moment. "And you're thinking that this means we get to do something stupid?"

"Me," Alex said. "I get to do something stupid. Because if I'm in custody but you're out, I've still completed my mission. And Uncle Lew gets his little summit, for whatever reason his little summit is so fucking important. And if you get that stupid bird out with you, then you've completed your mission, too. And everyone is happy. And if by some miracle I pull this off and I'm not in custody, well, then that's even better. And let Uncle Lew maybe send Angie in on the next suicide mission. And wouldn't it be funny if she's competent, too? Let him run out of nieces and nephews before he has to tell us what the fuck he's thinking."

"There's no way you're getting away with impersonating a Casphar general," Dale said.

"Why not?" Alex asked. "I'm supposed to get caught! *I am empowered!* I'm going to go get you your military escort!"

Vassily shrugged. "If orders look good. Confusion on planet. Maybe not check."

"Your Casphar sounds like you learned it in a Nostraspace boarding school," Dale said.

Alex pointed a finger at the ceiling. "I can work with that."

"How?" Dale asked.

"We'll just tell people I grew up on Yllas."

Dale arched an eyebrow.

"Do you think," Alex asked, "we have two native Casphar speakers on board who wouldn't mind risking arrest for the cause?"

Chapter 16

"Do good to people and you'll enslave their hearts."
        —Casphar proverb

As *Tri Sestry* approached *Anerchomeno Asteri*, the women on board had taken to sleeping in shifts on the floors, the sofas, and the various beds. More than half of them slept while others hurried to patch and alter the three Casphar military uniforms. The one Marco had worn had been modified with a general's sash made out of the headscarf of one of the women.

A square-jawed woman in her late thirties had Melanie's uniform draped over her own shoulders, pinned to her own shape. Ellemarie and two other sewers were fitting Anya into the uniform Kiera had stolen.

In the master cabin, Alex and Dale organized several stacks of suitcases. Melanie, still in secretary makeup, stood in the bathroom brushing blonde coloring into Kiera's hair. A woman's worker outfit that looked to have been hobbled together from spare parts from women of three different sizes lay on the counter beside the sink.

Vassily's voice made a ship-wide announcement in Casphar, then repeated it in Interstellar. "Approaching *Anerchomeno Asteri*."

The women working on uniforms hurried up their stitching.

Alex carried the black case into the master cabin, clicked its latches closed, and stowed it on the top shelf of the closet.

Anerchomeno Asteri drifted toward the jumpgate at a leisurely pace, close enough that its light plus the running lights of the enormous queue of ships trying to exit the system looked like a dim star in the distance. *Tri Sestry* angled alongside gently, then matched course and speed. After several minutes of flying alongside, *Tri Sestry* turned and began to back toward one of the docking rings on the side of the enormous liner's teardrop hull. The airlocks mated, and *Tri Sestry*'s gravity drive powered down.

The reception room on *Anerchomeno Asteri* was the mirror image of the one they had arrived in on their first voyage. A slender young man with thick curly hair stood behind the desk. His nametag identified him as Bahman.

Two Casphar marines stood just inside the airlock hatch, one with a crooked nose who held a tablet and an older one holding one of the two-wand scanners. Captain Mamatas stood behind them, wringing his hands.

The airlock hatch slid open. Vassily stepped through, clicked his heels while looking right past the two marines, and nodded to Captain Mamatas. "Captain Cheremetov of *Tri Sestry* delivering passengers. Permission to come aboard?"

"Of course," Captain Mamatas answered.

Vassily stepped aside. Alex and Ellemarie, both pulling an aluminum suitcase on wheels behind them, stepped through next. Without ceremony, they both squeezed their collars, and their papers appeared on the marine's tablet. The marine nodded. "We search suitcases."

Alex let go of the handle of his and walked over

to the desk. He squeezed his collar again, and Bahman
quietly started processing the list of tickets, his
professional smile not fading as he did so.

The older marine ran the two-wand device over both
cases, then gestured for Ellemarie to open them.

Just then, a wave of women from the ship crashed
through the airlock. Ellemarie and the marines were
swept up in it, carried almost all the way over to the
reception desk. Captain Mamatas dashed around behind
the desk to stay clear of it. Both marines screamed
orders over the din of chattering women. Marco,
lugging his crate in both hands and carrying a bag
over his shoulder, appeared behind them, making his
way toward Ellemarie.

The older marine stepped up onto Ellemarie's case
and barked an order. A confused hush came over the
mass of women. He gestured for everyone to stay where
they were. Then he hopped down and opened Ellemarie's
case.

The doll of Emperor Habid dressed as a miner sat on
top of several articles of clothing.

The marine squawked in horror and pointed at it.

"Yeah, we never did find the investors to put that
one into production," Ellemarie said matter-of-factly.
"Something about it being too disrespectful and the
investors not wanting to join Austin Montierthski
in... what was that place they said?"

No one supplied her with the name of the prison.

The marine rifled through the rest of her
possessions, then slammed the case shut. Alex was
back beside them. Ellemarie passed his suitcase back
to him to open for inspection.

The crooked-nosed marine looked over the crowd,
which had gone back to chittering noisily, before
shouting, "All luggage here. We check luggage, then
ID."

Captain Mamatas leaned over the desk. "We're checking ID with the tickets, if you'd like—"

"We check all passengers!" the crooked-nosed marine roared.

Not following instructions, the crowd surged forward, holding ID tablets out for the older marine, who was searching Alex's case. He hurried the search and closed the case. Crooked-nosed Marine grabbed his tablet, moved in between the crowd and the older marine, and began to scan ID tablets.

The older marine took out the two-wand scanner again and moved toward Marco, who was now in the middle of the crowd. He stopped to verify that one bundle was a baby and to scan both mother and baby before moving over to Marco. He pointed to Marco's crate. "Open."

Marco raised an eyebrow. "Okay, but I don't think you're going to like it."

Marco set the crate down in the middle of the reception room, unlatched the cover, and opened it. The porn collection lay on full display.

The marine went for his weapon instinctively.

A complete hush came over the room as every woman in the crowd—those whose IDs had been checked and those whose hadn't—turned to look. The crooked-nosed marine walked over, slack-jawed, staring at the contents of the crate.

Captain Mamatas came around from behind the desk, also staring with a fixed gaze at the crate. After a moment, Bahman looked up from his task and followed his captain around for a look.

"This..." the crooked-nosed marine started, stammering, "this... obscene!"

"Oh, so it is!" Captain Mamatas said with a hint of astonishment in his voice. "And completely legal on a Greekorp vessel."

"Is illegal!" the marine roared.

With all eyes on the porn, Vassily stepped away from the wall. Kiera, dressed as one of the workers, handed him the black case.

"Even when operating in Casphar space," Captain Mamatas said, "ships remain sovereign territory of their multistellar nation of origin. I have no problem transporting this as long as he keeps it out of public areas."

Marco ran a finger down the crooked-nosed marine's arm. "Look, I know why you're so worked up, and trust me, no one needs to find out."

The veins in the crooked-nosed marine's neck bulged, and his face turned red. He screamed at Marco in Casphar, spittle flying from his mouth.

Vassily set the black case down on top of Ellemarie's suitcase and slid back into position by the airlock.

"I don't speak Casphar," Marco said. "Is that a yes?"

The marine lunged. Alex and the older marine dove and restrained him.

"*Tri Sestry* is Nostraspace ship now," Vassily offered from by the airlock, looking like he had never moved. "Legal in Nostraspace. Time to notice and object was on planet, if porn ever on planet. Cannot see how it would be on planet. That would be illegal."

Bahman helped Alex and the older marine pull the crooked-nosed marine back over to the desk. After a moment, the crooked-nosed marine stopped ranting and trying to lunge, but Alex and Bahman didn't let him go. The older marine walked over and started scanning the porn with the two-wand device, moving images aside to verify that it was, indeed, porn the whole way down.

"If you don't mind," Ellemarie said to Bahman, "I'm checked in, and I really need to sit down."

Bahman nodded. Ellemarie took the handle of her case, now with the black case on it as well, and headed out into the lobby.

Captain Mamatas had rounded to stand in front of the crooked-nosed marine. He spoke clearly and sternly. "I am complying with the Casphar government's request—and I do mean *request*, because you have no authority here—to verify my manifest and ask for permission to check luggage. I am doing this as a courtesy. You have now exceeded the level of discourtesy I'm willing to accept on behalf of my passengers. I want to speak to your commanding officer. Now."

The marine lunged at Captain Mamatas. Mamatas didn't flinch, and Alex and Bahman's grip held.

"That was not a request, young man," Captain Mamatas said.

The older marine checked Marco's shoulder bag next, clearing it very quickly. He handed the bag back and pointed to the crate. "Is obscene. Do not return to Reggit."

"Oh, honey," Marco said, "you have no idea how far I'm staying away from this place."

The older marine kicked Marco's crate shut. "Any luggage?"

Vassily offered a small aluminum case, which the marine was able to search in a few seconds. Vassily held out a hand toward *Tri Sestry* and accompanied the older marine on board.

Captain Mamatas, meanwhile, continued his staredown with the crooked-nosed marine. Finally, he gave up and turned. "Very well, this party is cleared. Welcome aboard, everyone."

Bahman repeated the order in halting Casphar.

The crowd of women surged forward through the doors into the lobby. Marco and Alex stayed behind, Alex still restraining the crooked-nosed marine with Bahman.

The chatter of the women went silent as the door shut behind them.

The crooked-nosed marine shook his shoulders, snarling, and Alex and Bahman let him go, keeping their hands ready to grab ahold again should the need arise.

The door to the lobby opened again, and six armed ship's security officers arrived. The crooked-nosed marine glared at them, then at the captain, but accompanied them out without saying anything.

"I am deeply sorry," Captain Mamatas said to Alex.

"It's quite all right," Alex said. "We appreciate your hospitality, and we know that this isn't your fault. Casphar isn't exactly at its best right now."

Vassily and the older marine returned from *Tri Sestry*, laughing and chatting jovially in Casphar. The older marine took in the scene and looked at Captain Mamatas. "Is under arrest?"

Captain Mamatas gave an exaggerated nod.

"I will inform commander," the older marine said.

Captain Mamatas gave a more natural nod, with a hint of a polite smile.

The Casphar marine exited into the lobby. Captain Mamatas blew out a loud breath through pursed lips as the door closed behind him.

Bahman walked over to Marco. "May I help you get your case to your stateroom?"

"Thank you!" Marco said, moving to one side of it.

The young crewman moved to the other side, and together they hoisted. "So," he said as they moved through the door, "is that really your type? You know you can do a lot better."

"Oh, honey," Marco said as the doors closed, "it's been a looong trip to Reggit."

Captain Mamatas and Alex looked at each other.

Captain Mamatas started laughing first.

• • •

An hour later, Alex, Ellemarie, Anya, and one of the other women returned to *Tri Sestry*. The reception room was empty, and the airlock stood open. *Tri Sestry*'s airlock was closed and locked. Alex keyed in the combination and it slid open for them.

As soon as they were through the airlock, Alex pulled it closed. Ellemarie made straight for the lounge. Anya turned down the bed, revealing three perfectly pressed and presentable Casphar military uniforms. The three of them each grabbed one. Alex's had a complete general's sash. The other two were basically as they were when Melanie and Kiera wore them but with new ribbons added to the front pockets.

Vassily appeared in the doorway. Alex looked up at him. "Vassily, do you know Natalia, our other volunteer? She's one of Khadija's most trusted sewers, and she has military experience."

Natalia was a square-jawed woman in her late thirties. She had brown hair buzzed in a military cut, and she carried herself with more authority than her short frame should have allowed.

Vassily clicked his heels and nodded. He spoke to Natalia briefly in Casphar. She responded.

He nodded to Alex. "Let her be assistant who does talking. Real military experience hard to fake."

"That was the plan," Alex said, vanishing into the bathroom.

Anya and Natalia took their uniforms and headed past Vassily toward the other staterooms.

"We take *Tri Sestry*?" Vassily asked.

"There aren't any tenders currently docked," Alex called back from the bathroom, "but there's one other possibility that has presented itself. Ellemarie is checking on it."

"Fuel very low," Vassily said.

"That fact isn't lost on me," Alex called back.

Ellemarie reappeared, shuffling back toward the airlock. "Orders are inserted," she reported. "The rest will be less conspicuous if I borrow *Asteri's* computer." She yanked open the airlock and exited.

Anya and Natalia returned a few minutes later, dressed in the Casphar military uniforms and looking the part. Vassily smiled and took Anya by the shoulders.

Ellemarie returned, closing the airlock behind her. "Reception Room 9. Not luxury, but apparently the two it brought over are here for the duration."

"Captain Mamatas isn't likely to let that one out of the brig," Alex called back from the bathroom, "and I imagine the other one isn't allowed to leave him here. Now make sure that Dale, Melanie, and Kiera are in your or Marco's sights from now until we hand them over to the Don."

"Good luck," Ellemarie said, pulling the airlock open again. She stepped through and closed it behind her.

Alex emerged from the bathroom. He had shaved his moustache and given himself a regulation Casphar military haircut. The effect was that his face looked rounder but his jawline appeared more hollow and pouty. The uniform he wore fit perfectly, and all in all, he looked more like a Casphar general than the generals in the emperor's situation room had.

Alex looked at Anya and Natalia. "Do either of you speak any Interstellar?"

Both just stared at him. He repeated in Casphar. Both shook their heads, and Natalia spoke.

Alex nodded. He looked at Vassily and spoke in a low voice. "Are you confident in both of them? I don't like working with operatives I haven't screened."

Vassily nodded. "Anya learned lesson. Arrested for reporting protest. Casphar logic. Only criminal knows criminal plans. She will make good, loyal Nostraspace citizen."

"And Natalia?"

Vassily looked at her and spoke. She scoffed briefly then spoke curtly back to him.

"No loyalty to Casphar," Vassily reported.

Natalia spoke in extremely hesitant Interstellar. "Husband. Jail. Me." She motioned with a thumb over her shoulder.

"Crimes of family," Vassily explained. "Not allowed in military if married to criminal."

Alex nodded and spoke to both of them in Casphar. It was a long speech, rousing in tone. Both women smiled. He ended with, "Now, let's go."

• • •

Alex, Anya, and Natalia marched across *Anerchomeno Asteri*'s lobby like they owned it. A few people turned to look at them as they passed, but the hubbub of life aboard the ship continued without paying them much mind. The ship was crowded, and three military officers, even one of significant rank, were no more conspicuous than anything else on board.

Reception Room 9 was next door to the one they

had arrived in on their inbound trip. The door to
it was locked. Alex pulled a small, clear chip from
his pocket and placed it between his thumb and the
thumbprint reader. He pressed against both firmly.
After a moment, the lock beeped, and the door slid
open. The women went in first, and Alex followed,
pocketing the chip again.

The airlock stood open. Beyond it lay a Casphar
breaching pod.

Natalia strode toward it and jumped without
hesitation. As she left the ship's gravity, her feet
ran in the air and her body twisted. She touched
gently on the curved backside of the pod and turned
around, hovering in midair. She held out a hand.

Alex jumped next. She caught his hand and guided
him in. Anya stepped into the airlock and studied
the door for a second before pulling it shut behind
her. She jumped across next. Alex had her arm as
soon as she left the ship's gravity. She looked green
momentarily, but she closed her eyes and breathed
deeply, and it passed.

Alex closed the outer airlock door, then pulled
himself back into the pod. It was small, but there
was ample room for three people in it. Alex found the
handle for the hatch and pulled it closed.

The controls for the pod were on the inside of
the hatch. Alex found the power switch and had the
pod turned on almost immediately, but he took several
minutes to study the controls before attempting
anything else.

When he was ready, he checked with the two women.
Both nodded, and he slipped his hands into the control
sleeves. The O-ring connecting the pod to the airlock
retracted. The hull made a popping sound, and the pod
launched away from the enormous liner.

Anerchomeno Asteri continued on toward the jumpgate. The tiny breaching pod, barely noticeable next to the liner's heft, turned and headed back toward Reggit.

The journey took two hours, but eventually the little pod approached the spearhead-shaped cruiser that had intercepted *Tri Sestry* earlier.

Natalia pulled the communications headset on and spoke into the microphone. Listening, she relayed information to Alex, who flew in silence.

Without atmosphere, distances were very difficult to judge. Objects in space simply appeared to grow larger as they got closer. The cruiser grew and grew.

Then, without warning, the control panel went blank.

Alex pulled his hands out of the sleeves, floating once again, as he no longer held on to anything.

The pod pivoted around them. Alex put a hand on the back wall and turned himself around. A circular depression in the side of the hull loomed in front of them.

The pod pivoted again, turning so the window looked out into the nothingness of space. The thrusters mounted on the pod fired and propelled it, round end first, toward the depression in the ship's hull. The pod touched the hull of the cruiser and slid down into the depression.

Inside the pod, gravity came back suddenly. Alex landed on his feet, staggering. Anya and Natalia both fell, but they were up again immediately.

The cruiser pulled the pod inside. A large double door in the hull slid shut as soon as the pod was inside. The pod sat inside a large airlock. Platforms appeared and extended from hatches on either side of it. They met in the middle, right in front

of the pod's hatch. As they joined to form a broad
bridge, the hatch opened.

Natalia stepped out first. She moved to one side of
the pod's hatch and stood at attention. Anya copied
her on the other side of the pod's hatch.

One of the hatches in the side of the airlock
opened. Three men in white uniforms ran in and fell
into formation across from the pod's hatch.

Alex stepped out of the pod. He surveyed the scene
imperiously. Then he looked at Natalia and gave a
curt command.

She saluted and repeated the command. The sailor
closest to the hatch they had come from stepped
forward and turned to face the hatch. Alex, Anya, and
Natalia fell in behind him, and the other two sailors
brought up the rear. The group proceeded out of the
airlock.

The interior of the cruiser was a network of
interconnected bridges—most leading to breaching pods—
and cylindrical chambers filled with bunks. Below the
bridges, the gravity drive glowed an eerie amber-
green, its light reflecting off the varied metal
surfaces to create a diffuse light that filled the
entire ship.

The sailors led them to the exact center of the
ship, toward a spherical compartment held in place by
four bridges pointing fore, aft, port, and starboard.
The sphere was easily sixty feet in diameter, and
conduits came out of it in every direction. A hatch
in the side of the sphere opened automatically as
they approached, and the sailors led Alex, Anya, and
Natalia in.

The sphere had twenty people working in it,
workstations scattered around. Holographic displays
in the walls made the sphere itself invisible from the

inside, a 3-D representation of the space around the ship stretching off into infinity instead, creating the impression that the control center of the ship was an extruded-mesh platform floating among the stars.

Everyone present snapped to attention. A woman in a white captain's uniform stepped over and saluted.

Alex saluted back, then waved to Natalia. She reached into her pocket and handed over three green cards. The captain flipped through them, nodded, and pocketed them. Then she turned to point out one of the simulated lights in the distance.

The view zoomed, revealing the jumpgate. It was in the process of transmitting a small group of nonaligned spacer vessels all at once. A queue, several hundred ships long, stretched back from the gate, its borders defined by four strings of temporary buoys, each blinking red and amber. Ships of all shapes and sizes hovered, waiting, sometimes with as little as a hundred meters between them.

Natalia spoke, waving her hand. The view zoomed back and then zoomed in on *Anerchomeno Asteri*.

The captain raised an eyebrow.

Alex nodded and spoke quietly.

The captain chewed a lip briefly, then nodded. She turned and barked out an order.

The cruiser banked in space and began to pursue *Anerchomeno Asteri*.

CHAPTER 17

"There are three competing theories for the
origin of the jumpgates. First, and most
prominent, is the "Earth theory," which
postulates that the gates were all built by a
single world expanding outward. Second, the
"multiple origins" theory, which insists that
independent populations on the various planets
were in contact with one another and shared
the knowledge of how to build gates, allowing
each world to build its own. Finally, there
is the highly speculative "ongoing existence"
theory, which assumes that the gates predate
humans, and we merely learned to use them.
Although I intend to argue for the Earth
theory, the fact that rational arguments can
be made for all three of these theories and
that none of them completely fit the known
facts only serves to underscore just how much
we have yet to learn about jumpgate history
and technology."

   –Leslie Wesson, *The History and
   Technology of Interstellar Travel*

The jumpgate shone like a beacon. In front of it,
a cylindrical battleship and a blocky troop carrier
hovered on guard. The queue of spaceships, now over a
thousand ships long, stretched back from the gate.

Swarms of breaching pods moved from the troop carrier to the front of the queue, and from those to the ships farther back in the queue.

Anerchomeno Asteri, with a spearhead-shaped cruiser low along her port side, ignored the blinking buoys and headed straight for the gate.

Ellemarie and Dale stepped onto the observation deck. Dale had changed into formal Nostraspace attire, complete with purple cape, and carried the black case, two small stoppers inserted in the latches to keep them from closing the case completely.

Ellemarie was dressed more modestly in a simple shirt and pants, leaning on her walking stick more than usual. They made their way over to a window.

Dale set the case down in front of the window. Ellemarie took a seat on it, looking forward at the approaching jumpgate. "Looks like a party."

"This is the fun part," Dale said. "The Casphar really, really don't like foreign ships getting special treatment."

On the cruiser, Alex, Anya, and Natalia stood on the command deck, taking in the scene on the holographic viewers.

A communication window appeared amongst the stars with the face of Captain Mamatas in it. "Good afternoon," he said. "I have the troop ship ahead requesting that I stop to be searched. Your orders were to go directly to and through the jumpgate. Do I comply?"

The captain of the cruiser looked up, then looked over at Alex. He shook his head and spoke curtly.

Natalia stepped forward and stood beside the captain. She addressed Captain Mamatas in Casphar.

The captain of the cruiser spoke. "We have general on board. Direct orders. Tell captain, contact."

Captain Mamatas nodded, and another communication window opened with the face of a severe-looking captain in it. He had a pronounced, hooked nose and a beard, and he had his hair covered with a tied-back scarf. "All ships ordered stop for search," he said.

The cruiser captain spoke in Casphar. Natalia spoke in Casphar then.

The hook-nosed captain shook his head. Alex stepped forward and barked something terse.

Natalia stammered as she spoke more extensively to the hook-nosed captain.

Captain Mamatas interjected. "Forgive my limited Casphar, please. My ship is quite massive. If I do not start slowing now, I will not be able to stop."

"No stop," Alex said with a thick Casphar accent.

Captain Mamatas did a subtle double-take. Then he nodded, and his communication window went away.

The cruiser captain and the hook-nosed captain continued arguing. Alex stepped back.

Anerchomeno Asteri continued straight for the jumpgate. The cruiser dipped down below her keel, then accelerated to take a position directly in front of her, pointed bow aligned to run the troop ship through. Breaching pods made space, several of them turning back toward *Anerchomeno Asteri* as she passed.

The jumpgate's ring pulsed and then glowed blue. The stars visible on the far side of the gate changed.

The troop ship pulled up, just enough to leave room for *Anerchomeno Asteri* to pass underneath her.

The cruiser slid through the jumpgate. *Anerchomeno Asteri*, her wide body barely smaller than the jumpgate ring, followed.

On the observation deck, Ellemarie and Dale watched as the glowing blue ring passed, one set of constellations on one side of it, another set on the other. As the enormous bulk of the ring passed them, Dale leaned forward and pressed against the window to look behind.

The Santa Maria jumpgate still had the space warp between its posts. Through the warp, on the Reggit side of the jumpgate, the troop ship banked around and lined up with the jumpgate, immediately on the pointed tail of *Anerchomeno Asteri*.

The troop ship accelerated, steering into the jumpgate.

On the observation deck, Ellemarie stood up.

Dale took the case she had been sitting on. He popped the obstructions out of the latches, then closed it.

The jumpgate posts went dark.

The space warp vanished, the Reggit side through it replaced by the local constellations.

The troop ship, partway through the gate, was sheared in two. Her bow shot forward with a burst of outgassing atmosphere, the aft remaining behind at Reggit. Several bodies flew out into space from the bow section. It rocked and began tumbling toward *Anerchomeno Asteri*.

A collision alarm sounded throughout the liner. "All passengers, shelter in cabins or designated safe areas immediately."

Dale tucked the case under his arm. He, Ellemarie, and the two dozen other people on the observation deck made for the hallway amid gasps and murmurs of concern.

On the cruiser, the captain barked an order.

Alex, Anya, and Natalia quickly exited the command deck and made their way along the catwalk outside.

The cruiser pulled up. A flash of spatial distortion from the gravity drive sent it in an arch over the top of *Anerchomeno Asteri* and then between her and the careening bow of the troop ship. The broken-off section was as tall as the cruiser was long and several times wider than the cruiser's widest point.

Like an open box in the wind, the troop ship's bow tumbled, expelling debris and more human bodies.

The cruiser's nose angled in.

The careening bow came around again, the open end facing the cruiser. The cruiser accelerated slightly, its pointed bow moving inside the troop ship's hull. The inner hull of the troop ship connected with the top of the cruiser's nose. The cruiser spun like a compass needle, but the gravity drive caught it. Both the cruiser and the severed bow came to a stop.

Anerchomeno Asteri slid out of harm's way.

Aboard the cruiser, a klaxon sounded. Alex, Anya, and Natalia lay on one of the catwalks, clinging to the sides. Near them, a marine hovered, thrown from another catwalk, now floating weightless in the void above the glowing gravity drive below.

Natalia was on her feet first. She hauled Anya to her feet and took her hand.

Anya stared for a split second before realization crossed her face. With her other hand, she took Alex's hand.

Natalia jumped. She went weightless immediately. Her trajectory carried her toward the weightless marine. Anya stepped off the catwalk after her.

The marine reached out. As Natalia careened into him, he grabbed her in a bear hug.

Alex yanked. The three weightless bodies came back to the catwalk. Anya landed easily on her feet. Natalia and the marine went down in a heap on top of each other.

The marine laughed. He let go of Natalia, stood up, and hugged Anya. Then he dragged Alex to his feet and hugged him, too. Then, noticing Alex's uniform, he snapped to attention, then retreated.

Alex pointed in the direction of the breaching pod they had come in. Natalia shook her head and pointed in a different direction. She turned and headed that way. Alex and Anya exchanged a glance and followed her.

As they passed the various cylinders that contained bunks, all were sealed closed. In one of them, someone inside knocked, but they kept going directly past it.

Natalia led them to an armory. A dozen marines and around sixty sailors who were on the catwalks when the ship went into lockdown were lined up here. As each approached the armory, which was basically a smaller version of the other cylinders around the ship, they were each handed a weapon by a pair of arms on the other side of a small hatch. Natalia got in line. Alex and Anya followed.

Marines in line received large rifles. Sailors received small sidearms or narrow rifles, based on which version of the white uniform they were wearing.

When Natalia got to the front of the line, the quartermaster inside sized her up quickly, then handed her a sidearm. He did the same for Alex. Anya received one of the narrow rifles.

After checking her weapon, Natalia pointed in the direction of the breaching pods. She took off at a run. Alex and Anya sprinted to keep up.

• • •

Anerchomeno Asteri continued on toward the DiYesu Family gate, Santa Maria's sun burning like a bright star in the distance, the planet itself lost in the sea of stars.

Ellemarie and Dale had returned to the stateroom, which was packed with women from the factory. Marco, Melanie, and Kiera were asleep on the floor amid a dozen other sleeping women. More women milled around with the young children. Dale tucked the black case into the closet. As he did so, the communications panel on the wall by the door blinked. Ellemarie went over to it and answered. A young woman in a crewmember's uniform appeared on the screen. "Captain Mamatas for Sir Alexander."

"He's not available at the moment," Ellemarie said.

Captain Mamatas appeared on the screen. He leaned forward confidentially. "Does he happen to be impersonating a Casphar general at the moment?"

Ellemarie pursed her lips, then leveled her eyes at Captain Mamatas. "You do not need to worry, Captain. You're on the right side of this, and the Don has your back."

"I certainly hope so," Captain Mamatas said. "Because the Casphar ship that's on patrol in the area is moving to intercept, and they're sending out every breaching pod they've got."

Dale stepped over behind Ellemarie. "Can you get me a priority channel to the jumpgate in front of us?"

A window popped open on the screen. Dale pulled the tablet down, launched the keyboard, and typed quickly: Alex, his partners, and I are fleeing civil unrest on Reggit, transporting Nostraspace-protected civilians. Casphar jumpgate is down. Casphar patrol in DiYesu space attempting to board *Anerchomeno Asteri*. Request assistance. Dale Carsoni.

He pressed his finger against the screen to authenticate the signature, verified the routing to

Polairmo, then transmitted. He switched back to the link to Captain Mamatas. "If Greekorp and DiYesu will let a Nostraspace military vessel use their gates, I believe we'll have help within four of five hours."

Captain Mamatas grimaced. "We are going to be boarded long before then."

• • •

Aboard the cruiser, a ship-wide announcement echoed through the cavernous interior. Natalia stopped in her tracks. Behind Alex, Anya swore. They both stopped on either side of Natalia. Alex checked all around. They conferred quickly in hushed tones.

When they looked up, a marine stood in front of them. He held out his hand.

Alex handed over his sidearm. Anya and Natalia followed suit.

The marine pointed back in the direction they had come from. Alex grimaced and turned around. He started walking. Anya and Natalia flanked behind him. The marine followed, his gun pointed at their backs.

• • •

Dale strode out of the lobby elevator. Captain Mamatas stood in the cavernous space, giving orders to his security force, a group of about a hundred men and women. They had brought in tables, which were overturned and facing the doors of each of the reception rooms that lined both sides of the enormous lobby. Some were taking up positions behind them, long red stun guns at the ready.

Dale came up beside Captain Mamatas. "That won't work. Casphar marines will cut through that line like pudding. And they won't hesitate to kill. Your people will have better cover on the bridges."

Captain Mamatas turned and looked at Dale. "Spiro Mamatas. Captain, he."

"Dale Carsoni. Mister, he," Dale answered. "Nostraspace Secret Services. I came on board under the name Bruno Shostakovich."

Captain Mamatas's eyes narrowed. "I should object to being used by the Don in this manner."

"If we get out of this alive," Dale said, "I'll make sure the Don gives you a nice pension."

"And my entire crew," Captain Mamatas said.

Dale studied the bridges overhead. "If we survive this, the Don can buy the whole ship. Are any of your security team Deaf?"

"Two," Captain Mamatas said.

"You'll want them on point," Dale said. "Assuming the Casphar care about civilian casualties, they're going to come in with gas bombs and sonic weapons. Your Deaf people can vanish in the smoke and then hit them from behind, because they won't have to retreat from the noise. They'll still feel it, but they should be able to withstand it better than the rest of us."

Captain Mamatas nodded and relayed orders in two local languages. He turned back to Dale. "Are you the only undercover operative on my ship?"

"I can bring down one more," Dale said, "plus you could ask Vassily Cheremetov, who is exactly who he says he is. We're here if you need us."

"Still my ship, still my command," Captain Mamatas said, "but we could use every trained soldier we've got."

• • •

Aboard the Casphar cruiser, crews were working to manually open the emergency hatches on the various crew cylinders. Alex, Anya, and Natalia walked along the catwalks past them, the marine who had captured them still behind them, directing their turns. They moved past the command sphere, which had already had its hatches restored, and continued aft to a small cylinder behind it. The marine motioned to its open hatch. Alex stepped up to it.

The captain sat inside, behind a utilitarian desk. She motioned to three chairs. Alex took the center seat. Anya sat on his left and Natalia on his right. The marine placed the weapons he had confiscated from them on the captain's desk, then stepped back to guard the door.

"I am wondering," the captain began in clear Interstellar, "why Captain Moridi pursues us into jumpgate. I am not noticing private message he sends me until after immediate crisis is past. I learn he has done facial recognition on you, Sir Alexander." She tipped her head and raised an eyebrow.

Alex held his hands out, palms up.

The captain shook her head. "Should have known. Accent is ridiculous, even for man from Yllas. Would you like to explain why?"

"I know it sounds like I'm making excuses," Alex said, "but the truth is I was just trying to get my people out."

The captain held a gaze on him for several seconds, one corner of her mouth tugging downward. "So I check my orders. Should have been my first warning. No orders come from command in crisis. But orders still look legitimate. I check sources. Orders come from command. I check ID. No General Polanski in any branch of service. So you make up ID, not kill general to impersonate."

"No," Alex said. "That wouldn't have been my style."

"Ship through jumpgate," the captain continued, "yet you still stop to help marine trapped in microgravity bubble. Why?"

Alex opened his mouth to respond, then paused. He closed his mouth again and shrugged. He considered for a moment before answering. "I'll be honest, Natalia here took the lead on that, but it seemed to the rest of us like the obvious thing to do. I've been around gravity drives long enough to know that those bubbles can be unstable, and he could have plunged at any time."

The captain looked at Natalia.

"She doesn't speak Interstellar," Alex said.

The captain switched to Casphar.

Natalia raised both eyebrows at the question, then answered in a few matter-of-fact sentences.

The captain asked another question. She got a two-word answer from Natalia. The captain then looked at Alex with a raised brow. "She sews dolls?"

"One of my best sewers," Alex said. "All my employees are the best."

The captain drummed her fingers on her desk. "So Nostraspace can insert orders direct from command, can make ID tablets and order cards that fool even me. How many spies in military right now?"

"Oh, I wouldn't know that," Alex said, his voice earnest. "I'm sure my uncle likes to keep tabs on what's going on, but he certainly wouldn't tell me about it. If it makes you feel better, it's not our style to interfere."

"Riots have nothing to do with you?" the captain asked.

"Well, we didn't exactly do anything to stop them," Alex said. "Our policy has always been that if the people in another nation want to change their government, we remain neutral. I spoke honestly to the miners when Emperor Habid asked me to. I spoke honestly to Emperor Habid when he asked me to."

"And jumpgate goes down as soon as we exit," the captain said, nodding. "Coincidence?"

"I couldn't answer that," Alex said. "I certainly don't control the jumpgate, or I wouldn't have needed to pull this stunt."

"That is first answer that I do not believe," the captain said.

Alex pursed his lips, then shrugged.

The captain drummed her fingers again. "My planet burns, Sir Alexander. My commanders are silent. My emperor is silent. Now jumpgate down, and answers could not come through if commanders and emperor deigned to send. My orders are stop departures, stop people seeking safety. My question: Don can stop this?"

Alex swallowed visibly, glancing at Anya and Natalia before answering. "I'm not a diplomat. I can't answer for the Don."

"Not asking will Don stop this," the captain said, leveling a gaze at him. "Asking, *can* Don stop this?"

Alex grimaced. "I believe he could. I don't think you'd like how, since it probably means sending in a military force to restore order."

The captain nodded. "Right now, Don has more respect in Casphar Empire than Emperor Habid." She pulled a DSC out of her desk and laid it in front of Alex. "You ask."

Alex took the DSC, typed and transmitted a login request through the DiYesu Family jumpgate ahead, and began to compose a message:

<u>Onboard Casphar cruiser *Aiez* between Santa Maria gates. Severe civil unrest on Reggit. Have received a very unofficial,</u>

<u>low-level request wondering if peacekeeping assistance is</u> <u>available. Please advise. Alex.</u>

He waited a minute for the login validation to come back, and he transmitted. "Assuming they do the two-gate bounce at Polairmo, he should have that in a few minutes."

The captain nodded. "You made Austin Montierthski doll?"

Alex started at the question. "Our company did, yes."

The captain shook her head. "Very poor taste."

They sat in silence for fifteen minutes until the DSC buzzed with a response. Alex verified his identity with a password, then opened it. It had proper authentication from Sixcrystal Station, the Nostraspace gate at Polairmo, the Greekorp gate at Polairmo, the Greekorp gate at San Jose, the DiYesu Family gate at San Jose, and the DiYesu Family gate at Santa Maria. It read simply: <u>Ask the captain if you may</u> <u>use their secure message network.</u>

Alex showed it to the captain. She shot up from the desk, sending her chair toppling backward. "Don is reading our secure message network?"

"Apparently?" Alex said, sounding genuinely surprised himself.

The captain thumped her fist on the desk, muttering something that might have had Habid's name in it. She moved over to the bulkhead and slid a panel open. Inside was a large screen with a keyboard attached. She touched the screen, entered a password on the keyboard, and stepped aside.

Alex came over and typed in the pertinent addresses, then wrote: <u>The captain has been kind enough</u> <u>to let me send you this.</u> He transmitted.

Alex stepped back. The captain folded her

arms and waited. While they stood in silence,
the quartermaster stopped by and removed the three
weapons.

Finally, a response came. It read: <u>Yes.</u> A string
of nonsense characters followed. Then: <u>If that makes
no sense and your cousin isn't kicking and screaming already,
start taking apart whatever he's bringing home until it does.</u>

• • •

Vassily and Melanie were just emerging from the
lobby elevator when Captain Mamatas, looking at his
tablet, muttered a few choice words in Hellin.

Dale stepped up to Captain Mamatas. "May I ask?"

Captain Mamatas turned his head toward Dale and
wrinkled his nose. "The captain of the Casphar ship
ahead says, 'Surrender vessel.' Then the commander of
the DiYesu jumpgate says, 'No transmission of any ship
not cleared by Casphar captain.' Now, message from
the Don himself says, 'Turn *Anerchomeno Asteri* and
return to Casphar jumpgate. I will help if I can.'
And I am wondering, what is it you have gotten me
into, Mr. Carsoni?"

Dale shifted his weight. "Obviously, Captain,
it's your ship. But turning around will slow those
breaching pods down quite a bit."

"And he who swims in the protein vats gets eaten,"
Captain Mamatas said.

Vassily and Melanie arrived beside them.

Captain Mamatas looked at them both. "You," he
said to Vassily, "you are Casphar."

"Yes," Vassily said.

Captain Mamatas then turned to Melanie, who was out
of her makeup though still dressed in Casphar attire.
"And you? Kon?"

"Proudly," said Melanie.

"And you both now work for the Don," Captain Mamatas said slowly. "Tell me. Have you ever regretted that decision?"

Both were silent for several seconds. Melanie answered first. "Never for very long, but Patcorp will have me back any time I want to go."

Captain Mamatas looked at Vassily.

"Only when he send me back to Casphar," Vassily said.

Captain Mamatas wrinkled his nose again, then nodded. He typed an order into his tablet. "I am turning *Anerchomeno Asteri* around. We will return to the Casphar gate."

• • •

A blunt-nosed shuttle departed the Casphar cruiser *Aiez*, slipping out of a set of double doors on the aft section of the ship. It skirted nimbly around the breaching pods and emergency tubes making their way to the wreck of the troop ship. It turned toward the DiYesu jumpgate.

On board, Alex, Anya, and Natalia stood close together in the limited floor space behind the pilot.

Then the pilot began cursing in Casphar.

Alex leaned forward. "Is she coming back toward us?"

• • •

The lights in *Anerchomeno Asteri*'s lobby were out except for the dim glow from the elevator shaft and guide lights in the floors of the balconies and bridges. Security personnel were scattered along the bridges, with a handful standing backs against the walls between doors to the various reception rooms. The overturned tables remained, but with no one sheltering behind them. Vassily, Dale, Melanie, and Captain Mamatas stood conspicuously in the center of the lobby.

The lobby echoed with irregular hollow thumping sounds.

"That's the first of the breaching pods attaching," Dale said.

"This would be a lot safer if we were under cover," Melanie said.

Captain Mamatas shook his head, his round cheeks squeezing in. "My government will want to see that we tried to discuss the situation."

"Just don't resist when I knock you to the ground," Melanie said.

The thumping sound was joined by a creaking sound.

"That's the airlocks being forced," Dale explained.

"That means they will need to be repaired," Captain Mamatas said.

Vassily scowled. "More damage before this done."

Captain Mamatas inspected his tablet. "They have entered Reception Room 31."

The group rounded the elevator, and Mamatas pointed to one of the reception room doors. Security forces shifted positions on the bridges. Two of the security people stationed against walls ran over to flank that door.

Dale handed earplugs to Vassily, Melanie, and Captain Mamatas. They all inserted them.

Captain Mamatas entered a command on his tablet. The door to Reception Room 31 opened.

Three marines, looking surprised, stood inside.

"Good afternoon," Captain Mamatas said, his voice amplified throughout the lobby. "When I spoke with your captain, I informed him that I am not in Casphar space and therefore would not be complying with your request for an additional search. Permission to come aboard is hereby officially denied. Please return to your own vessel."

The marines pulled masks over their noses.

Melanie tackled Captain Mamatas. Dale and Vassily hit the deck right after her.

The lobby outside the reception room exploded in a cloud of smoke.

A piercing screech shot out from the smoke.

Even with the earplugs in, Vassily, Dale, Melanie, and Captain Mamatas clamped their hands to their ears, each of their faces contorting into hideous grimaces of pain.

The screech stopped abruptly.

The smoke began to clear. The two Deaf security guards stood proudly over the unconscious bodies of the three marines, stun guns in their hands still glowing.

Mamatas rose, still grimacing, and checked his tablet. He redirected the two Deaf security guards to another door.

Vassily, Dale, and Melanie sprinted toward the three downed Casphar marines. They removed the weapons from the unconscious bodies, then yanked the face masks and ear protection off of each.

Meanwhile, the door the Deaf security guards were beside opened. Captain Mamatas retreated behind the elevator. Another smoke bomb went off. The sound guns did not go off this time, though. As the smoke cleared, the Deaf security guards were already on their way to another door, and three more security guards were stripping equipment off unconscious marines.

Vassily led Dale and Melanie to another door. They stopped outside it. Vassily held up three fingers and counted them down.

The door opened, and all three sprang through.

Three marines were in the process of jumping through the airlock from a breaching pod.

Vassily fired a smoke bomb. Dale fired the sonic weapon.

Melanie dashed into the smoke, wielding a stun weapon like a harpoon.

The smoke vanished from the airlock with a huge pop and a whoosh.

Melanie, off balance, caught herself on the edge of the airlock, which stood open to space. The breaching pod careened away from the side of the ship, the marines falling out of it and flailing in the vacuum.

Air rushed out of the room, knocking Dale to the floor. Vassily bent his knees but stayed upright.

Melanie dragged herself back. She landed on the button to close the airlock door. It slammed shut.

The three of them stood gasping for air.

"Note," Melanie said at last, "those O-rings pop right off if you accidentally hit them instead of your target."

Dale dragged himself to his feet. "We need to get back in the fight. Their tactics aren't going to stay nonlethal for long."

The three of them staggered back out of the reception room.

• • •

The blunt-nosed shuttle from *Aiez* sped toward *Anerchomeno Asteri*. Alex, Anya, and Natalia now huddled even closer to the pilot.

The pilot spoke in clear Interstellar, "Shuttle Two from cruiser *Aiez* to *Anerchomeno Asteri*. We're returning three of your passengers. Requesting docking."

The swarm of breaching pods closed in around *Anerchomeno Asteri*. Alex leaned forward and looked out the window. "It looks like they're busy."

"The captain did not give me the option of bringing you back with me," the pilot said.

"I don't suppose you can call off the attack," Alex said.

The pilot just shot him a glare and repeated the request for docking.

• • •

All the security guards on the lobby floor were now armed with confiscated Casphar marine weapons. Captain Mamatas stood guard over a collection of unconscious marines near the elevator, stun weapon in his hand, shocking any who stirred back into oblivion. In the other hand, he monitored the tablet and pointed teams to whichever reception room was in the process of being boarded.

Dale ran up to Captain Mamatas. He pulled back his ear protection and spoke, winded. "They're going to start shifting tactics soon. Either they're going to start coming in with real weapons firing, or they're going to start attaching elsewhere and cutting through the hull."

"We're monitoring the outside of the hull," Captain Mamatas said. "We should have some warning."

Another smoke bomb went off. Blind gunfire echoed from the other side of the cloud. Dale hustled Captain Mamatas behind the elevator shaft. Several stun weapons fired into the cloud simultaneously. The cloud swirled and partly cleared as the bolts moved through it. Several more stun weapons targeted the marines and took them down.

Captain Mamatas, looking at the tablet, pointed a team at another reception room.

"Wait!" Dale said, looking over the captain's
shoulder.

Mamatas turned to look at him.

"That's Alex!" Dale said.

Captain Mamatas looked down at the tablet again.
On it, a video feed showed Alex, Anya, and Natalia
entering through the airlock.

Captain Mamatas waved to get the attention of the
security guards he had just dispatched. He signed
a phrase with exaggerated arm and face movements
across the lobby to them. They nodded and repeated
the instructions to those around them. Instead of
charging the door, they took up postures of readiness
and waited.

The reception room door opened. Alex, hands up,
advanced slowly. He spotted Dale and Captain Mamatas
and jogged over to them, Anya and Natalia behind him.
Dale held out stun weapons to each of them. Anya and
Natalia each took one.

Alex shook his head. "Looks like you're handling
this, and I've got orders." He dashed past them and
into the elevator.

Mamatas redirected everyone's attention at two more
reception rooms. Dale filled Anya and Natalia in on
the strategy.

Alex arrived on an upper deck and ran across
the bridge, past two security guards, then onto the
balcony. He reached the stateroom door, knocked first,
then used his thumbprint to open it.

The room was packed. The bed had nine women on it,
all seated with their knees clutched to their chests.
Ellemarie occupied one of the few chairs in the room.
Marco and Kiera sat on the bathroom counter. Every
centimeter of floorspace had someone either seated or
standing on it.

"Where's the case?" Alex asked.

"Closet," Marco answered.

Alex checked the door was secure behind him, then with long-legged steps made his way through the crowd of people. He slid the closet open. The case sat on the floor. He grabbed it, lifted it over his head, and reversed course back to the doorway. He let himself out onto the balcony.

One security guard was on the same balcony as he was, but a fair distance farther aft. As the door closed, he set the case down on the ground, knelt next to it, and pulled a hard copy of his message from the Don from his pocket.

Alex reread the message: <u>Yes.</u> Characters from no known language. Then: <u>If that makes no sense and your cousin isn't kicking and screaming already, start taking apart whatever he's bringing home until it does.</u>

Alex opened the case. The two-headed falcon stared up at him with four porcelain eyes. He lifted it out of the protective padding.

With a sharp smack, he brought it down on the edge of the case.

The falcon's back cracked. The heads, just below where the necks joined, tipped forward and snapped off.

Alex examined the pieces. Shoved inside, one in each head, were two crystals. They glinted back at him, the left one black, the right one magenta. Alex reached up inside and pulled them out.

Each crystal was a half sphere, cut with tiny triangular faces, and sat on a steel ring, carved with tiny symbols.

Some of the symbols matched the gibberish in the Don's message.

Alex studied the crystals closely.

Pulling one of the pins off the sash of his uniform, Alex turned the magenta crystal over and pressed the pin against the first mysterious symbol in the Don's message. With a tiny click, the rest of the ring changed shape as tiny switches under each symbol all snapped to the outermost position.

Below, another smoke bomb went off and gunfire erupted.

Using the pin, Alex pressed each symbol on the ring in the order they were listed in the Don's message.

Back at the Casphar gate, the lights on the gate blinked back on. Then the posts glowed blue again. Sleek and aluminum, a Nostraspace cruiser emerged from the gate. The space warp vanished behind it, and it banked around toward *Aiez* and the wreckage of the troop ship.

Alex repeated the procedure on the black crystal's ring. Then he pocketed both. He put the bird parts back into the case, closed it, and sauntered back toward the elevator.

Below, several security guards were wounded, but they still seemed to be holding off each boarding party as it came on board.

Alex spotted Dale below the bridge he was crossing and called down, "Dale!"

Dale looked up.

"Show them this!" He dropped the case down to him. Dale shuffled his weapon over his shoulder as he caught it.

"We don't need it anymore!" Alex said. "Open it!"

Dale set the case on the floor and popped the latches open. He opened it, blinked, then laughed. He rose to a standing position, holding the falcon's heads in his left hand and the front half of its body in his right hand.

"I hope you're going to explain to me why you did that!" Dale called, not looking at Alex and instead turning to face the door to the next reception room.

"I'll let Uncle Lew do that!" Alex called back.

Dale strode over to the door to the reception room, set the broken statue down just outside it, then joined the security guards positioned beside it.

The door to the reception room opened. A marine lunged forward, about to fire a smoke bomb, and stopped dead in his tracks. He stared down at the broken statue.

"That's right!" Alex yelled down. "Stand down!"

Two more marines, apparently at a run before the door opened, piled into the marine in the doorway. They tumbled forward and landed in a heap beside the broken falcon.

The security guards swooped in and disarmed them.

"Surprisingly effective!" Captain Mamatas yelled up to Alex. He glanced at his tablet. "And it looks like help is on the way!"

At the DiYesu gate, a new ship had arrived. It was a wedge-shaped Greekorp frigate, brightly painted with a yellow beak on its bow and red feathers on the delta wings. It drifted momentarily forward as the gate deposited it between its goalposts, then accelerated toward the approaching *Anerchomeno Asteri*.

Then, all at once, the swarming breaching pods broke off and pulled away.

An eerie silence came over the lobby.

One of the captured marines rose slowly to his feet. He called out in a strong voice, "New orders. We remain with comrades or we remove all comrades. Ship to continue to gate."

All eyes fell on Captain Mamatas.

Captain Mamatas looked around. "All weapons are

to be placed in a pile over here and left behind. You may retrieve your comrades and leave the way you came. Also take the two who are in the brig with you, if you wouldn't mind."

• • •

Two hours later, *Anerchomeno Asteri* was through the rectangular Nostraspace jumpgate at Polairmo, transmitted directly from the Casphar gate at Santa Maria by a small team of Nostraspace jumpgate technicians who had arrived on the cruiser.

A swarm of news media craft were there waiting, hovering below the posts and dangerously close to the thirty-story habitation block. As *Anerchomeno Asteri* arrived, they swooped up and began circling the jumpgate, barely staying off the main space lane.

Periodically, one darted in for a closer look at the large liner. Various logos painted on the sides identified some of them. Others appeared to be larger drones sent up uncrewed to get footage of the arrival.

Captain Mamatas was still supervising the cleanup in the lobby when word came through on his tablet. He marched up to Alex. "Sir Alexander, do you have any idea how the media came to be so interested in our arrival? Particularly since this is not the gate we were scheduled to use?"

Alex arched an eyebrow and looked at the video feed on Mamatas's tablet. "Maybe someone at a jumpgate passed along your communications?"

Captain Mamatas's wide cheeks pursed, and his nose crinkled. "Those communications had to pass through Greekorp gates. You do not know much about our culture if you think that."

Ellemarie approached, leaning unsteadily on her cane. "Or, somebody on board sent a message ahead alerting them. Scared passengers, locked in cabins while being boarded, wanting to get word out to family. You know."

"Strange," Captain Mamatas said, "but all the inquiries I'm receiving are asking about our heroic rescue of Nostraspace citizens from civil unrest on Reggit."

Ellemarie smirked slightly. "Well, a scared passenger may have provided some context."

Captain Mamatas pointed at Alex. "You are speaking to them."

Within twenty minutes, the lobby was buzzing with media drones. Dale, Melanie, and Kiera had made themselves scarce, but the rest of the team and all the women stood behind Alex, now dressed in formal Nostraspace attire again. Six actual human reporters stood in front of them.

"It's easy to call us heroes," Alex said, "but the truth of the matter is that all we did was run away when things got bad. If you want a story of real heroes... well, I wish I had a list to give you.

"It started as a peaceful protest on Reggit. Princess Aiez came out and asked to meet with the leaders. I don't know how much you know about Casphar culture, but when a totalitarian dictator asks you who the leaders are, most people would shrink away. Three people stepped forward, putting their lives on the line to speak for the concerns of the people. One of them I can name. She worked for us, but decided to stay behind to help her people. Khadija Alsadat. She... She is a hero.

"Two other people stepped forward, too. An older miner and a businesswoman. I don't know their names. We may never know their names. At the rate people were being killed when we escaped, we may never know if they even lived. Those are the heroes. The ones whose names we'll never know.

"Princess Aiez. She gave her life trying to find a peaceful solution to the people's grievances. Killed by her own father. She defied him in an effort to help people. She didn't run away, hide in the palace, wait it out. Hero.

"We were escorted by the very brave crew of a cruiser that bears her name. This, despite the fact that the government was trying to arrest us. When we were nearly in a collision, that captain bravely put her little cruiser between *Anerchomeno Asteri* and the hull of a troop ship. She protected us. Hero. Definitely a hero. And I don't know her name.

"And look around here. The *Anerchomeno Asteri* security force held off a boarding by Casphar marines. Casphar marines against civilian security armed with stunners. Many of them are hurt. Seriously. Heroes, one and all. And I haven't learned a single one of their names. And I doubt any of you would have thought to ask.

"So, no, we're not heroes. We're just people who knew the right thing to do was to get as many people out as we could.

"The real heroes are the ones whose stories we'll never hear, whose names we'll never learn, who fought the tiny battles that went unnoticed. We'll never know everything that went down in this fiasco. So, let's celebrate all the heroes.

"And let's make sure that their acts of courage, sometimes the ultimate act of courage, won't have happened in vain. Let's rebuild Casphar and make it a series of worlds where all citizens are heard, valued, and free to prosper."

CHAPTER **18**

"Cynicism is the price of survival."
 —Lewis LaCour, Patcorp politician

Alex stepped off the shuttle onto the battleship. It had been two months since they had returned from Reggit. His moustache had regrown, and he'd put some weight back on. He swept out into the corridor and made his way toward the conference room.

Kiera Twight was waiting for him inside. Gone were the battle scars and the borrowed clothes. Her face had filled back out, and her curves were fuller. Her hair fell in a flawless sheet down one side of her face before sweeping back up, then was tucked into a tiara. She wore a jewel-encrusted cape over an elegant suit. She smiled formally. "Sir Alexander, welcome."

Alex sat down. "Have we gone formal now?"

Her smile turned wry. "Hostess duties. I'm supposed to be practicing. You're actually going down to Sixcrystal Station."

"Oh?" Alex asked. His new DSC buzzed, and he checked it. "Oh!" he said with pleasant surprise in his voice.

"News?" Kiera asked.

"A message from a cute brunette I abandoned in my bed to come here. Didn't remember her name until I saw it here. I may actually see her again."

"Yeah," Kiera said, "your uncle's requests for audiences are rarely well timed."

"So how are things?"

Kiera nodded, sighed, and lowered herself into a chair opposite Alex. "Good, I suppose. I don't like being out of the game, but this is a good gig. Your uncle's a handful, but I'm not complaining."

Alex nodded and leaned forward. "You do know you're one in a long line, right?"

She smiled. "Luckily for me, and unfortunately for him, I'm smarter than most of them were, and I know the game."

Alex grinned. "And you're a better assassin. I'm amazed Colonel Brawley lets you near Sixcrystal Station."

"I'm searched every time I go down. I'm not joking. I really am."

"I believe you."

"Oh," Kiera said, "we got word today that your friend Khadija won the election. We're swearing her in as the new governor of Reggit next week."

"It's a pity," Alex joked. "She was a damned good foreman. Now I'm going to have to make her a partner if I want to keep her."

"She's going to be a force to be reckoned with," Kiera said. "Someone seems to have made her think that we're some sort of messiahs."

"We are," Alex said. "If we don't screw this up, I suspect the Casphar people will be more loyal than we are. Are you still going ahead with the trial of Emperor Habid?"

Kiera nodded. "Trial by a jury of his own people. We're providing his legal team and the judge to preside, but his fate is entirely in their hands."

"Smart," Alex said.

Kiera nodded. "Your uncle isn't stupid."

They drifted off into silence. They didn't talk about Dale. They didn't talk about their shared experiences. They looked out the conference room windows at the blackness of outer space.

The screen on the wall blinked alive with an airlock number. Kiera rose again. "That would be your shuttle down."

"Are you coming with me?" Alex asked.

Kiera shook her head. "This is a family matter."

Alex took her hand, and they lingered for a moment before he let go and headed to the airlock.

The shuttle down was a smaller model, with a single pilot and seats for ten passengers. The pilot was a small woman, olive skinned with a long nose, and clearly Casphar. Alex greeted her in Casphar. She smiled. "Nostraspace citizen now. Thank you, Sir Alexander."

"The royal shuttle is quite an honor. You must be one of the best pilots in the Casphar fleet."

"Trained as pilot," the woman said, as the automated undocking procedure began. "Casphar military decided skills more useful elsewhere."

"Oh?" Alex asked. "What did they have you do?"

"Cook," she answered.

The trip down only took five minutes. Sixcrystal Station loomed larger and larger as they approached, the faceted domes glinting sunlight from one side and vanishing into darkness on the other.

The shuttle approached one corner where three tubes came together, each forming half of an X that supported a dome. The cone-shaped airlock stuck out from the joint, red and green marker lights identifying it, and three pairs of lights—amber, cyan, and purple—marking the airlock hatch itself.

The shuttle spun around, and the automated docking procedure brought the airlocks effortlessly together.

"Thank you," Alex said to the pilot as he stepped out of the shuttle.

The shuttle's airlock ramp extended out and into the Sixcrystal Station airlock, connecting to an extruded-aluminum walkway that glowed from beneath with a tiny gravity drive. The walkway up ahead bent sharply upward and vanished into the three-meter-diameter tubes that led to the Evening Dome.

Two other tubes with walkways came in below to the left and right, bending to join the walkway Alex would use in a hollow triangle, each also glowing with its own little gravity drive. If the shuttle had docked at a different orientation, one of these would be "up," and would take him to either the Noon Dome or the so-called Cylinder Dome, named for the cylindrical operations center mounted beneath it.

Alex stepped off the shuttle's ramp, wobbling slightly as he shifted to the different gravity of the walkway. He proceeded up it, pausing briefly to take the step onto the uphill portion. He planted his first foot flat, then bent his knee and brought the other foot flat. As he did so, he straightened up and stood upright, the uphill portion now serving as "down" and the airlock swooping "uphill" behind him. He walked the 200 meters to the elevator.

The Evening Dome elevator let out into a small "building" constructed of a mix of aluminum and real wood. The doors opened to a vista designed to impress visitors. Alex did not react to it as he stepped out and onto the stone path through the thick grass beyond it.

Sunlight filtered through the trees, soft lights on slender poles along the path aiding with illumination.

The dome stretched 300 meters in diameter and rose more than fifty meters above at its highest. Overhead, a few facets caught the light of the suns directly and flashed light down as Alex proceeded up the path, checking the various patios that had been set up to serve the function of different rooms.

No staff was visible. Alex found his uncle seated on a plush sofa under a canopy of eucalyptus trees. Alex strode over and knelt.

"Alex," the Don said, "so good of you to come."

"I wouldn't have missed it," Alex said. "I got to talk to Kiera on the battleship. She seems to like it here."

"I wanted to thank you personally for bringing her back to me," the Don said. "I wasn't sure your cousin would do so."

"Dale can follow orders," Alex said, rising. The Don motioned him over to an overstuffed chair nearby. Alex sat. "But I don't think he'd ever go much beyond his orders."

"You, however, went well beyond orders, bringing me these." The Don pulled back his cape, revealing the two jewels Alex had retrieved from the falcon pinned to his waistcoat just below a third jewel, identical to the other two, except this one was yellow. "Do you know what they are?"

"We sort of parsed that they control the jumpgates somehow," Alex said. "I assume the yellow one is the Nostraspace line?"

The Don nodded. "Black is the ring-style Casphar gates. Magenta is the post-style Casphar gates. There are only ten of these. Not many people know what they are or what they do. You're now one of only sixteen people in the empire who does. I trust you understand how important discretion is."

"Of course," Alex said.

"Heretofore, discretion was never your strong suit," the Don said, pulling his cape back down over the three jewels.

"I'd like to think I'm growing up," Alex said.

"Your mother doesn't think so," the Don answered. "But you not only showed tenacity on Reggit, you showed creativity. That impressed me a lot."

Alex nodded and licked his upper lip before asking, "The plan was for us to be captured, wasn't it?"

The Don tipped his head to one side. "Let's just say it was one of the scenarios I had planned for. I'll be honest. You delivering the Casphar Empire, asking to be annexed, was *not* one of the scenarios I had planned for. I'd like to know how you did it."

"I've been thinking about that myself," Alex said. "And I think that the only thing I did that anyone else wouldn't have done is I treated people like family."

The Don nodded. "Including letting Ellemarie and Vassily walk all over you."

Alex swallowed visibly and nodded. "Including that."

The Don chuckled. "When I was young, we called that screwing up with style."

Alex swallowed again.

"Don't worry," the Don said. "I'm not promoting you."

Alex sighed and visibly relaxed.

"I am going to ask that you avoid any more unscheduled press conferences, however."

Alex flushed and pointed back toward Polairmo. "Ellemarie—"

"Is a pain in my ass, too," the Don said.

Alex shut up and shook his head.

"If," the Don said quietly, "you should ever again have an opportunity to bring me more of these crystals—without causing an international incident, mind you—you should take that opportunity. So long as you can do so without letting too many people know just how vulnerable a nation's jumpgate system really is. Whoever controls the jumpgates controls the multistellar nation."

Alex nodded. "And they're apparently fairly easy to detect."

The Don smiled and pulled a blue wand out of his inner pocket. "Confiscated from your cousin, who was under the impression he would be allowed to keep it after his mission."

"Sounds like Dale."

The Don turned on the wand and pointed it at himself. As he moved the wand down his chest, it went off as he pointed to the bottom of his ribcage, blinking blue and chirping. The Don pulled his cape back to reveal that it was pointed at the black gem, not having gone off for the yellow or magenta ones.

"In theory, it would also detect the old Hundye gates, but I'm not in a rush to take on the Suturiku for that one. We tested it for the Patcorp gates, but either it doesn't work or they don't keep the key where we think they do. Here." He handed the wand to Alex. "A souvenir. Never let it fall into anyone else's hands."

Alex gulped and slipped the wand into an inner pocket.

"Now," the Don said, rising, "I believe we're having dinner in the Midnight Dome today."

They walked together to the edge of the dome. The grass gave way to a steep concrete embankment that sloped down to the base of the dome, steps cut into it leading to a hatch in the tall aluminum side.

The dome sat on a three-meter-thick platform over their heads as they each grabbed a handlebar above the hatch and swung their feet into it. They went weightless as they passed through the tube, falling at a forty-five-degree angle away from the Evening Dome, and emerging feet first into the gravity of the Midnight Dome, set at a further forty-five degrees down.

The Midnight Dome was aglow in soft blue light emanating from the roofs of hundreds of small aluminum buildings scattered across its shock-absorbent floor. The formal dining room glowed with internal lighting a hundred meters in front of them.

Dinner was just the two of them. They discussed family affairs: who was dating which clawing upstart, how much money was being squandered by no-good relations, which purchases for official residences were too extravagant.

The same pilot was waiting for Alex after dinner. She smiled as he entered the shuttlecraft. "Did you have a nice dinner, Sir Alexander?"

"I did, thank you," he said. "I hope you got something to eat."

She nodded. "The food in the staff dining room in the cylinder is quite good."

"I'm glad."

The automated departure sequence cut them loose, and the shuttle headed back toward the battleship.

Alex looked out the window in the airlock and watched Sixcrystal Station recede, glinting in the sunlight and hiding in shadows as always.

His DSC buzzed.

He pulled it out. The message had stamps from the Reggit and Nostraspace-Polairmo jumpgates authenticating it.

It was from the manager of the bank:
<u>Trial of Emperor Habid starts in two weeks. Have investors. Ideal time to launch Habid-as-Miner doll.</u>

END

ACKNOWLEDGMENTS

There is a popular narrative about writers that says we work alone. If you'll excuse me for stealing a line from one of the masterpieces of twentieth-century cinema, this is both true and misleading. It's true in that, yes, we spend our time alone with a computer doing most of the work of writing the book in our own heads. But it's misleading in that it implies that writing a book is not a highly collaborative process, with many, many people involved. I did not write this book alone, and there is a lot of additional credit that must be given.

First and foremost, I need to acknowledge that this story universe began as a tabletop roleplaying game I built using the Hero System (5th Edition). I owe a debt of gratitude to the good folks at Hero Games who created a robust way to create all sorts of original worlds. My co-GM the first time I ran it, Phil Adler, did large swaths of the worldbuilding—to the point where I'm honestly not sure any more what parts were originally his and what parts were originally mine—and deserves a lot of credit. I promised to buy him a Tesla if this book makes millions of dollars, so tell your friends to buy lots of copies.

The players in that original game also steered the story in unexpected directions, as players always do. Some of those unexpected twists survive in my plot. The armored personnel carrier, for example, was 100% player and 0% me (except that in the game it was a tank). Some of my characters were very strongly inspired by the characters my players built and inhabited. This book would not be what it is without them. My thanks go to my players: Judy Adler, Andy Ashcraft, Jeff Barrett, Lee Bennett, Chris Boltz, Shawn Heslin, Jackie Kashian, Daniel LaCour, Helen Jane McKee, Eli Micu, Chad Neptune, Anders Paulsen, Lisa Peters, Tucker Russell, Christina Schroeder, Eric Spuur, and Sean Young.

Turning a game into a workable novel involved a lot of informal mentoring from folks who'd been down the path before. Here I'm very grateful to the members of the Science Fiction and Fantasy Writers of America (SFWA), Codex, and the Outer Alliance. All three organizations

are filled with generous individuals who will happily
answer questions, help brainstorm, or serve as cheerleaders
through the painful slog in which you feel like the novel
will never be finished and will never be any good if it is
finished. Also, all my writer friends on Slack. I'd love to
say, "You know who you are," but the truth is, you probably
don't. Those casual conversations I may not even have been
actively participating in fixed more problems that I can
possibly count. Every writer should hang out in a community
of writers, even if it's all virtual, and I appreciate my
"friends at the pub."

It would also be remiss of me not to thank the wonderful
faculty I worked with in my formal writing education: Steven
Church, Alex Espinoza, Corrinne Clegg Hales, John Hales,
Howard V. Hendrix, Randa Jarrar, Tim Skeen, and Lisa Weston.
Across many genres, they showed me how it's done.

Once a book is written, the contributions of others
don't stop. There are many drafts and revisions, and we
writers rely on first readers to help us determine what works
and what doesn't. These people often function as informal
editors and noticers-of-plot-holes. Chris Boltz and Carol
Keller filled those roles for me, and I am grateful.

My husband, Chris, had the unenviable task of reading
every iteration and functioning as an unpaid global editor.
We live in a community property state, so this book is half
his regardless, but he deserves much more than that, and he
deserves more than the thanks I can give him here. He has
always been supportive of this crazy plan of mine to write
books for a living, puts up with all my neuroses, and lets
me keep adopting cats. I don't know why it's de rigueur
for writers to have cats, but he lets me have cats, despite
the fact that we're both allergic to cats. Thank you, and I
love you.

And, of course, there are professionals involved in all
this. For editorial services, I worked with the wonderful
people at Pikko's House. I had a marvelous line editor,
Crystal Watanabe, and a great copy editor, Therin Knite.
Trust me on this, writers, even if you also work as an
editor, never try to edit your own work.

So although writing this book was mostly me, alone, with
a laptop (and at least one very helpful cat), I was never
far from a network of people who were helping me with it.
It's a solitary job, but not a lonely one, nor one where

mine is the only voice, the only mind that matters. This
book is all of ours.

     And there's one final person I need to thank: You. As
someone who is reading this book, you're participating in
the final step of the process. You're letting the words I
wrote enter into your brain, where your imagination brings
them to life. You are my ultimate collaborator, and the
story that plays out in your mind is, necessarily, different
from the one in my mind, or in the mind of anyone else in
these acknowledgments. My job is to give you the blueprint
for your imagination to spin you an amazing story. Thank
you for doing that. I couldn't do it without you.

About the Layout

The layout of this book was done by Jim Keller and was based on the latest research on how to improve readability for dyslexics, striving to balance that with maintaining readability for everyone else. We at Lightning Cellar Publications would love to learn how this experiment worked. Please feel free to discuss the layout design in all your reviews and conversations about this book.